LAWYERS, GUNS, AND MONKEYS

LAWYERS, GUNS, AND MONKEYS

TONY GLEESON

WILDSIDE PRESS

To the Holy Trinity:
McBain, Westlake, Block

ONE

Curtis Stryker still couldn't get over his recent good luck.

I've got a car!

The balding tires were sliding just a bit on the slippery streets and a slight drizzle of rain was seeping in through the driver's-side window. *Okay, it's a beater, but it runs! It got me all the way here from Bartontown, and since I've got a car, I've got a job!*

He peered out the windshield between the half-hearted sweeps of the ragged wipers at the street signs. There should have been some morning sunlight by now, but the rainclouds hid the dawn in sludgy darkness that his headlamps just barely penetrated. He still wasn't familiar with a lot of the city but the GPS on his phone so far hadn't failed him. He was close; all he needed now was Obrigato Drive and then Mockingbird Lane.

Five days in town and I've got a nice place to stay and a cool job!

I was even able to afford a great breakfast this morning–pancakes, sausage and eggs–and still have time to make my morning pickup!

Curtis, it had to be said, had a great attitude about life.

Bartontown, he knew, was a dead end, pure and simple. To stay there would have been to end up like all his friends, continuing to work in a big-box store. He had bigger and better ideas. He'd come to the city as a last resort, but now he had a game plan.

He'd been fortunate enough to meet Celia Smithers, and even more fortunate that she'd taken a liking to him. After spending the first two nights in town sleeping in his car while looking for lodging, he could afford, he'd seen a notice for a basement room in her apartment house and after a conversation, she'd not only accepted him as a tenant but offered him a job with her courier service. That's what she called it, a courier service. Curtis made the mistake of referring to it as a messenger service and she'd sternly corrected him: "We are not messengers. We are *couriers*. We serve an important function. Our clients are counting on us, and not incidentally, they're paying for being able to count on us. We never let them down."

He spotted the green street sign for Obrigato Drive in his headlights and turned right. His car bumped along the rough pavement. It hadn't been patched or resurfaced in a while and he had to avoid potholes. This was a strange part of town, an older neighborhood, kind of rural looking and more run-down than some of the well-kept suburban neighborhoods he'd already driven through. There were lots of trees and shrubbery. It kind of reminded him of the area upstate where he'd grown up, about which he had decidedly mixed feelings. He'd decided he preferred living here in the city, with its tall buildings and all those people on the street. It was different and exciting. This less urbanized section of town did not appeal to him.

Curtis happily considered his developing game plan. Mrs. Smithers had urged him to go ahead and get his GED. A kid who'd never finished high school, she cautioned, wasn't going anywhere. She'd already given him the information about classes at the local school to prepare him for the exam. He was a smart guy, she told him, with lots of potential. With the proper prep, he'd have no trouble passing the test. Then he could apply for Community College and after a year or two could transfer to the University. She made it all sound so easy. She asked him: what was he interested in pursuing?

He'd thought about that. Even though he hadn't finished high school, he'd always been pretty good with numbers.

Maybe, she said, he might like learning to be an accountant. There were plenty of opportunities for a good one. Why, he could even learn some bookkeeping with her on the job if he showed any aptitude.

Aptitude. Curtis loved those words she used. They made everything sound full of promise. *Potential. Opportunity.* Nobody had ever talked like that to him in Bartontown.

But to start with, what she needed was a courier "out on the scene." The fact he had his own car made that possible.

How lucky could a guy be?

* * * *

The rain seemed much lighter suddenly. Maybe it was because he was under all those trees, or maybe it was really letting up. Some rays of morning light were starting to peek through the leaves and break the darkness.

Obrigato Drive dead-ended, three small streets branching out from it. He could read the large rustic wooden signs from left to right: Mourning Dove Lane. Scrub Jay Way. Mockingbird Lane.

Almost there!

There was a row of mailboxes along the turnaround and Curtis could quickly see why. The three bird streets were rutted gravel roads, just driveways really, shrouded in foliage that concealed the homes at the end of them. He turned his car onto Mockingbird Lane, which curved around through an overgrown thatch of bushes and trees. He could make out the lights of a house about a hundred feet in.

He glanced down at the large important-looking manila envelope on the seat next to him. This was one of the coolest features of his job, the famous and important people they serviced. This envelope bore the return address of what had to be a *very* prestigious lawyer. Curtis had already seen the billboards all over town with the guy's face and name. Mrs. Smithers had said Mr. Applegate was a *major* client and he should expect to be picking up a lot of *vital documentation* from him, just as he had done this morning from Mr. Applegate's associate.

Mrs. Smithers just had a way of making everything sound important, even glamorous.

Branches swiped against the car as he crunched and bumped his way through the gravel, puddles and mud of Mockingbird Lane. The road opened to a turnaround in front of a low one-story house with attached carport. The lights in the house glowed golden amber, a small bit of warmth cutting through the dark blue coldness of the morning.

Curtis brought the car to a halt, killed the engine, grabbed the envelope, and opened the car door. The turnaround had been blacktopped but that was years ago, and it had fallen into disrepair, with missing and broken hunks. There was no rain coming down, but he saw he was going to have to carefully negotiate his way around the dirt and mud puddles. It wouldn't do to deliver an important set of documents with his shoes or pants legs all covered in mud. He had the image of Smithers Courier Services to uphold.

There were three low concrete steps leading to the front door, and he noticed the door itself was ajar. The lights came through the crack in the doorway.

He didn't see a doorbell, so he knocked on the door.

"Hello!" he announced smartly, as he had been taught. "Courier service!"

The door nudged open with a slight squeak.

I'll be glad to get this one over with, he thought. *I don't like this part of town so much. Kind of weird vibes around here. The rest of the day will be better. The rain's stopping, the sun will come out, and I'll be driving around the part of the city I'm starting to know. Maybe there'll even be time for me to get my application in for the GED class and start fixing up my room.*

Yes sir, things are really looking up. The rest of the day is going to be great.

Curtis knocked again and said "Hello?" The door pushed open a little further. He ventured a couple of steps over the threshold.

The day was not going to be great.

TWO

If the guard was being especially careful and aware with his present charge, it was to be understood. He was no stranger to big guys or dangerous guys but this inmate, damn, if he'd been any bigger he'd be real estate. So, the guard kept a careful distance and a vigilant eye on him, and a hand on his baton, as he conducted him through the passage to the security door.

He need not have worried. Had he been more attuned to the man's body language, he might have gotten a clue: this was a man finally deeply at peace with himself, more so than he had ever been in his entire life.

His name was Sylvester, although nobody called him that. His employer and coworkers referred to him as Tiny, and he was fine with that. He'd found his place and his calling with them; it was his world and his life work.

His work was, you might say, cleanup and disposal, and he'd discovered he was really, really good at it. He'd been highly instrumental in the astronomical rise of his boss, one Yancey Rybus, to the top of his profession: undisputed dominance of the drug market throughout his entire metropolitan area.

Right now, as the result of a recent unfortunate encounter, both he and his boss were in custody, but that was of no matter. He knew that Yancey was smart enough and connected enough to get himself out.

If he himself ended up staying behind bars, as he had come to assume, that was all right, too. After a lifetime of unbearable inner rage, he'd finally found a peace that surpassed understanding, and it wasn't going away. It was worth the price. He was pretty sure nobody would ever understand, but for the first time, he had the most priceless gift a human being could possess: his mind and his soul were at rest.

Why he was being led to a visitors' room, he wasn't quite sure. He hadn't spoken to anybody and did not intend to do so. He'd refused to see the lawyer that had been sent to see him twice before, but this time the lawyer had insisted. So here he was, doing his best to fit onto a chair on a drab, harshly lit room across from a stranger in a dark suit. He crossed his arms and stared placidly at the man.

"I know you don't wish to talk with me, Mr. Famoaana. I'm not going to ask you to say a word to me, if that's your preference, but if I could get you to listen for just a few minutes, it would be appreciated. I'm here on behalf of your employer. He recognizes your loyalty and service and is highly grateful to you." The man opened a leather portfolio that lay on the table in front of him, took out a sheet of paper, and slid it across the table. "He has one proposition to put before you—one last favor, you could say. Can you just hear me out?"

Tiny remained impassive and simply stared across the table. The man in the suit took that as a cue to continue. Tiny took in his words, impassive like a great stone monument. Finally, he cast his gaze down at the sheet and slowly, carefully, perused it.

* * * *

The same gentleman in the expensive dark suit, now sitting across the table from another figure in orange prison scrubs, couldn't help considering the irony in the scene. He hadn't felt fright in the presence of that absolute mountain of a man earlier this morning, but this meeting was different. He considered the irony: he was the one who could get up and walk out of this room when he pleased, and yet he was the one who was feeling intimidated and trying his best not to show any sign of it.

The man in prison garb was every bit as confident and frightening in here as he would have been outside. He was Yancey Rybus, the notorious Ice Man himself, still kingpin of his entire city. He might indeed be even more dangerous inside, since he was desperate to maintain that control despite the recent events that had brought him here. If he'd harbored suspicions to the point of paranoia before this, he had even more reason to mistrust everyone around him now, even his hand-picked attorney.

One concern remained a constant, now as before: displeasing Yancey Rybus was something to be avoided at all costs.

The gentleman in the suit felt a certain sense of relief that on his daily visit today he had brought reasonably good news. Nobody ever wanted to bring the Ice Man bad news.

Rybus sat back, arms folded, looking for all the world like he was holding court back in his customary headquarters above his nightclub. He maintained his infamous composure, never showing anger or even raising his voice.

"So, Randall, bring me up to date on what's been going on. How soon am I going to be getting out of here?"

"It's safe to say you'll be out of here shortly, Mr. Rybus. The wheels are in motion. I facilitated our friend's plea agreement with the prosecutor this morning."

Randall could, for a rare moment, read his employer's expression. It didn't need to be said aloud: *he actually spoke? That would be a first.*

"It was a written document, nothing verbal. He looked it over, listened to the explanation, and signed it. I'm confident he fully understands what it states in full: that he acted on his own initiative in all the incidents, that you had no part in them and no knowledge of them. The bottom line is that it's sufficient to exonerate you from all the remaining charges against you."

Rybus nodded, sitting in thought for a long moment.

"He's always been a cipher, Randall. True enough, he's always been dependable, but I've never *understood* him, which is why I had some hesitancy about this plan. Of course I'm happy it's working out, despite my misgivings, but I still must wonder why. *Why* would he do that?"

Randall shrugged. "His loyalty is singular."

"That would seem to be the case. But up to now he's simply been silent, just doing his time, refusing to commit. He wouldn't implicate anyone, but he wouldn't affirm or deny anything he might have done either. Until now. He's going down for a long, long time, maybe for life. He's not worried about his safety, that's for sure. Who in their right mind is going to fuck with him? He's got no family ties so no concerns there. But tell me, Randall, what's the upside? What's he get out of this?"

"He listened to reason when it was presented to him. Certainly, the DA was happy to accept the plea. It clears everything up nice and neatly, and it is, after all, an election year when everyone wants smooth sailing, no snags, no controversies. It's a happy solution for everyone."

Rybus brought his palms together and smiled wryly. "I suppose we should simply accept he's taken on the sins of the world."

"And this also addresses, in detail, the matter of our, um, *other* friend's involvement," Randall continued. "It assumes full culpability for the incident for which *he's* being held as well, so he's also exonerated. It was stipulated that his weapon was taken, without his knowledge, wiped clean after the crime in question, and returned surreptitiously. Consequently, there will be no reason to continue to hold him any longer either. He, and his associate who was arrested along with him, will be released."

"That's going to mess with his head when they tell him. I wish I could see it. I still don't totally understand how and why this worked out. But no matter, if it comes to pass. Just as long as I get out before him."

"You can count on it. He'll have no idea what's up until the moment he's sprung. And we're ready for that moment."

"There remains one major problem that's a matter of some concern to me, Randall. That final stumbling block, if you will, that we discussed earlier."

The lawyer knew exactly the remaining problematic individual to which Rybus referred. A different approach would be called for there, but he had it covered.

"That solution," Randall said smoothly, "has been put into motion as well."

The Ice Man allowed himself a slight smile. He never allowed himself to be totally at ease; nothing was ever 100% sure, after all. But it was nice when things *seemed* to be falling into place as planned.

THREE

"I think you know what to do with this," Barclay Vickers said to the two younger men standing nearby. Antoine and Alex looked so similar, they could have been brothers. Hell, for all Barclay knew or cared, they *were* brothers. He didn't have any interest in the personal stories of the men who worked for him. He just needed to know he could depend on them, and so far he'd been able to depend on them quite well.

In fact, they were cousins, and both delighted to be taken under his wing. They both nodded gravely. One of them–was it Alex?–said, "We'll take care of it, Mr. Vickers."

They bent down, one on each end of the unmoving body of the kid on the pavement, and picked him up, lugging him farther back behind the alley with a learned expertise that was becoming second nature to them both.

He hoped this would be the last one for now. This "maintenance" was a drag on his time.

Barclay re-holstered his automatic underneath his jacket and turned to walk back up the alley to the street. The two younger kids waiting out on the corner stood stock still, wide eyed, looking so scared that if he said "Boo" at them, they might fall over or take off running. They were just barely into their teens. Made him feel downright old. But that was the best age to start teaching them, Barclay believed. Get them young and train them right.

"What's your name, young man?" he asked the taller one.

"Kenny," the kid stammered.

"Well, Kenny," Barclay drawled with a smile, clapping a hand on the kid's shoulder, "this is your lucky day, 'cause I'm giving you this corner now. You and your partner here, what's your name, son?" He turned to look at the other kid.

"B-Bodie."

"B-B-Bodie it is." Barclay turned back to Kenny, still smiling, his hand remaining on his shoulder. "You, and your man Bodie to back you up, you now got the responsibility for this corner. What do you think of that?"

"Great," Kenny said eagerly. "Yeah. Sure." He glanced over at his companion, who seemed to beam from being called a *man*.

"The thing is, that word *responsibility* I mentioned. I take that very seriously." Barclay reached his free hand into his jacket pocket and pulled out a roll of bills, holding it up in front of the kid's eyes. "Every day the numbers better be right. No shorts. Understood?"

He looked back and forth at both kids as they energetically nodded their heads. He re-pocketed the roll and finally removed his hand from Kenny's shoulder. "You know how this works out here, right?"

"Sure. Watched Chazz all the time. He was teachin' us so we could help him out."

"Uh huh. I hope Chazz didn't teach you anything about keeping a few stray bills in your pocket. Because, as you see, that was a problem for him."

"No, no, nope. Nothin' like that. Had no idea he was doin' shit like that, honest."

"You know, I believe you, else I wouldn't be promoting you like this. I'll be keeping an eye on both of you. Maybe this is a steppingstone to better things, *if* you play it straight. Now, I'm going to go over the routine that you always stick to and a few quick rules. You listen carefully, then if you got any questions, you ask them, and then I leave you on your own. Got that?"

It went smoothly. It usually did. Barclay liked it when that happened. It was important to bring his boss back home to a tight, sweetly running operation.

FOUR

The man behind the wheel of the oil truck had a red beard flecked with grey and a brown tee shirt stretched over an enormous belly. Both beard and shirt were smeared with spots of barbecue sauce from the two double cheeseburgers he'd just gulped down at his last stop, washed down by a large chocolate milkshake.

That sharp pain that had started running up his left arm worried him.

With an uncomfortable belch, he resolved to himself that this was it, that now he was going to start taking his doctor's admonishments seriously and change his diet. Maybe, in fact, he'd better cut the day short and give his doc a call. He was glad he'd decided to take the arterial road alongside the freeway; traffic here was light, and he was making good time. He gunned the accelerator, trying to ignore the growing pain in his chest and left arm.

* * * *

The prisoner transport van wasn't exactly a stretch limo ride.

It was in bad need of a suspension overhaul. The bench Lydia sat on was hard and she jounced around as if in a brain-rattling theme park ride. She stared down at the other end of the enclosure where another woman, in olive drab scrubs like herself, bumped around on the bench across from her.

Whoever came up with these fucking prison uniforms? Pretty funny. Reminds me of the last time I had to go to the ER. We look like doctors or nurses or something.

The other prisoner was just a girl, really. She looked about nineteen or twenty. Like Lydia, she wore shackles connected by chains to each other and to the chain around her waist. The girl glared at her across the aisle from the back of the van. Her eyes still simmered with anger and resentment, but Lydia could see the signs. They were well on the way to just looking dead.

That's not gonna be me.

There were no windows, so she had no idea where they were or how far they'd gone or how much farther until they got to the Costa County facility. That was the jurisdiction where she was going to be arraigned and tried.

She was looking forward to this. *Stay stoic*, she told herself, *take this one step at a time. Keep your eyes on the prize.*

She idly fingered the little silver disc that hung on a short thin chain around her neck. She'd conned the prison authorities that it was a religious medallion, the only kind of personal jewelry they allowed inmates to keep inside. Well, it did have what looked like a Madonna on one side and her initials, LM, on the reverse.

In reality the female figure on the disc was no saintly figure, and Lydia was about as far away from religious as you could get. She didn't rely on any fairy tales in the sky; the only thing she'd ever been able to rely on was Lydia. But the necklace did hold a special meaning to her. It had been given to her, in happier times, by the man she despised most in the world right now, the one who had some major payback coming for his betrayal.

She considered how important she really was in the order of things. The most feared and dangerous individual in her city, the stone-cold man so elusive and slippery that it was said he made Teflon seem like Velcro, had to have her on his mind right now.

The greatest danger to Yancey Rybus was not one of those big nasty gangsters but a woman named Lydia Montgomery, and nobody was more aware of this fact than she was.

It all came down to a question of how she was going to use that fact to her best advantage.

When she had been tight with Rybus's number two, Theo Charles, she'd been privy to information, all kinds of information. Theo and the rest underestimated just how aware and perceptive she'd been, picking up a snippet of private conversation here, grabbing a glance at a piece of confidential material there, and she'd put a lot together. She would, she sometimes told herself, have been one hell of a private investigator. Or even a police detective.

The thought of herself as a cop made her shake her head.

As it turned out, perhaps Lydia hadn't hidden her curiosity as well as she thought. She'd never fathomed the reasons that Theo one day had just cut her loose. Possibly he'd just gotten tired of her. He cut her what he considered to be a very generous departure gift along with a clear message: take the money, don't come back, keep your mouth shut.

It further turned out Theo was nowhere near the genius he'd set himself up to be. He'd have been smarter to remove her from the equation altogether. Fortunately for Lydia, he hadn't.

So, Lydia had plotted her revenge, which included an even bigger payday for herself. Things hadn't worked out according to the plot, ending up with her accomplice dead and Lydia being arrested. Brick, the big dummy, wasn't any unsurmountable loss; she considered it collateral damage. The arrest charges were minor, compared to the bargaining chip she held with her extensive knowledge of the entire Rybus organization. Prosecutors on several levels were salivating at the prospect of breaking open the drug operation. She would skate out of custody with a sweetheart deal while Yancey, Theo and their whole crew would be put out of commission and neutralized as a threat to her.

But there'd be ample opportunities for further personal enrichment as well. For one thing, she was sure she could wangle a lucrative book deal. True crime books were the rage. A movie or streaming TV deal was not out of the question either.

Best of all, she'd also be free to track down the cool million that she'd squeezed out of Rybus.

That cool million, she was sure, had been intercepted by Theo in his attempt to rip off his own boss, and in the process kill Brick. He'd tried to palm it all off with an elaborate fairy tale about a guy named Musgrave, a master manipulator who'd stolen Yancey's money, but that was clearly bullshit. She was positive Theo had the money salted away safely, and not far away.

That was where that one little unforeseen development had come up, resulting in a body found in the tailgate of an abandoned car in a small town downstate, in Costa County, that traced back to Lydia.

There was no way Lydia could deal her way out of a murder rap. Even Lana Morvan, the high-profile attorney she'd brought in on her case, agreed with that, though she was convinced she could mount an effective defense, and they were in the process of doing so. But it meant that it was in Lydia's best interests to withdraw her offers of information and clam up.

Lana concurred, telling her that they would deal with the murder charges first. Once those were out of the way (and she seemed confident they would be), everything else could be back on the table again.

Lydia wasn't sure how her attorney could be so confident, considering the evidence in the case included bullets in the body from her Glock and her fingerprints all over the car. But that's why she was going through the money she'd gotten from Theo to have Lana on the case. Lana, she had to admit, had an impressive track record with skating the guilty. Once this was over, *if* she was free, she'd be starting at square one, financially speaking, but the potential payoff would be a *lot* more than what she had now. It was an investment.

From the first day she'd arrived in lockup, she was ferociously angry and craving vengeance. Displaying a buzzed, bright yellow scalp, seething venom without any concern for who caught it, she'd instantly gotten the tag as someone to avoid. It was a good move. Through her time in custody so far, that hadn't completely prevented her from getting into a few scrapes, but she'd held her own in those and other inmates had stopped bothering her. Lydia wasn't worried about Rybus getting to her inside. She wasn't really worried about anybody messing with her down in Costa County either. In fact, she figured it was a blessing to have her case heard down there, where she'd probably mostly have to deal with meth heads in the lockup population and Lana could make short work of those hick prosecutors in the courtroom.

She continued to work the medallion between her fingers as her mind churned. She was a survivor. It was all going to work out. Nobody was going to get away with trying to take advantage of her and she looked forward to taking them down first chance she got.

Her reverie of bile was interrupted, rudely and abruptly, by a deafening impact against the side of the van. Lydia and her travel companion were hurled out of their seats and tossed and spun until she lost any sense of orientation. Up and down and sideways had all changed places. The details in the darkened van whirled around her like some murky kaleidoscope. She felt like a chew-toy doll being tossed around by a big dog, jerking on the end of her chains in every which direction. It was when she felt a sharp pain around her temple that the darkness started getting darker and things shut down.

FIVE

"Where the hell are we, anyway? I've never even seen this neighborhood before, have you? This doesn't even feel like the city!"

Detective Leon Simpkins yawned and stretched in the passenger's seat of the sedan. "As a matter of fact, Arthur, I have indeed been here before. Strange little forgotten neighborhood. Used to be a private estate. The family fell into scandal and bad times, the property went to ruin, got seized for taxes, was parceled up and sold. People jumped on them for cheap and kept the kind of woodsy rural look. The properties are smaller than they look from the street because of the trees and foliage and so forth up front. But the homes themselves are small, with no back yards to speak of, since they're right up against the hills and the county line. They've pretty much remained as they were when they first built on the subdivided lots. There were some zoning issues and other legal nonsense that prevented resale and redevelopment. Word is that's in the process of being changed by the wheeler-dealers. My guess is, give it another year or two, and this is all going to be hot real estate with high rise condos."

Art Dowdy whistled softly as he followed the GPS instructions and turned onto Obrigato Drive, the car in a virtual crawl as he looked around like a lost kid. "I did not expect that lecture, Professor. So how did you become such an expert on all this?"

"A while back I was looking into possibly buying some investment property, so I did a little look into areas around town. Wish I could have gotten in on this one, just for the promise of a quick resale when the developers start coming out of the woodwork. See those magnificent old trees along the street? Oaks. Sycamores. Beautiful. Appreciate them, Arthur, while you can. How much you want to bet they'll all be cut down and uprooted in another couple years?"

"Yeah, the damn trees, between that and the rain, can't see shit around here! Are you sure this is the right way? Could this GPS be screwed up? Where the hell is this Mockingbird Lane?"

"Art, is everything okay? This is more words than I've heard from you in a week."

It was true, Dowdy was notoriously taciturn and dour. His nickname on the unit was the Mortician, a moniker he didn't greatly appreciate. He sighed, still anxiously sweeping his gaze in every direction.

"I guess my mind's wandering. A little difficulty with my daughter. No big deal."

"She's gotta be, what, sixteen now?"

"Fifteen. She came in *way* late last night. The ex is on the warpath and called me early this morning, wants me to have a talk with her."

Leon patted him on the shoulder in mock sympathy. He had a son and daughter of his own. "Tough age. It'll work out."

They made quite the disparate pair, as just about everybody at Personal Crimes had remarked at one time or other: the tall, handsome, personable Black guy and the short, sour-faced ash-blond guy. Their nicknames on the unit were the Emcee and the Mortician. Nothing, it would seem, in common, except for the job. Maybe that's why it worked. They'd been partners for some time and both they and their Lieutenant seemed fine with keeping it that way.

Art exhaled in exasperation. "What the hell! So, this street just dead ends? Where are we supposed to go?"

"Take it easy, partner. Look: street signs, little side streets. I thought you were a *detective*. Shouldn't you be noticing things like that?"

"Leon, you know I love you, right? But..." Art extended the middle finger of his right hand. Leon grinned.

"You did happen to notice the black and white parked there, or did you miss that too? Pull up next to them."

"Fuck you very much, I did see him."

One of the uniforms was next to the police cruiser, waving them to pull over alongside. Leon rolled down his window. He vaguely recognized the patrolman, a blondish long-timer named Radley, and greeted him with a nod.

"Easier to park out here, Detectives. Leave some room for the vans. It's just a short walk down the driveway to the house."

"So the techs haven't arrived yet?"

"Nope. Coroner and SID are both on their way. The kid who called it in is still in there. He's, like, still in shock. He's just been sitting on the stoop since we got here."

"A kid, you say?"

"He looks like a teenager. Just a warning, he blew chunks all over the front of the house. It was pretty bad." Radley shook his head. "Got a probie partner I left back there with him. She got quite an eyeful inside the scene too. Kinda shook her up as well."

"Lovely," Leon muttered, mostly to himself.

Art turned the car around the narrow circle and pulled it to the curb.

The wet gravel crunched underfoot as they carefully threaded their way under the overgrown bushes and tree limbs, keeping an eye out for any possible evidence they might need to point out to the crime lab techs when they arrived. That didn't look promising. Not much of a chance of tire tracks or footprints and nothing obvious dropped on the ground.

"At least the rain's stopped," Leon observed. His voice broke the damp, heavy stillness of the air.

"My shoes are gonna be a mess," Art said.

They approached the lone address on Mockingbird Lane, their eyes sweeping the premises. It was a one-story wooden house, not much more than a cottage, with three steps leading up to a small, covered porch. Lights still burned through the windows and the partially open door. A carport had been built onto the side of the structure, a slab of concrete covered by a wooden canopy. Two aging vehicles sat on the slab: a beat-up Chevy Blazer and an old sports car that had seen better days.

"Wouldn't have expected to see that," Leon murmured, pointing at the orangey-red sportster. "Porsche 944. Must be at least twenty-five years old."

"Every now and then you see that," Art replied quietly. "Someone picks one up because it was once a fashionable status car and now it's cheap because it got neglected and went to shit. Probably always needs some work or other."

It was still odd to see it sitting next to the Blazer, which couldn't have been much younger itself.

There wasn't much more to see in the small front yard, a blacktop turn-around that had gotten chewed up over time and encroached upon by untended grass and foliage. An older Toyota, likely the kid's car, was parked to the far side of the turnaround. Somewhere nearby, a dog was barking.

"There's our boy," Leon nodded with his head.

The uniform, a young female officer, was crouching next to him, her hand on his shoulder. The kid sat motionless on the top step of the porch, head down between his knees, his arms laced around his legs. He was gripping a manila envelope in both hands. He heard the crackle of their approaching footsteps and jerked his head up, his eyes wide. The officer stood up, acknowledging them.

They had their IDs and badges out as they came closer.

"It's okay," Leon said reassuringly. "We're detectives. How are you doing, are you all right?"

"Oh my God," the kid said, returning his gaze to the ground. "Oh my God." He took two deep breaths, more like gasps, and said, "I never saw nothing like, like that." Even wrapped around himself like that, he was visibly trembling as if shivering from the cold.

"Watch your step," the officer said, pointing down at the glop on the cement stoop.

"Have you been inside yet?" Art asked her, pulling out a pair of nitrile gloves from his jacket pocket. He noted the name on her badge read OCHIDA.

"Just inside the doorway," she replied hesitantly. "That was enough. I didn't want to risk compromising the crime scene, and I figured it was more important to stay with him."

She looked like a probie, new on the job, and more than a little uneasy. Art figured whatever was in there might have been almost as shocking to her as to the kid. The difference was that she'd get accustomed to this kind of thing pretty quickly. Hopefully the kid would never have to.

Can't wait to see this one.

He stepped around them towards the front door. He eyed the large hunk of puke on the stoop and diligently stepped around that as well. He figured he could make a pretty good guess at what the kid had eaten and that it hadn't been all that long before.

"I'm sorry about that," the kid stammered. "I couldn't help it."

Art displayed his prowess at multi-tasking, slipping on the gloves as he did his dance around the mess. He gingerly pushed the door open just enough to step inside, looking around attentively to ascertain what he might need to avoid for the crime scene techs.

Leon bent down to talk to the kid. "So, tell me what brought you here this morning."

"I, I was delivering this." Shakily, he held up the envelope. "I'm, I'm a courier. For Smithers Courier Services."

Leon, who had also pulled on a pair of the same kind of nitrile gloves, reached out to take it. For a moment the kid wouldn't loosen his grasp.

"Let me take a look, okay?" Leon said quietly. The kid opened his hands. The envelope was legal size and thick, probably holding at least a dozen pages. It was addressed to Halley Donner at One Mockingbird Lane. The return address read The Law Offices of Marshall Applegate Esq.

Leon shook his head. He knew the name.

"Okay, so you came here to deliver this and what happened?"

"I, I didn't know the door was, was open. I knocked and, and announced myself. And the door pushed open so I, I stuck my head in and, oh my God there they were."

"Leon," Art called back. "Think you'd better come in."

"Hang on, okay? I'll be right back." Leon handed the envelope to Ochida and asked her to stay with the kid.

The door opened directly into a low ceilinged, wood-paneled living room that extended to the right. A powerful mixture of aromas hit Leon: wood polish, stale cigarette smoke and beer, the lingering odor of onions… and other, more malevolent ones. Blood and decomp.

Art had taken out a handkerchief and was holding it over his nose. "Sorry, I shoulda warned you. This is a ripe one."

The window had been covered by some kind of patterned sheet strung over a long curtain rod, but it had come loose, allowing the morning daylight to mix with the amber incandescent light of a still-burning metal floor lamp. The result was an eerie colored cast over the room.

The two figures lay back on the blood-spattered sofa, their heads snapped back unnaturally over the top of the seat back. Both the man and the woman wore Pendleton shirts, now stained dark with blood in the chest areas, over jeans and boots. They leaned against one another in an unsettling pose, shoulders together, his right arm resting across her left, heads nearly touching. Both mouths gaped open in faces that no longer invited recognition. They had both been shot directly into the mouth, probably after having first been shot in the chest.

The predominant theme in the tableau was blood, lots and lots of blood.

"I don't blame the kid," muttered Art quietly.

Leon's gaze swept the room.

"What are you thinking, partner?"

"One killer. Good chance they knew him—or her. There's one chair that's been drawn up across the coffee table from them." Leon indicated the wooden chair that stood askew, pushed back away from the low wooden table. "There're two other matching chairs still tucked away over there in the corner." He pointed to beer bottles in front of the two vics. "I'd say we can rule out a home invasion. They were all sitting and talking when the killing began."

Art nodded. "Cold as ice. Came as a surprise to the both of them. The shooter was able to shoot them each in the chest first, maybe even not even getting up out of the chair, knock 'em back against the sofa...*then* get up and finish them off up closer."

Leon nodded gravely. "Pretty cold indeed. And efficient. Put a bullet in each of their heads, up close and personal." He pointed around with two fingers. "There's no drink in front of where that third person sat. Maybe the visitor showed up unexpectedly, but in any case, they weren't being particularly social. This was some kind of serious business."

The unfinished wooden table was littered with various knick-knacks along with a closed laptop computer and a large glass ashtray filled with butts. One additional item caught Art's attention. It was a hinged-top box, of polished wood—darker, much nicer wood than the table on which it lay—that lay open on its side near the bodies. A fine dusting of white powder lay inside the box and on the table around it.

"Maybe they were using something different to be sociable."

"Or maybe that was what they were talking about. Maybe whatever was in that box left with the killer."

There was a closet off the living room, with the door open. A few objects had tumbled off the shelves into the room: round things that looked like they were made of white foam rubber, longer items that looked like they were made of plaster. To the left was an open passageway, through which they could see the kitchen. That probably also led to the bedroom and the back door.

"Leon, have you noticed," Art noted, taking a few steps farther back, "the carpet's noticeably wet in places. Look here, and here, and especially over there by the door."

"You're right, Arthur, so it is."

"Whoever came in, maybe they didn't take off their raincoat or whatever, just dripped all over the rug, and then walked around a bit before they left." He leaned towards the kitchen. "Whole bunch of dishes in the sink back there."

The one time he'd get on a yakking streak was when they were at a crime scene. He'd go into something akin to a free association thing, bumping down some dead ends and backing out again, gradually pulling out shards of observations that would begin to fall into place. It was a good sign. Leon had learned, when Art got a head of steam up, you let him run with it.

And Art was off and running. "So, the vics had finished dinner. From the stale stink of things, I'm guessing burgers with lots of onions. They're kicking back with their beers. Maybe they got the blow out for a toot. I'm guessing it's early evening. I bet that TV was on." He jerked a thumb at the flat screen mounted kitty-corner past the windows, then pointed to the remote lying askew on the table. "Their visitor interrupts them. It's someone they know, so they let 'em in. The TV gets turned off. Visitor pulls up a seat. Doesn't get a beer. Maybe *that's* when the blow comes out. No. Strike that." He pointed to the open closet. "It got taken out in a hurry. All that crap got knocked out on the floor. If they'd brought it out for themselves or for a friendly social snort, wouldn't you think they'd have taken the time to do it neatly? I'm thinking the shooter hunted around for it and found it after blowing them both away. Maybe actively looking for it, maybe just, you know, serendipity while looking for something else. They were looking for *something*, which they may have found pretty quick. Clearly didn't take any time to straighten up, didn't even close the door shut on the way out." Art took a deep breath and kept turning his head, looking all around the house.

Leon had known his partner long enough to sense when he was coming down from his rant and it was safe to turn it back into a dialogue. "So if there was a box full of powder, why not just take the whole thing? Why take the time to empty it?"

Art screwed his mouth up into a wry grin and tilted his head. "Maybe he—"

"Or she."

"Or *she* was carrying something else they found and needed to put it in something easier to carry? Just freestyling here, you know?"

It was all conjecture at this point. Forensic evidence would help them unravel the tale. But Art's "freestyles" now and then afforded them some insights instead of a journey down a blind alley.

They heard the crunch of tires on gravel.

"Sounds like SID is here. Now it's a party."

They stepped outside to greet the two Scientific Investigation Division techs, who had parked their van just before the broken blacktop apron. Officer Ochida was already helping the courier kid to his feet and leading him off to the side out of their way. The techs, a man and woman in their standard blue windbreakers, cases and kits in tow, nodded to the detectives as they mounted the steps.

Leon swept an arm pointing to the ground. "Watch your step. The puke's not part of the crime scene, it's from the witness." Both of them made a face as they took giant steps to avoid the gunk. They stopped to pull on shoe coverings and gloves before plunging into the house.

More gravel crunching: the County Medical Examiner's van, pulling to a halt behind the SID vehicle. Exiting the vehicle: the man with the basset hound face, the venerable Mickey Kendrick. They had the A team in on this one.

"Detectives," he intoned as he trudged up the blacktop with his kit in hand. "Lovely day." He noticed the vomit and also did a two-step around it, stopped at the threshold and stared into the living room scene. "Maybe not for everybody."

"Let us know when we can come back in," Leon said to the gathered multitude carefully crowding into the house.

"Half hour," one of the techs called back. "Then you can do a walk-through."

Leon turned his attention to the messenger, who was now standing next to Officer Ochida a short distance away, but still looking shell shocked. They stepped down to the blacktop and approached the kid.

Ochida handed Leon the envelope.

"I'm supposed to deliver that," the kid murmured. "I'm a bonded courier. I can't give it to anybody else."

"We can bring it back and explain everything," Leon said gently. "Your employer will understand, given the circumstances. Okay?"

The kid looked up at him. There still wasn't much light in his eyes as he struggled to process what had happened. "I, I guess that would be okay, huh?"

"Son, is there someone you know who could come pick you up, maybe drive your car home?"

"I don't really know anyone here. I just, I just moved here."

"What's your name?"

"Curtis. Curtis Stryker. That's Stryker with a *y*."

With a Y. Well, there was a little bit of light coming on. That was a good sign. "Where do you live, Curtis?"

Stryker cited an address. "I just moved here from Bartontown. Mrs. Smithers, she's who I work for, rented me a room."

"Okay, how about I call her and see if she can come pick you up? You shouldn't be driving right now."

"She's gonna think I screwed up," the kid intoned, not quite focusing his gaze on Leon. "Can't make her come all the way over here. I need this job."

Leon laid a hand on his shoulder. "Curtis, she is not going to think you screwed up. I'll explain you just walked into a terrible crime scene. It wasn't your fault. You did absolutely nothing wrong. Now, do you know her phone number?"

He stammered out a number and Leon tapped it into his phone. An officious receptionist picked up with a brisk, "Smithers Courier Services." Leon asked to be put through to Mrs. Smithers, identifying himself but not his reason for calling.

Cara Smithers' voice gave her away as an inveterate chain smoker. She expressed almost motherly concern for her young charge and told Leon she and her assistant would be on their way to Mockingbird Lane in short order to pick up Curtis and his car.

Art stepped up to them and said, "Let's check out the rest of the property, Leon. With all the rain I doubt we're going to get any footprints or tire prints."

Leon waved the envelope at him. "I'm going to go drop this in the car and I'll join you."

He walked back down Mockingbird Lane, around the two vans, noting that his partner was right: the rains had removed any chance of evidence of entry or exit. But maybe the shooter had come around the side of the house or into the car port.

Officer Radley was talking to someone who had pulled up their car, directing them away. They pulled around and drove back down Obrigato. He looked up as Leon opened the side door to their car and dropped the envelope, label side down, onto the seat.

"Damned lookie-loos," he said, shaking his head. "This neighborhood, it figures."

"Not sure what you mean," Leon replied, shutting the car door. "Looks pretty peaceful around here."

"It would look that way, wouldn't it? We've had a half dozen calls out here in the past year or so, all to Jack Donner." He jerked a thumb back down Mockingbird Lane.

Leon recalled the name on the package from the lawyer. "What do you know about them?"

"Jack and Halley Donner. Jack's a low life. You'd think living here, removed from your neighbors, there wouldn't be any trouble, but their neighbors called in complaints. Loud music, louder arguments. Working on his car late in the night. We busted Jack for possession once, likely could have done it more often if we'd had more probable cause. Got him once on possession of stolen property but he skated."

"It would seem sound travels pretty well in this area. Any idea who phoned in the complaints?"

"Nope, we just followed up on the calls."

"Have you tried to canvass any of the neighbors yet? Maybe somebody heard the shots last night."

"There've been two people driving through but neither of them live along here. If you'd like, my partner and I can start knocking on doors and asking."

Leon considered that and decided he'd rather that he and Art interviewed the neighbors. Maybe some of them knew something else about the victims that might be of help.

"I'd rather you kept the scene secure out here. But tell me more about the Donners."

"Not much more to tell. Jack was a suspect in a couple break-ins and thefts, and he did some dealing. As far as I know, he didn't hold any kind of regular job. Halley, she didn't seem to be involved in Jack's shit. She tended not to be around when we answered a complaint. I heard she had some kind of freelance business, selling stuff like cosmetics or oils or something online. I'm not sure about her."

"You said he did some dealing. Any chance that Jack was involved with some of the wrong people up the chain?"

Leon understood it was a perilous time to be dealing any kind of substances, with the Rybus organization currently ruptured and their top figures in custody. Yancey Rybus had run a tight ship, and while his drug businesses were rampant throughout the city, at least drug-related violence had been drastically reduced. Now all bets were off.

"Someone you might want to look into, a guy named Dougie Barn-feather. He's got something to do with the organization. Jack turned up in his company a couple times, or so I was told. Jack was a small timer but like a lot of knuckleheads, he didn't know how small time he was and was trying to social climb. Anyway, that's all I got."

Leon thanked Radley and told him to be on the lookout for Cara Smithers. He locked his car and headed back down the damp gravel driveway, ducking around the overgrown bushes on either side.

Art was standing in front of the house, hands in pockets. Leon could hear the dog barking in the background again.

"Gate to the yard's locked and there's a big dog on the other side. Doesn't look like anyone else has gone back there and I'm sure not going to. The cars are locked up tight. I don't think there was any entry or exit except through the front door."

"Well, let's see if we can take a look in yet."

The SID techs had quickly taped off the areas where they were working. One of them pointed to extra shoe coverings and gloves at the doorway and waved them in. They were busy photographing and fingerprinting surfaces, one along the open closet and the other along the table. Art and Leon slipped into the coverings and gloves. Mickey, hunched over the man's body on the sofa, looked up at them.

"Come on in and join the party. The main show must have been short and sweet. Looks as if they both got plugged in the chest from, oh, right over there." He gestured to the seat that had been pulled out across from them. "Then they each got one in the mouth up close and personal. I'm estimating this was last night, around maybe seven to nine. I can pin it down more when I get them back on the table." He pointed to the sofa next to the man, where a ragged leather wallet sat. "That was in his back pocket."

Leon took a few steps forward and picked it up carefully.

"Driver's license. John Wesley Donner. Credit card, expired date." He raised his eyebrows. "And about three hundred dollars in cash."

Art carefully stepped around the techs towards the passage to the back. They were all adept at the ballet involved with multiple investigators trying to stay out of each other's way at a crime scene. "I'd say the rest of the place hasn't been tossed, but it's kinda hard to tell. They weren't great housekeepers."

He stopped at the open closet. Its shelves were haphazardly packed with various items, some of which had spilled out onto the ground. They appeared to be medical items: foam neck collars, plaster arm casts that had been cut open. A pair of crutches were jammed into a corner of the closet.

"That looks like where the drug box came from," observed Leon. "Got pulled out in a hurry and took all this stuff with it."

"Someone was accident prone," mused Art.

Leon pointed to a shoe box that had also been knocked aside on the shelf and was now partly open. "Whoever it was, they only wanted whatever was in the wooden box, if they overlooked that." The box held unruly stacks of money in what looked like all manner of larger denominations.

"Not to mention the heat." Art pointed to another shelf, where a Glock automatic sat.

"These folks were careless, leaving money and weapons around like that. I'm not picking up that these were the sharpest tools in the shed."

Art stepped toward the kitchen. "It's like, what, twelve hours later, and it still reeks of onions in here. Phew." He passed a rack in the short hallway where a rifle and shotgun stood vertically. He peered into the stacks of dishes, still covered with food scraps, in the sink and on the counter, and grimaced. "Careless doesn't begin to describe it. Oink, oink. They just did not give a shit."

Leon peered into the small bedroom connected to the right. "One of them cared enough to make the bed, at least. It doesn't look like anyone's gone through anything in here."

Art carefully sidled to the door that led from the kitchen to the back yard. The dog's barking was louder from here. He flipped the dead bolt on the door and cautiously opened it. It was a small yard, mostly concrete with patches of grass and weeds. The dog stopped barking and perked up its ears at Art.

"There he is. Big white beast. He's on a chain under an overhang over there. At least he wasn't out in the rain all night."

"Better get Animal Control over here to take care of him. Or is it a her?"

"Forgive me if I'm not gonna get close enough to see." Art stepped back into the kitchen and relocked the bolt. "I'm guessing their visitor didn't come back here or out in the yard. But let the lab gang do their thing."

They devoted more time to perusing the closet and the living room, making note of things to call to the attention of the lab techs and for anything they felt should be taken for evidence, including the laptop, the money, and the drug box. Finally Art said, apparently trying out the idea to himself, "We should get out and talk to the neighbors while they're still around."

"Good idea, partner. Pick which side you want."

SIX

"Yeah, I'd hear all sorts of stuff coming from there now and then. But, you know, it's cool, never a major bother. I'm a musician, and I got my den acoustically paneled, so not only does none of my sound get out, but not much really gets in, you know?"

The "den" in which Art stood talking to Phineas Weingartner was in reality a converted garage, and it was full of instruments and recording equipment. Probably, Art reflected, Phineas had spent more on the equipment than on everything else in the house combined, including Phineas himself. The guy was one of those people to whom a comedian once remarked the sixties had been good, an aging hippie with long curly hair balding on top, vintage band-tour sweatshirt and jeans. Clearly it was more important to him to house his gear in the garage than his cars, a rusty vintage VW bus and an actual hearse that had been painted burnt orange and sat in the driveway. Phineas' property abutted the Donners, divided by a high redwood fence that had seen better days.

"I'm especially interested," Art continued patiently, notebook at the ready, "if you heard anything coming from there yesterday evening, say around seven to nine?"

"Oh, man, I was working on a new project. Ran out and grabbed a bag o' burgers and then worked right through past midnight. Had the headphones on, wouldn't't'a heard a thing."

"So," Art persisted, "you didn't hear or see anything from your neighbors?"

"Hey, it's live and let live, you know? I purposely keep myself sealed off from the nabes. This is a nice funky hood, the kind of place a cat like me is lucky to live, with all my music projects and such. Hear no evil, see no evil, you feel me?"

"Never any noise problems directed against you by any of your neighbors, then? Maybe there's somebody who likes to call in complaints?"

"Well, now that you mention it, used to be a little problem with the dowager princess who lives two doors over. She dropped a dime on me a couple times which is why I installed the acoustics." He gestured around the room at the speckled beige-grey panels that covered the ceiling and walls. "Never a peep since."

"You know your neighbors at all?" Art asked. "Or is that part of *live and let live*?"

"I'm not what you'd call social," Phineas drawled. "See one of 'em now and then coming or going, just nod hello. Mostly when they're driving out. These houses are pretty private, you know?"

"Any chance you might have heard anything about, oh I don't know, drug dealers or anything going on?"

Phineas got a huge grin across his bearded face. "Shit. Is that what this is all about? You tellin' me somebody got popped for dealing? Hey, nothin' I know anything about." He crossed his chest with both hands. "Only thing I ever partake of these days is, you know, natural wines and the noble weed from the Colina Street dispensary. Which is legal."

"Yes, sir," Art sighed. "I am aware that's legal now. I'm not asking if you yourself have done anything illegal, I'm asking if you're aware of anything going on that—"

"Like the poet said, good fences make good neighbors. I have nothin' to do with the locals and they got nothin' to do with me."

Art paused momentarily at the thought this guy knew poetry, at least Robert Frost. Would wonders never cease.

"Any chance you've got any kind of a security camera here, maybe one of those ones on the front door?"

"Nope. Never saw the need."

Art pocketed his notebook, deciding there was nowhere to go with this one. "Thank you, Mr. Weingartner, sorry to have taken up your time."

"Hey, while you're here, maybe you'd like to hear my most recent mix. Bet you'd like it. It's deep retro. You look about the right age—"

Art couldn't get out of the garage and back out to Obrigato Drive fast enough. He wondered if everybody on this street was nuts. Then he hoped that Leon was having better luck on the bird streets.

Leon, as it turns out, was discovering who'd called in the noise complaints.

* * * *

"My goodness, no," Helena Corkendale was telling Leon, her eyes sparkling happily. "Clarence and I don't own this property. We've rented it from Mr. Gale for, how long now, Clarence?"

Clarence Corkendale was a somewhat dourer presence, sitting gloomily in the maroon patterned easy chair with the wide padded arms, upon one of which his wife was perched. "Thirty-three years."

The two of them looked well into their seventies. Their house was small, neatly kept, but felt even smaller since it was filled with antique furniture.

While Helena seemed absolutely delighted to have a visitor call, Clarence looked as if he was counting the seconds until their visitor departed.

"Mr. Gale owns the three bird street properties and lives in the one on Mourning Dove. Or rather, he did. Unfortunately, he passed away recently."

"Rumors are," Clarence muttered, "his damned grandkids are going to sell off all the properties now."

"Oh, Clarence, *language* please. And those are just idle rumors. We've been able to stay here all these years, I can't believe they'd just throw us all out. We've not yet even met the grandsons." She turned back to Leon. "Are you sure I can't get you a cup of tea or a glass of lemonade, Detective?"

Leon, who was sitting in a similar overstuffed chair with matching maroon pattern, smiled. "You're very kind, Ma'am, but no thanks. I just have a few quick questions for you if you don't mind. Were you home yesterday evening, say around seven to nine or so?"

"Oh, yes. We hardly ever go out at night. We had an early dinner and were probably watching television. We get that streaming service with all the British mysteries that I love. We were watching the Inspector Cholmondeley Files. Have you ever watched that one?"

'I'm afraid not, Mrs. Corkendale." When Leon got home to his family at night, the very last things he wanted to encounter were more murders and mayhem.

"I think that actor Simon Wyre is just marvelous. He has such charm and confidence as the Inspector."

"Too handsome to be a real detective," snorted Clarence.

"Clarence!" Helena gestured towards their guest. Clarence actually harrumphed. "No offense, Constable. This Hollywood stuff, you understand. Don't you find it all unrealistic? They never get it right, do they?"

Leon covered his mouth with his hand to hide the smile and cleared his throat. "Well, police work is generally a little more tedious in real life, yes sir. But I'm afraid I'm not familiar with the show. Did either of you hear any unusual sounds coming from your neighbors over on Mockingbird Lane last night?"

Helena sighed heavily and rolled her eyes. "Oh, those people. Have they been at it again? I can't say I heard anything. It was raining fairly heavily and there was thunder. Not to mention we've taken to raising the volume on our television since those incidents."

"Incidents, ma'am?" Leon leaned forward.

"One or two of our other neighbors are sometimes loud but that couple were the worst. They're such inconsiderate, *noisy* sorts. Loud arguments out in front of their house. The man working on that car of his late at night, revving the engine, running power tools of some sort or other, when decent people are trying to sleep. And just lately, that dog. The poor thing has been barking all weekend. They even left it out in the rain last night."

"Have you ever spoken with them about any of this?"

"And probably get shot?" Clarence interjected.

"Heavens no. But we've called your people many times to come out."

"By 'my people,' you mean the police."

"Yes. And you've come out several times to talk with them."

And apparently, Leon mused silently, every time it was Radley who wound up coming out.

"Do you think your neighbors realized who had called in the complaints? Did they ever say anything to you or indicated in any way—"

"No, not really. We only encountered them rarely, when we'd both be coming or going, and they never even acknowledged us. Dear me, it sounds as if they've really done something serious this time, have they?"

Leon hoped she could handle it. "I'm afraid they're dead, ma'am."

Helena's eyes widened, but in delight rather than shock.

"You don't say! You're investigating a honest to God murder! And you're here in search of suspects and clues!"

"We're just checking to see if anybody heard anything, Mrs. Corkendale. No suspects yet."

"You'll have to come back and tell us when you find out whodunit!" she exclaimed happily. She reached over and patted Leon on the sleeve. "And never you mind Clarence. I think you're every bit as fetching a detective as Simon Wyre."

* * * *

"I'm afraid I can't be of any help. Nobody was here last night. Nobody's lived here since my grandfather died."

When Leon had trudged up the third driveway, Mourning Dove Lane, he had encountered Willis Gale dropping a plastic trash bag into a garbage hopper. Willis looked to be in his early thirties, with a mane of light brown hair and an air that hardly screamed of "How To Make Friends and Influence People." Leon had produced his ID and asked the question he'd come to ask.

Willis turned his back on Leon to return to the house. It was no bigger than the other two bird street homes but made of brick with stucco trim. The yard looked well-kept although now a bit overgrown.

"My condolences on your loss, sir," Leon called after him. "Mind if I ask you a couple more questions? I won't take much of your time."

Willis spun around, looking not grief stricken but very put out. "He was old. It was his time."

"Can you tell me anything about your neighbors on Mockingbird Lane?"

He pulled a face. "I don't know. I don't live *here*. In fact, I was never here until we had to take care of this, this *mess*." Amazing how a slight arm gesture could convey such contempt. "In fact I haven't been near this place since I was a little kid. So, what's happened, one of the Tobacco Road inhabitants causing a stink?"

"Actually, sir, two people were killed last night."

"You don't say. I'm not surprised. Well, I can't help you, Detective. You did say Detective, right?"

"That's correct. Detective Simpkins. How often have you come here since your grandfather passed away?"

"Well, that was a couple weeks ago. We came to town to see the property about a week ago and either my brother or I has been here every couple of days since, clearing out the junk and figuring out how we're going to sell it." Willis stopped and shook his head, seeming to soften just a bit. "I don't mean to be snarky. Old Bart was kind of a hippie weirdo. He lived his kind of beatnik life. Accumulated all kinds of junk, old books and papers and records and stuff. And he apparently accumulated weird people renting his properties too. He seems to have left all of it to my brother and me; nobody else is left to give it to. So, we're trying to deal with it."

"Did your grandfather have much contact with the tenants?"

"Not that I know of. They mailed him their rent every month, checks or more often money orders. I don't think they ever communicated, unless there was some problem or complaint and then they'd call and he'd send somebody over to do whatever, I don't know." Willis looked at Leon. "So somebody got killed?"

"On Mockingbird Lane, yes sir."

"Was it, like, a robbery or something?"

"We're trying to figure all that out."

"Huh," he said, not really seeming all that disturbed by the idea. "Well, as I said, I can't help you. Sorry."

Willis spun around on his heel once again and almost trotted back to the house. Leon shook his head and turned around as well, heading back down the driveway.

That, he mused, was about as dead of an end as one could find.

There must have been some back story to that family. He could live happily without ever learning it.

* * * *

As they returned to the Donner house, Cara Smithers and her assistant were just pulling up. Leon decided she even looked like an inveterate smoker, carried the aroma, and her voice was even huskier in person. She gushed solicitously over Curtis Stryker as if she were his actual mother, shepherding him into her car while her assistant took the keys to Curtis's own vehicle to drive back. Curtis, who felt somewhat better at this point, protested he could drive himself back, but his boss/ landlady would not hear of it. Not a word was mentioned about the envelope intended for Halley Donner that had started the morning's festivities before they departed. Officers Radley and Ochida would remain to keep the scene secured and await the arrival of Animal Control to pick up the dog, which was still barking in the back yard.

Leon and Art trudged back down the gravel drive, taking one last look around before getting into their car. The Obrigato Drive turnaround was now deserted and very quiet.

Art pointed around the street and shook his head. "The weirdest part of this? No cameras. What was the last time you remember that there were no cameras at all?"

"And no witnesses. Nobody heard anything."

"Heavy rain, so no tire tracks, no footprints. Nothing."

"Let's hope for forensic evidence. Meanwhile, what have we got?"

"Bupkes," Art said, ducking down to get into the driver's seat. "We got bupkes."

SEVEN

"Well, speak of the devil."

Art pointed out through the windshield at the garish billboard they were approaching. It screamed in large Gothic letters:

MARSHALL APPLEGATE

LET ME FIGHT FOR YOU

YOUR SETTLEMENT COULD BE MUCH LARGER THAN THE INSURANCE COMPANY OFFERS!

There was the conveniently easy-to-remember telephone number with area code and 123-4567 and a dramatic photo of the man himself, in dark suit and bright red tie, scowling heroically and aggressively pointing a finger out at the viewer in such forced perspective that it felt like it could poke a driver in the eye.

"Can't wait to meet him in person," Leon yawned.

"You said the address says Suite 2314, 785 Zeiterfeld Street?" Art had this unnerving habit of peering out the windshield as he drove, like a geriatric driving to the market. He made exasperated sounds at a couple jerk moves being made by the drivers around them.

Leon held up the envelope. "That's what the return address says here."

"That can't be right. Suite 2314?"

"What's your point, Art?"

"Come on, you remember Zeiterfeld, right? We've been there. It's a two-block long street that dead ends between San Andreas and the freeway. It's a bunch of little buildings with stores and apartments and like that. I bet there's nothing higher than three stories there. Well, I'll give you four, maybe."

"Now that you mention it, yeah. I'll double-check that." Leon had his phone out and was tapping Applegate's name into a search engine. "Uh huh. Marshall Applegate, Attorney at Law. He's listed here as being at 18064B San Andreas." He continued tapping onto the screen as a map came up. "That's about a block away from the Zeiterfeld address."

"Why am I thinking that 'Suite 2314' is a mailbox drop around the corner from his office? This guy really is a high roller."

Art's hunch turned out to be correct. 785 Zeiterfeld Street was a store-front in a two-story building. Painted in a prosaic typeface on the display window was the name "U Send U Receive" and a list of offerings including shipping drop-offs and mailboxes. He drove on, turning onto the much wider and busier San Andreas Boulevard.

"What was that number again?"

Leon looked down at the screen. "18064B."

"That would mean... that mini mall on the left."

Art hung a left into the parking lot of a large tract mall. He stopped and they craned their necks to read the signs on the store fronts.

Laundra-Max, Wash and Dry.

Snak Shack Mini Mart convenience store.

Cafe Corner Coffee.

Marshall Applegate, Attorneys At Law.

Art shook his head. "Well, whattaya know."

"I'll give him this," Leon smiled. "He's got the biggest space in the entire mall. It looks like he expanded into the spaces on both sides. Mr. Applegate must be doing all right."

"Must be how he can afford the billboards and the late-night ads," Art muttered, turning towards a parking space.

There was a bored receptionist checking her cell phone at the desk when they walked in. She looked up, saw their extended badges and IDs, put the phone down and smiled brightly.

"Yes, officers, how can I help you?"

"Detectives, actually," smiled Leon. "Simpkins and Dowdy. We'd like to speak with Marshall Applegate, please."

"I'll see if he's available," she said sweetly, picking up the receiver of the desk phone, pressing a button and then speaking quietly.

"He'll be right out," she said, hanging up the receiver.

About two minutes later, a man who could only be Marshall Applegate bustled out of a rear door and strode forward to greet the deputies. He was a thick man with dark thinning hair and a combover, wearing a dark blue striped suit, bright aqua shirt, and possibly the same bright red tie from his billboard. He extended his hand to each of them with a toothy grin.

"Detectives, this is a surprise. You are detectives, is that correct? I'm Marshall Applegate."

Leon re-introduced them and asked if they could speak in private.

"Why, why, of course. Umm, I'd ask you back on my office, but, well, I'm in the middle of painting and redecorating, you know how it is? So let's go in my conference room over here. Sigrid, hold all my calls, would you?"

"Certainly, Mr. Applegate," Sigrid replied, the boredom back in her voice.

Leon and Art exchanged amused glances. They wondered whether there were going to be all that many calls to worry about or whether this was more for their benefit. You had to love this guy.

Applegate led them to another side door that led to the extension into the next mall space. The room was long and unfinished, with the glass window fronts that looked out onto the parking lot covered with long Venetian blinds.

"We've just expanded into these new offices and, as I said, the remodel... so please forgive how things look. Let's sit at the conference table here." He gestured to a polished walnut table, that held a desk telephone, with six chairs arranged around it. The only other furniture in the room were three file cabinets and a breakfront that held a coffee maker and a box of doughnuts.

Leon had to admit, the table was a nice one. Applegate had spent a few bucks on that at least.

Once they were seated, Applegate said, "Now how may I help you, Detectives, um, Simpkins and, um, Dowdy, did I get that right?"

"Yes you did, sir." Leon handed the envelope to him. "I believe you sent this to Ms. Halley Donner?"

He took the envelope, staring at it mystified. "Yes, this was to be delivered *only* to the addressee, my client. How did you get it?"

"Your client was Halley Donner, then?"

"Well, yes, as I said." Applegate gestured at the address label. "Wait, what do you mean *was*?"

"I regret to inform you, sir, that Halley Donner was found dead this morning by your messenger."

Applegate just stared at the letter for a long time, his lips moving soundlessly. Finally, he looked up at Lee and then at Art. "What happened?"

"They were murdered, sir, both Halley Donner and her husband."

"Oh my Lord. Where? How?"

"In their home. As I said, your messenger who was trying to deliver that letter was the one who found them."

"Killed in their home? A burglary, a home invasion? How were they killed?"

"The investigation has just begun. All we can tell you right now is that they were killed while they were home. We were hoping you might be able to help us with some information."

Applegate had begun to fiddle with his hands, looking back and forth at them, his head twitching like an insect.

"Of course. Of course. My God. This is horrible."

"To start with, you were representing Halley Donner in some legal action, may I assume? You were sending her some kind of documents?"

"Yes. This is about a deposition I was going to take with her. I represent her in a lawsuit that's going to be coming to trial. Well... I guess now it's *was* going to be coming to trial."

"Can you tell us about that lawsuit, Mr. Applegate?"

"There is confidentiality involved here, Detective. You know, I'm not supposed to..."

"Sir, your client is dead. She's been killed, and quite violently."

"Attorney-client privilege continues after death in this state, surely you understand."

"I'm aware of that. But I repeat, we're talking about a murder, a most disturbing one. If you can help us shed light on this and apprehend the killer, it would be of utmost importance."

"This case hasn't even begun yet. We were still in preliminaries. I mean, you don't think it could have anything to do with her death, do you?"

"I have no idea. You understand, I'm sure, we must look into every possible angle. We aren't asking for any privileged communication with your client, just the matters on public record. And your case is moot now in any event."

Applegate nodded thoughtfully, staring down, for an awkwardly long period of time. Finally, he looked up and sighed. "I could be on very dubious ethical grounds here, you realize."

Leon and Art exchanged another look. Somehow, they didn't think ethical considerations were a major stumbling block all that often with this guy. This was for their benefit. He made a good show of pondering the intricacies of the problem for some time, then nodded forcefully.

"Well, you're right, it would become public record. It's a liability case, a negligence suit."

"Was she suing or being sued?"

"She was the plaintiff. She was injured on the property of the defendants."

"And just who were these defendants? What happened?"

"Wayne and Abigail Pendleton. My client was attacked by an animal on their property and in the process of trying to get away, was struck by Abigail's vehicle as she backed out of her driveway. Their insurance didn't cover the full extent of her injuries, so she came to me to seek the proper compensation for her medical expenses and pain and suffering. We were, as I pointed out, still in the preliminaries of the case."

"Wait, now. Attacked by an animal... *and* hit by their car?"

"That's correct."

"An animal, you mean, like a dog?"

"Actually? It was a monkey."

Art actually spoke. "Excuse me? A monkey?"

"They have a pet monkey that was allowed to run loose on the premises." The lawyer stared placidly at them both, as if what he'd just told them was the most ordinary thing in the world.

"How long ago did this accident, when she was injured, happen?"

"Let's see... I'd have to look up the exact date, but it was between three weeks and a month ago."

"Could you do that, please, look up the details for us, maybe provide us with the information from the documents you were preparing?"

Applegate considered that for a moment, regarded the severe stares on the faces of the two detectives, then said, "Sure, I guess." He picked up the phone on the table, pressed a button and then said, "Sigrid, could you make copies of the Donner file and bring it in, please? No, just the most recent case. Thank you." He hung up and said, "Shouldn't take long. Can I offer either of you a cup of coffee while you're waiting?" He idly gestured to the side table. "I think there are doughnuts left. They might be a little stale..."

"No thank you, sir." Leon was smiling again, now in a strained manner. "I'm sorry, I couldn't help hearing, do I get the impression you've represented Halley Donner more than once?"

"Yes, she has been my client previously."

"Also on lawsuits?"

"Other liability concerns, yes. And once I defended her on a criminal charge that got thrown out."

"It might help us to look at those earlier cases as well. This is all public record now anyway, isn't it? So you'd just be saving us the time that we'd spend looking it all up anyway. In the interests of justice. I'd say we'd appreciate that help."

Applegate hesitated, his eyes shifting, calculating the situation. Then he nodded thoughtfully, his face brightening. "I'm always happy to be recognized as a friend of law enforcement, you can be sure." He picked up the phone and buzzed Sigrid once again, adding the files to his request. "Of course, I'll need to give everything a once-over and remove anything I deem confidential."

"Of course," Leon continued. "Oh, and we're going to need to contact any family the Donners have. Can you help us out with that?"

Applegate shook his head. "I only dealt with Ms. Donner but neither of them, as I understand, were in touch with any next of kin. I'd suggested to Ms. Donner that they might want me to assist them both in writing wills, but she said there was really nobody to leave anything to. She was divorced several years ago. Her husband moved away and to my knowledge the two have never since been in touch."

"The fact that you brought up the idea of writing a will, perhaps you figured they had some reasonable assets?"

"I doubt they were exactly well to do, if that's what you're getting at. I don't think they owned any real estate property, for instance. They were renting their current home. I knew nothing of any assets. But it's my experience that people generally have something of value, even if it's only sentimental. I always suggest that having some kind of will is a good idea."

"But she did pay you for your services. There must have been a bank account or something?"

"The liability cases were taken on contingency. She did pay me my fee for the criminal case, in cash. I'm afraid I was not privy to their financial information. I'm guessing you won't have much trouble uncovering that on your own."

"I suppose more what I'm getting at, Mr. Applegate, is if there could be a financial motive in their deaths?"

"I haven't the foggiest idea, Detective. Afraid I can't be of any help on that one."

Leon wasn't all that sure just how much help Applegate was on any of it. At least he'd provided them a starting point. They concluded the interview shortly thereafter.

As Art pulled the car out of the mini-mall parking lot, Leon looked down at the envelope of photocopies—and a small stack of business cards that Applegate had eagerly thrust upon them as they said their goodbyes—and sighed.

Art made a wry face. "Would you call Mr. Applegate something of an ambulance chaser?"

"And you know, here I figured a lawyer with big garish billboards and late-night commercials would be of a higher class. Just goes to show, Art, you never can tell."

"I guess this kind of explains the crutches and the 'horse collar' we found at the house, huh? Halley Donner seems to have had some insurance hustles going on."

"She had, let's see, four in all with Applegate, counting the latest one." Leon pulled another paper out of the envelope and skimmed it quickly. "And that criminal case he represented her in appears to involve attempted insurance fraud. Looks like a swoop and squat."

The scam was all too common. There were several variations on the game, but they all involved a driver waiting for a car behind them to get appropriately close, then suddenly slamming on their brakes on some pretense, causing the intended mark to rear-end them. There would be a hurried, uncomfortable confrontation in which the scammer would try to assign blame to the victim and intimidate them into giving them some cash there and then to avoid legal and insurance hassles.

Apparently, in this case, Halley Donner had picked the wrong mark, a lady who'd been instantly suspicious. She had her phone out and was calling the cops before Halley was even out of her car.

"I wonder if that was her first try at that," Art mused. "Or how many times she'd gotten away with that one before it caught up with her."

Leon continued to peruse the paper. "These usually involve a partner, a driver one car ahead, who slips in ahead of them on signal and taps their brakes to give the scammer a pretext for braking hard and getting hit. Then they scoot away."

"Yeah, yeah, I know all that."

"I'm not seeing anything mentioned here about an accomplice. She was prosecuted as a solo. And then the charge got dropped."

"Huh," said Art, speeding up to make it through a yellow light. "Wonder why?"

"Whoa! Take it easy there, partner. I don't want us to be involved in a smack up ourselves."

"So, you can drive next time."

"I think I'll do just that." Leon returned his gaze from the windshield to the paper. "To answer your question, looks like the victim withdrew her testimony."

"Now, why am I thinking intimidation? Ot maybe bribery?"

Leon snorted. "Now wouldn't that be shocking. Certainly been known to happen."

"Might have backfired on Halley."

"You're thinking, something to get someone angry enough to come after her? One more thing to look into."

"Our girl Halley was quite a piece of work, it would seem. And she paid her lawyer in cash. And we haven't even yet looked into Jack. I'm guessing he's every bit as sketchy."

Leon sat quietly for a few seconds. "By the way, there was something when I talked with Radley back at the scene. Maybe it's nothing."

"Please elaborate."

"He's had contact with the Donners on a few calls. He seemed to be trying to steer me away from Halley and more toward Jack. He mentioned a gangster that Jack hung out with, Doug Barnfeather. It just seemed a little odd."

"One of the Rybus fraternity?" Art asked. "Right now, they're in quite a pot of shit, the way things look. Since Yancey got picked up, everything's going to hell."

"He sounds more like an outsider. If Jack was maybe thinking it was a good time to get involved in the drug market, it's a dangerous time to be doing it. Looks like we got ourselves an awful lot to sort through in a hurry."

"How do you want to divvy this up?"

Leon wrinkled his brow in thought for a moment. "I'd really like to look further into Jack. Maybe he was the target of the killer, maybe not. If he's got a drug connection, maybe somebody over in Narcotics can offer something. How about you take Halley, and I'll take Jack?"

"I can't wait to start going through all those insurance scams," Art deadpanned. "We might have a long line of likely suspects."

"Well, I'll be happy to jump back in with you on Halley after I check out Jack. In the meantime, you can put those awesome organizational skills to use laying out our strategy."

"Do I sense some sarcasm?"

"Not at all, partner." Leon sat back and closed his eyes. "You really are great at organizing. Much better than your driving skills."

EIGHT

The unit was called Personal Crimes. Years earlier, it had officially been called Special Crimes and before that had gone by the prosaic but accurate title Robbery-Homicide. At some point, the Department had decided the name Personal Crimes bore more gravitas. They still dealt with basically the same types of crime, almost entirely felonies: homicides, severe assaults, robberies, hate crimes. Simultaneously, the unit that handled burglaries and similar non-violent crimes, currently housed in a similar squad room one flight up from them, had gained the moniker Property Crimes. The veterans of either group would likely have remarked that there had been little difference beyond the name changes.

The activity, as always, was hectic throughout the room. Leon and Art were at their computers, trying to establish a set of leads, beginning with whatever records existed on Jack and Halley Donner. Jack had three minor arrests, one arising from a bar fight, one for possession of a controlled substance, and the third from possession of stolen goods. None had resulted in prison time. The only incident on Halley's official criminal record was the collision scam.

There seemed scant personal information or history to be gleaned on either of the Donners. Both Jack and Halley were basically ciphers. The only time either one of them seemed to surface was when an opportunity arose to make a quick buck, and honest documented employment seemed to be off the menu. The online sales enterprise of Halley's that Radley had mentioned must have been under another name, because nothing of the sort came up under her own name search. If either of the two ever had bank accounts, it was going to take some digging to unearth them. Leon and Art submitted requests for DMV records but knew those would not be forthcoming for at least another day. Tax return requests were going to take somewhat longer.

Halley's first two litigations had been settled by the insurance companies before trial. The newest, the one they were calling the monkey case, seemed different; it looked as though she had no intention to settle this one but was ready to go to court. Art's attempts to locate and contact the individuals involved in the three suits came up empty all three times. He uttered a few choice epithets as he hung up his desk phone.

"One's a big box store that put me on hold for ten minutes before I hung up. One number isn't picking up and seems to be disconnected. And no answer at the monkey folks, Wayne and Abigail Mercer. At least I've got addresses on all three since she pulled her liability scams on their actual properties."

Leon was leaning back in his chair, cradling the receiver of his own phone on his shoulder. He raised his eyes to his partner. "Maybe you'll have better luck with the cold-footed witness from the swoop."

Art looked at the notes he'd written on his pad. "Moira Legge. Only found one of those in the online directory." He began tapping a number into his own desk phone. He impatiently tapped his pen on the desk as he listened to the rings. Finally, he hung up and scratched a note on his pad. "Well, at least her phone seems to be working, there's that. Still, I'm four for four."

"If it makes you feel any better, I'm not doing so well myself. I'm not finding any friends or known associates of this guy."

"Actually, no, that doesn't make me feel any better." Art stood up. "I'm gonna do better knocking on their doors. I can still do at least a couple of those before quitting time."

"Good hunting. I'm going to make a call to Narcotics and see if anybody's heard of Jack or this Barnfeather guy. He doesn't seem to be in the system."

"Gonna call your buddy Gene Gehm?"

Gene had once worked in Personal Crimes before transferring to Narcotics. He had never been a favorite of either of theirs, but they'd maintained decent relations since.

"My buddy, yeah, right. He's a good start."

Art trudged off towards the elevator. One of the humorists across the room started whistling the funeral march. The Mortician was on the move, at his traditional operating speed.

Leon got through to Narcotics and to Gene Gehm without difficulty and after the briefest of social niceties, got to the point.

"We picked up a double homicide that might have some drug connection, possibly with the Rybus crew."

"I can't say that would be a surprise right now," Gehm replied. "Since Rybus and his fraternity brothers got picked up, the shit's been hitting the fan in his organization. Who you got?"

"Ever hear of Jack Donner? Or his wife, Halley?"

Gehm paused to think. Leon could hear his jaws working around a wad of chewing gum as his brain presumably whirled more silently.

"Nope, neither name rings a bell with me off hand."

"How about Doug Barnfeather?"

"That one sounds more familiar. Just why, I'm gonna have to think. I'll ask around, do some digging. Can I get back to you tomorrow?"

"Sure, Gene. The earlier the better. Much appreciated."

"Talk about the shit hitting the fan, did you hear that Rybus was released this morning?"

"Seriously? No. No, I hadn't." His colleague Marlon Morrison had apprehended Rybus and several associates a few weeks earlier. Solid evidence of multiple murders had seemed to insure they weren't going anywhere.

"No idea how that could have happened. Some legal maneuver. Quite the master escape artist, that one. Things are really going to get interesting now. And Marlon's gotta be royally pissed. Anyway, as you can imagine, it's sheer chaos around here at the moment. I'll see what I can do for you. Gotta jet, Leon."

Leon hung up the receiver and swiveled back and forth in his chair pensively. It seemed an inefficient use of what time he had to be looking too deeply into this Barnfeather guy just yet. All he had to go on was a random comment from Officer Radley; maybe that was where he should be asking any further questions.

One other thing came to mind. There had been a fair amount of alcohol around the Donner house. Leon wondered if they might have spent any time in any bars or clubs in the immediate area. It couldn't hurt to check.

* * * *

Gene Gehm figured he'd slammed the receiver down just a little *too* hard, not that anybody bustling around him in Narco, including his partner Olivia, was going to notice or care. The anxiety level was high right now, what with the craziness in the organization and the news that the Ice Man himself was coming back.

Several detectives had been attempting an updated command tree now that many of the known figures had been put away. Interest was high in a new rising star, Barclay Vickers, who had seemed to assume control in an unusually violent and high-profile manner. Rybus's top lieutenant, Theo Charles, and his top enforcer, Sylvester Faamoana, had both been scooped up along with Rybus himself, leaving the rest of the chart a guessing game as to who was taking charge. Now their speculations would need to be revisited as the head man himself returned.

How in hell had the Ice Man slipped out of an open-and-shut murder rap? Apparently, his executioner, Faamoana, had signed a full confession exonerating his boss. Gene had to hand it to him, an unexpected move. Rybus must have come up with some strong enticement. What the hell, one more count of homicide first degree on top of how many others, what did it matter to the guy? How many more lifetimes could he spend behind bars?

Rybus's return was particularly concerning to Gene, for personal reasons. He'd been hoping, desperately, that he was finally out from under what the Ice Man held on him. It was hardly a sure thing but at least he had hope.

One small, simple mistake.

Well, Gene had to be honest about it. His newfound sobriety, after all, depended on his honesty with himself as well as with others.

It wasn't a *simple* mistake.

It wasn't a *small* one either.

And it really wasn't even *one*. He'd been on the road to ruin in gradual steps and then came the one, grandiose *coup de grace*.

Ultimately, he'd cleaned up his life and got it back on track. But there was this creep, this lowlife, who still had this *one thing*, this one *big* thing, on him, and it had turned Gene into his asset in Narcotics.

That creep had finally exited his business courtesy of one Yancey Rybus, who absorbed his predecessor's assets. One of those assets, unfortunately, was Gene Gehm.

Rybus was considerably more demanding; things went downhill from there, into the stuff of nightmares. With Rybus finally behind bars, Gene had begun to believe he could finally be free.

But now the Ice Man was back on the streets. He certainly had lots of bigger things on his mind at the moment, but there was no doubt that sooner or later Rybus's attention would swing back to his assets inside the Department. He wasn't sure how many that might be or who. What he cared about was that he was one of them, and Rybus was not one to waste a resource.

Gene had had a long time to think about what he'd need to do, if and when it came down to it. He was going to have to take down the Ice Man.

Now all he needed was a way to do it.

NINE

The Pendleton household was in a nice section of town north of the University, hardly a mansion, but a good-sized comfortable-looking Crafts-man style abode with a big porch, surrounded by a well-manicured lawn and shaded with stately mature oaks and sycamores. There was no car in the driveway and the house looked unoccupied. Nobody answered the bell or his follow-up knock. As Art was doing his Mortician walk back down the drive, a woman's head popped up over the hedge from the adjoining property.

"Nobody's home," she drawled. "Can I help ya, young man?"

Art pulled out his badge and ID. "Any idea when they might be back?"

The lady adjusted her glasses and read the ID. Her suspicious scowl softened. "Detective? Oh my! They're out of town. I'm watching the place for them. They'll be gone for another week."

"Can you tell me how I might reach them, Ma'am?" Art asked, sounding incredibly weary.

"I guess it would be okay for me to give you Abigail's cell phone, you bein' a detective and all. Is there some trouble?"

"Just a routine inquiry into something we're working on. Thank you for your help."

"I'll go get it for you, sweetie. Hang on." The head disappeared behind the hedge and shortly thereafter reappeared, along with a hand that passed a slip of paper over the trimmed greenery. "They're visiting Abigail's mom, Ruthie, in Duluth, all three of 'em. Took Amelia out of school for the trip."

"Amelia would be their daughter, I assume?"

"Yep, such a sweet little girl. She's about ten. She still feels so bad about Gummy."

"Excuse me, Gummy?"

"Gummy Bear! The monkey! He's such a cutie, with that sweet face and all, but he is a wild animal, after all. Been a bit of trial for them, I'm afraid."

Nothing like a neighbor in the know who liked to dish. Art played along.

"That would be the monkey that was involved in the incident?"

"You must mean the insurance case. What a situation. I bet Abigail wishes her father had never given Amelia that monkey. But Amelia loves him to death."

"What do you know about that insurance case exactly, Miss…?"

"That's *Mrs.* Mildred Spahn. You can call me Millie. Abigail was backing out of the driveway, and she bumped this lady walking down the street. Abigail swore she looked every which way and didn't see anybody, but there she was, like she appeared out of nowhere. Abigail also swears up and down that she was pulling out slow and braked immediately but the woman fell over and started hollering bloody murder like she'd been hit at high speed. Abigail got out of the car and that's when the real hell—excuse my language—broke loose. She had Amelia and the monkey in the car. Gummy was in a cage but somehow, he got out, and when Amelia opened her door, Gummy jumped out and ran around to see what was going on. The woman started screaming that Gummy had bit her. Next thing anybody knew, she was demanding insurance information in between moaning and groaning about her injuries and such."

"Did you happen to see any of this?"

"No. I heard the ruckus and came out to see what was going on. That woman was really hollering at the top of her lungs. So, I just saw the aftermath, if you will, her lying on the ground and wailing at Abigail, who was just standing there over her. Later Abigail told me all about it. By that time her insurance company had gotten involved."

"What did this woman look like, do you remember?"

"Oh Lord, I don't remember her much. Dark hair, maybe forty? What I *do* remember is that she was *loud!*"

It certainly sounded like Halley Donner, and it certainly sounded like an insurance scam.

"What else can you tell me about the rest of the family?"

"Wayne's some kind of contractor. He works some long hours. There's just the three of them."

"And you say Abigail's father gave them the monkey?"

Millie snorted. "Craig Mercer is quite the piece of work. You might say he and Abigail are estranged. Gummy was his cockeyed way of trying to work himself back into her good graces and get to see his granddaughter again."

"You said Abigail's mother lives in Duluth. Do I get the idea she and the father are separated?"

"Oh, for many years now. Craig's here in town. A drunk, a druggie and a deadbeat. Hangs out with his lowlife friends. You can tell the kind of judgment he's got, he gives his granddaughter a wild monkey and thinks it'll make up for being a terrible parent! I love Gummy but he was probably stolen to begin with. Not that I want to get Craig in trouble with the police."

Art waved a hand. "Don't worry, Mrs. Spahn, that's not my department that deals with that in any case. You said they've been away, since when?"

"Oh, let's see. They left Thursday, so that's four days ago."

"So nobody's been here since then?"

"Just me, when I come by to pick up the mail." She stared at Art over the hedge for a long moment. "So what kind of detective are you, exactly?"

"Personal Crimes."

"Is that, like, robberies and muggings and killings and serious things like that?"

"Yes, ma'am, that's right."

"So how are Abigail and Wayne involved in something like that?"

"As I said, just routine. They might be able to help an ongoing investigation."

Art saw no reason to tell Millie about the Donner murders. He figured she'd hear about them on television soon enough, and maybe put the incidents together. Time to move on to another litigation and another litigant. He thanked Millie Spahn and departed.

The Food Extravaganza branch was a huge, bustling store; it took Art about fifteen minutes to track down a manager who knew something about the Halley Donner lawsuit. In fact, she had been the manager on duty when the supposed incident occurred.

"We got two or three of those every year," she was telling Art as he followed her at a brisk pace around the store. She would constantly stop to check something on a shelf and check it off her computer pad or stop an employee to ask a question. "This one was a real piece of work. She claimed she slipped on a wet spot in the produce department. A while later, I found an open pickle jar stuck in the citrus. Turns out she'd grabbed a big jar of pickles and poured the liquid all over the tile and then staged the flop. Then just to be on the safe side, she'd also pried up a corner of one of the rubber mats so she could also claim she'd stumbled first, then slipped."

"And this wasn't settled by the insurance company?"

"Her ambulance chaser of a lawyer wouldn't accept the insurance company's offer. He was going to take the company to court. I had to go in to give a deposition at the lawyer's office. She showed up in a neck brace and a cast on her foot, hobbling in on crutches. An Oscar winning performance. The store decided to settle at that point. It was just easier for the corporate bigwigs to make it go away."

Art remembered the various medical paraphernalia they'd found at the Donner house. A regular cinematic prop house.

"Any idea how much they settled for?"

"I don't know but I heard it was less than she wanted. The company drew a line and said they'd go this far and no farther. It was still substantial, if it was more than the insurance would cover."

"Did that affect you or your job adversely? How did you feel about it?"

She sighed as she signed a clipboard for another store worker. "Nobody blamed me for it, if that's what you mean. Like I said, we get our share of scammers here all the time. We all try to keep an eye out for them and take certain precautions, but corporate gets it that we can't completely prevent it. Their attitude is it's part of the cost of doing business. Personally, I think it sucks. Those people are leeches and parasites, stealing from the store because they think it's got deep pockets. They don't care that this kind of thing affects all of us adversely: higher prices, lower wages."

"Anybody else here besides you who might have taken exception to this scammer in particular?"

"I guarantee you, we all think someone like her is dirt. Hey, that was a few months ago, what brings you here to investigate it now? Are you bunco squad or something?"

"I'm not even sure anyone actually calls it bunco," Art said, trying to avoid directly answering the question. "Just on old movies and TV."

"I got a better name for it," the manager spat, smiling nastily. "If you're dealing with that one, maybe you're on the Asshole detail."

Art pulled a wry face. "Oh, you can be sure I find myself on that one pretty often, Miss."

* * * *

Leon was beginning to think this had been a fool's errand as he parked in the lot of the fourth neighborhood bar, a place called the Short End. His footwork around a few areas of the city talking to contacts and informants had yielded absolutely nothing about Barnfeather or the Donners, and now his bar hopping hadn't done any better.

Leon's entry into the dimly lit tap room caused the handful of patrons to turn and look at him, but only briefly and without much curiosity. They all returned to their drinking and low conversations.

The smiling fifty-something woman in the tank top who was behind the bar looked at Leon with some interest as he sat down and produced his badge and ID.

"Looking for one of your coworker buddies?" she asked in a raspy voice.

"Would I find many of them here as a rule?" He smiled easily. She laughed.

"If you come by on the right night, I would say yes. We got our share of the city's finest. What can I get you, Detective Simpkins?"

"Maybe just an answer to a question, then I won't need bother you any further." He pulled out his phone and opened to the photo from Jack Donner's driver's license. "Would you happen to have seen him in here."

"Would his name be Jack, by any chance?"

"Do you know him?""

"I heard they found him dead this morning."

"News travels fast, it seems."

"Gin mills tend to be hotbeds of news and gossip. Yeah, he came in here now and then, enough that we knew his name. You know that old TV show set in a bar, where everybody knows your name?"

"In fact, I do."

"It had nothing on us. But it was his wife that we tended to see a lot more of. Halley. She was a regular."

"But not with Jack?"

"Oh, now and then, sure. They'd stop in, have a few drinks sometimes with some of their friends. More often it was just Halley, not Jack."

"By herself?"

"Sometimes. And a couple, three times with this other guy. And then there was that one incident."

"Tell me about it, what incident?"

She hesitated, then shrugged. "What the hell, they're both gone now. That's why you're here, right? You're looking into who killed them?"

"If you know anything that might help me," Leon said quietly and gravely, "please."

"Halley was in here with this other guy one night. They were just sitting, over at that booth back there, having a couple beers, just talking, very seriously. Then Jack came in and saw them and started yelling at them. The guy got up and tried to calm him down. I started getting worried so me and my partner Pete both came out from behind the bar and came over. Pete, he's a big guy, you don't mess with him, and he walked Jack out. That was the end of it. Halley and the other guy sat back down and went back to talking. After a while they left. Pete made a point of following them out to the parking lot just in case, but I guess Jack had cooled off and left."

"So, who was this other guy Halley was with?"

"No idea. Saw him once or twice before and never again after that. Story around was he was a cop, and he kinda looked it, but that could just be talk. As I said, we do get off duty cops in here."

"How long ago was this?"

"Oh, maybe, let's see, two, three weeks."

"And Halley didn't come back after that?"

"Neither of 'em did."

"You said they would come in with other friends. Anything you remember about them?"

"Different people. No regulars. Nobody really stands out. A few years behind the stick, they all run together, you know?"

Leon smiled again. She couldn't help but smile back. "Oh, come on," he cajoled. "A good bartender is like a good priest or a good therapist. They see a lot, even though they keep it in confidence."

"Well, now aren't you the honey tongued soothsayer, darlin'? Tell you the truth, there was one guy I remember came in with them a couple times. Lean, scary looking guy. Dressed all in black, shaved head, bushy mustache. Kinda gangster looking. The mood was not really friendly, but not unfriendly, if you get me? Just serious. Again, they were back in that same booth."

"And when was this, would you say?"

"Oh jeez. Maybe a month, six weeks."

"But you remembered their names, even though they weren't regular regulars."

"You sort of remembered Jack. Smiley, big talker. He was always trying to impress everyone, acting like he was involved with a lot of big stuff and big people. It seemed important to him that you'd remember his name. You tended to remember Halley for different reasons."

"How do you mean?"

"She gave off this vibe, I don't know, like don't mess with her? She always seemed on her guard, aware of everything and everybody around her. Felt as if you said the wrong word, she'd take extreme exception to it. You took note of her, all right, so you'd know to avoid her when you could."

"Anything else you remember about the other people Jack and Halley were with? Did the conversations seem friendly, or were they strained?"

"Nothing stands out. Nondescript people, which means they didn't spend a lot, and probably getting along, because back here behind the bar we tend to take note more often when there's a sign of discord, you know?"

Leon nodded. "Flying under the radar."

"They used to say no news is good news, but I'm afraid in your case it's not, sweetie. Sure, I can't get you something on the house?"

"Thanks just the same. Appreciate the information."

"Come back and see me again," she smiled sweetly.

Leon smiled back mischievously. "Can I bring the wife and kids next time?"

TEN

Yancey Allan Rybus was not fond of ostentatious automobiles, the kind favored by many in his crews. He understood the utility and psychology of powerful SUVs with large capacity, and he even owned a Cadillac Escalade for particular situations (although at the moment that was in impound), but in general he preferred his two muted-color Lexus sedans. They didn't call unwanted attention to themselves or scream "gangster" when they passed a police vehicle. They had comfort and the understated class that he had come to appreciate. He'd long since learned the value of a low profile in his line of work.

So, Yancey was pleased when he exited through the prison doors Monday morning to find his beige Lexus waiting, with his man Barclay quickly exiting the driver's seat and coming around to open the back door for him.

"Would you prefer to drive?" Barclay asked.

"Actually, I'd prefer you drove but thank you. And thank you for bringing the perfect car to take me to freedom."

Barclay, for the moment, was his new Number Two. He'd assumed operations the moment Yancey had found himself behind bars, and there had been immediate problems that he'd handled as best he could. All things considered, so far, so good. He'd be keeping an eye on the guy, that was a given, but he seemed promising.

Barclay Vickers himself had leaped at the chance to fill the vacuum left by the former Number Two. He was an intimidating guy and his rep among the crews was already that of a mean piece of work who didn't shrink from extreme violence: just the kind of guy needed in the situation. He'd been eyeing the position for some time, waiting his chance. When Yancey and the others had been arrested, the potential for chaos in the organization was high. Outsiders immediately probed for weaknesses. Insiders broke discipline. Barclay and a couple of his trusted boys had stepped in and set things straight, pronto. It was no time for indecision, weakness, or second chances. He quickly made a few examples, of the extreme variety, and made it clear policies and rules remained in effect.

The biggest problems he'd faced had been with the street gangs that Yancey had absorbed into his network as he expanded his hold over the city. There were more than a few young hotheads who needed to be shown the facts of life by an adult. Once a few of them had disappeared without a trace, the kids began to fall in line. Again, Barclay ruthlessly and efficiently got all his ducks in a tight row.

Once he'd re-established some sense of internal discipline, he began to address the outsider problem. He dispatched muscle around. Things got a little messy, but he believed that old saying about breaking eggs to make omelets. Then he opened a quiet channel to Yancey, asking for his marching orders, which were passed back to him. Barclay followed them to the letter, no questions, no deviation. In the process, some eggs definitely got busted. The grand omelet started to be put back together. So far, so good.

Yancey settled back in the comfortable seat as Barclay pulled away from the curb. He savored the familiar smell of his own car again. He could indulge himself a minute or two, just soak in his return to freedom, before getting back to work.

After a few minutes, Barclay ventured a comment: "Welcome back, Yancey." It was a particular privilege accorded the number two, to be able to get away with calling the boss by his first name. Yancey wasn't sure whether it felt a bit presumptuous yet, but in general Barclay had shown himself to be respectful and effective, so he'd let it go for now, a perk of the position. But everybody in his extended crew, Barclay included, was always on probation. The very skills that made people valuable tended to make them dangerous. The Ice Man trusted nobody, and recent events had only served to reinforce that practice. Indeed, it was "trust too far" that had brought everything to the morass he was currently trying to get himself out of.

"Good work on keeping the money going," Yancey said. "And for maintaining the proper order." He'd of course paid close attention to the regular status reports discreetly delivered to him in lockup by his lawyer. There had been bumps, as expected, but in general it seemed Barclay had done what was necessary to keep people in line and the enterprise, and most importantly the cash, flowing.

Barclay tried to hide his sigh of relief as he coolly acknowledged the compliment. Yancey continued. "There will be lots to review, of course. You'll need to bring me up to date on things in detail, and then we'll discuss what comes next, but first, what about T.C.?"

"He's being released shortly. It should come as a complete surprise to him. I'm guessing his lawyer will be picking him up since he's got nobody else at this point. We'll have eyes on him from the moment he leaves custody."

Yancey nodded. "He's not stupid; he'll know our people are watching. Observe from afar. Nobody comes near him. No contact. Let him wonder what's going on. He's going to think we want to hit him, so we'll keep him off balance. But I want to know exactly where he is, where he goes, who he sees, at every moment." He paused, looking out the window. "He's going to need funds very quickly. That would be the preferred, easier way, to follow him to the money. But he might be too smart for that to work. I'd prefer not to get heavy handed, but if nothing comes of this after a few days, then we pick him up and get him to divulge the location of the money in other ways."

"Understood."

"He's not going to be easy, Barclay. The people on him better be very good."

"I've got our best on him. I've done a lot of intel on him while he's been in lockup. There's really nobody left he can trust, so we'll stay on the lawyer, who might be his only reliable contact." Barclay decided to drop his other ace in the hole. "And then there's another promising source we're tapping as well."

"Now that sounds interesting. I'll expect regular updates."

"Of course. T.C. is not gonna lose us. He'll have to make his move pretty fast, and we'll be there when he does."

"Let us fervently hope you do, Barclay. Make me proud. Now, what about our dear Lydia? Where do we stand with her?"

"There was an unexpected turn of events involving Lydia earlier this morning."

"Do tell."

"She was supposed to be transferred to Costa County. She never made it."

Barclay decided there was no need to point out that a freak accident had removed the need to deal with Lydia. No harm in leaving the impression that he had engineered the event.

"Will wonders never cease." Yancey made a *tsk, tsk* sound, smiling grimly. "Poor, dear Lydia. I'm sure T.C. will miss her so. And since he no longer has to share the money they stole, all the more reason for him to head straight for it once he's out."

"When he does, we'll be on him. I've got every available pair of eyes on the lookout for him. Everywhere in the city."

Barclay was stretched much thinner than he could let on, and well aware that he couldn't keep that many of his crew on the street playing the detective game with T.C. He had to trust that T.C. would indeed move fast to retrieve the money, so they could devote that manpower back to the other urgent business at hand.

He also knew his show of bravado wasn't totally fooling Yancey either.

Yancey sighed, a man with the weight of worlds on his shoulders. "Another matter. Do we know where Vanessa was sent to *foster* care?" Yancey said it like it was a foul, distasteful word he'd rather not needed to be in his mouth.

It was a touchy situation. Where Vanessa was concerned, one had to tread *especially* carefully around Yancey. That asshole Barnfeather had complicated matters, but it could still be dealt with. Barclay just had to gloss over the details.

"We know exactly where she is."

"Good. When can I pick her up?"

"If you'd like," Barclay replied, trying to conceal his breath of relief, "We can do it right now."

* * * *

Theo Charles, a.k.a. T.C., former second in command of the citywide Rybus organization, looked idly around his cell, once again telling himself this wasn't so bad.

A chair, table, a shelf, some reading matter. He could put up with this for now. Even with the bars and the sub-optimal food.

In his estimation, he was much safer in here than out there.

He wasn't sure whom he could trust right now, not even his main man Felix, who'd known him most of his life and always had his back in the organization. Right now, he wasn't sure if even Felix hadn't bought what a lot of the others were thinking, that Theo had gone over the edge delusional and had put the organization into this mess. Yancey himself was convinced that Theo was a traitor and a thief, and that word had spread throughout the crews in and out of lockup. He was a marked man. Theo's only course of action was to avoid everybody and talk with no one.

He figured he could take care of himself for the moment. His rep as a badass was still strong and he was especially careful, scrupulously watching his own back. But sooner or later he knew he'd need his lawyer to get him out of here.

He wasn't sure how he was going to do that. But he had confidence. He'd always found a way to come out on top.

The problem with his deliberately enforced isolation was, he missed any word going around about anything: no rumors, no gossip. All he knew was whatever he could catch from a snatch of an overheard conversation here and there. It wasn't much.

He decided he was faced with two immediate legal problems.

The outstanding one was that the police had his Desert Eagle automatic and several slugs from it that had been taken out of the lifeless body of one Bradley "Brick" Brixton.

The other problem was his ex-girlfriend, Lydia Montgomery, currently also in custody, and the apparent fact that she was telling everything she knew about Yancey, Theo, and every other crew guy she'd ever met, to multiple law enforcement agencies in order to save her own hide. That would include plenty about him and his activities.

Two formidable obstacles to get around.

There was a third problem to solve, not a legal one but a money matter.

After Theo had found it advisable to cut her loose, Lydia tried to parlay her knowledge of the organization into a million-dollar payday by kidnapping and ransoming Yancey's beloved Vanessa. He agreed to pay up. Lydia enlisted that big dumb fool named Brick as her partner, but her plan all along had been for him to be her fall guy. Theo had deduced her real co-conspirator, a conniving mastermind who'd established a fake identity as a park employee named Webster Musgrave.

The two of them clandestinely intercepted the money drop at a remote park, making it appear to Yancey that his number two-man Theo had kept it for himself.

The frame worked well. It distracted from the real thieves, casting all the suspicion (and the vengeance of the entire Rybus organization) upon Theo. Nobody else believed Musgrave even existed, or that he had the million and was waiting for Lydia to happily rat her way out of custody and run off with him.

But Theo knew; he personally had run down the evidence, and he alone had all the answers.

It was going to be up to Theo to find his way out of custody, avoid getting killed by Rybus's associates, and somehow pick up the trail of the elusive Musgrave, whatever his real name was. The guy was clearly a pro, a virtual shadow.

If Theo could locate "Musgrave" and the money, he could return it and get back into the good graces of Yancey once again.

But Theo did not want to do that. He'd decided, in the light of recent decisions on Yancey's part, that the boss's shelf life was limited. With a million dollars, he could successfully challenge Yancey and take over the business himself. Hell, he was the one who'd really been running things anyway.

So, putting it all together, his course was clear, if not easy.

All he had to do was get out of here, dodge all his killers, find a diabolical shadow-man nobody else believed existed, and relieve him of one million dollars.

And then, if necessary, eliminate a few more people.

Yeah, no problem.

"Charles!" the voice rang out from the hallway. Theo stood up and walked to the barred door.

"Congratulations," one of the two bored guards said as the door slid open. "Grab your shit. You're getting out."

"What?" Nobody, not even his lawyer yesterday, had mentioned anything about an impending release.

"Come on, cone on," the guard said, waving his fingers. "Maybe you got all day, but we got things we need to do."

"How come I wasn't told before this?"

The bigger and meaner looking of the two—Theo seemed to recall his name was Bourbon, like the booze—shrugged. "How the fuck would we know? We just do like we're told. Like we expect you to do right now. Come on, Charles, this is our parting moment together, let's not ruin the romantic mood."

* * * *

"What the fuck is going on here? Why didn't you let me know I was going to be released?"

Theo had the words out of his mouth before he'd even gotten all the way into his lawyer's Acura. The attorney, Winston Montrose III, raised his hands over the steering wheel in supplication.

"I know, I know, I *know*, Theo. Nobody told me either. I was out of the loop. They just called me a half hour ago to tell me you'd be getting out."

"This is fucking bullshit! They blindsided me! Can they do this?" Theo slammed his door shut. Montrose pulled away from the curb.

"For sure this is highly irregular. Rybus must have pulled some strings inside. He wanted you out and he wanted it to be a surprise."

Theo tossed the bag, with his personal effects and his copies of the forms they'd made him sign, into the back. He looked very carefully in every direction. The road was empty. If there was anyone waiting on him, they were well concealed.

"Where shall I take you?"

Theo'd had some time, at least, to think that one out. There was one place he'd be safe for the moment, but he couldn't let Montrose take him there directly. He gave terse directions and hunkered down in his seat.

As they drove, Theo spoke quietly. "So, the impression from what I heard as they processed me out is that Tiny is behind my getting out, is that right?"

"Yes. He signed a confession taking full responsibility for killing Brixton. Said he took your weapon, did the deed, wiped it down and replaced it without your knowledge. He also absolved Yancey Rybus of any responsibility in the other deaths. He said they were totally his own idea."

"Are you fucking kidding me! So, Yancey is out too."

Montrose nodded. "Released this morning."

"Tiny, the guy who never talks, signed a *statement*. Damn." Theo shook his head. "Well played, Yancey."

"I just got some more news," Montrose continued. "There was an accident this morning. A fatal one."

"Who died?"

"Lydia Montgomery."

"Are you shitting me?"

"Oil truck hit a police van that was transporting her. She got burned up."

Theo felt a momentary twinge of regret for the woman who'd once shared his life and, he had to admit, given him one hell of a ride. It passed. Then all he could think of was *one problem solved, two to go*.

After directing Montrose through a circuitous trip around the city, they approached his destination, and the moment looked opportune. Theo did a quick visual sweep all the way around, reached back and grabbed his bag.

"Wait until the last possible moment, then hang a hard right into that little park there. Slow down long enough for me to jump out. Then keep driving around for a while. You know what to do next. I'll be in touch."

Montrose nodded. "Don't worry, I'll stay public and very visible. They're not going to try anything with me. Good luck."

"Just the same, stay safe. Thanks, my man."

The lawyer took the sharp turn and slowed sufficiently for Theo to open the door and roll out into the roadside foliage. Then he gunned the Acura. Theo slid into the bushes and waited. He didn't have long. About half a minute later, a black Charger screeched around the corner and accelerated with a roar. He'd never seen it behind them, not for a moment.

These guys are good!

He gave it another five minutes before he ventured out from beneath the shrubbery and hightailed off across the field to his destination about a quarter mile away.

Theo kept a few places around town, but this was one that he made sure nobody else knew about, with one exception, but she was no longer in the picture. It was a small condo bought through a front without his actual name on any records or documents. One attractive feature of the building was that it backed against this park and could be accessed without going to the street. Theo warily scaled the back fence and made his way to the entrance to the gated underground parking garage. He tapped in his key code and slipped in as the door opened.

He had two tandem parking spots in the garage and kept a nondescript grey Toyota Camry parked in the deeper one. His Navigator had been impounded on his arrest and he'd have to look into getting it back, but for the moment he was content to leave it in the police garage. If he tried driving around town in that, he might as well paint a large red target on it. The whole purpose for this crib was to remain undetected if necessary, and right now it was necessary. In a small magnetic box underneath the carriage of the Toyota, he found the keys to the car and his apartment. Pocketing them, he headed to the door to the stairwell.

Once in his apartment, he locked the front door and headed back to the bedroom. He was going to need a piece, and his Desert Eagle was now in a police evidence locker. Even if Tiny took the rap, he wasn't getting it back. Luckily, he kept weaponry here. He rummaged in one of the dresser drawers and pulled out the case holding his Beretta M9 automatic. From the top shelf of his bedroom closet he pulled down a box of shells. He wasn't going to be more than a few steps away from either from here on out.

He dug around some more and found the prepaid mobile phones he'd picked up a few months ago at a convenience store, still in their packages, along with an envelope containing some other items. When he set up this safe place, he'd doubled down on the possibility of needing it as a refuge. It was easy enough to set up a company with a DBA and open a bank account and a credit card. None of it would be foolproof against, say, the IRS, but it would make it harder to be detected or traced by the kinds of people that might try. He could remotely order food and other necessities and have them dropped off without any physical contact.

For now, his second problem was under control, while he worked out the third and most difficult challenge: finding Musgrave and the money. He knew he only had a limited window to work that one out.

* * * *

Barclay brought the Lexus to a stop half a block away from the end of the street, struggling to maintain a placid exterior and not to let loose a string of obscenities, even under his breath. He saw yellow tape strung across the drive, and worse, he saw uniforms and a black and white police cruiser.

That fucking Barnfeather.

"What's going on?" Yancey asked from the back seat. "Do not tell me that's where Vanessa's supposed to be?"

Barclay didn't have to answer, which was fortunate, considering how stupefied he was.

"Turn around and get the hell out of here. Now. But be cool."

Barclay didn't need to be told not to call attention to themselves. He smoothly pulled into a driveway along Obrigato Drive, waited about thirty seconds to not be obvious, and then backed out into a three-point turn. He drove cautiously, without any apparent haste, back out to the main drag and away from the activity.

They were several blocks away before Yancey spoke. "What exactly was that all about?"

"I don't know," Barclay said, fighting to keep his voice level. "Something must have gone down there."

"All that yellow tape. All that activity. I'd say that was something quite serious. Something involving a death."

"I've got no idea, Yancey. I'll look into it right away."

"Just whose place was that, anyway?"

"It was a safe house, trusted people."

Tell him as little as you can get away with until you sort this out.

"Vanessa had better be all right. This disturbs me, Barclay." Yancey readjusted himself in the seat and cleared his throat, staring out the window.

"I'll start looking into it right away."

"I've got a better idea. The club is still a going concern, isn't it?"

"Absolutely."

The Hometown Club, ostensibly a bar and night club, was actually the functional headquarters for the Rybus organization. During the recent troubles, despite visits from the authorities, Barclay and his loyal allies had quietly kept it going as their nerve center. The owner on paper, Worthy Lewis, had most ably kept up the front of the joint as a straightforward bar and night club without as much as a hiccup, and Barclay had seen to it that the upstairs headquarters had been swept clean of anything conceivably incriminating. Investigators' early efforts had been energetic but futile, and they'd quickly given up.

"Then take me there. I'll need to look up some of my Department assets. If there was some kind of police activity at that house, the odds are they transported Vanessa somewhere. There must be somebody among those assets who can provide me with the details to find her, somewhat faster than you'll be able to." He took a deep aggravated breath. "That's assuming no harm has come to her."

Barclay swallowed hard. "I'm sure she'll be all right."

"I'm very interested in how you can be so sure about that. Suppose you tell me more about this arrangement you set up."

It wasn't lost on Barclay that Yancey was using first person, singular, suddenly. Not even the royal "we." Not a good sign. He frantically thought about the answers he needed to give the Ice Man to keep from digging himself any deeper into this hole.

And worst of all, he somehow had to completely keep out of the story any reference to that dumb shit who'd gotten him into this.

Fucking Barnfeather.

ELEVEN

"Detectives, I appreciate that you got here so quickly."

Mickey Kendrick always looked morose, in that hound-dog sort of way, but today he looked particularly so. And tired. Very tired.

Jilly Garvey carefully picked her way through the mud and debris down the incline. Her partner Dan Lee was about ten feet behind her, having locked up their car on the access road above. "Hello, Mick. Tough day?"

Kendrick waved a hand. "Don't ask. Started out bad and just went downhill from there."

They stopped at the bottom of the hill and surveyed the scene. Charcoal black was the predominant color and "burnt" was the predominant aroma, amplified by the dampness that still hung in the air from the previous night's rain. Various workers, in jumpsuits, gloves and masks, were poring over the whole area, extracting whatever items they could, sorting them on tarps thrown over the muddy ground. The charred remains of a tanker truck lay on its side in the mire, along with the twisted wreckage of a Ford transport van.

Jilly reflexively ran a hand through her short red hair, looking slightly disoriented.

"This accident looks every bit as bad as it sounded when we got your summons this morning."

"Oh, it's a perfect gem, isn't it?"

"So just why, exactly, are *we* here?"

"Because, Detective Garvey, it's a crime scene."

"My understanding, Mick, was that the trucker had a heart attack, plowed into the transport and took it down the hill, where everything caught fire."

Kendrick nodded stoically. "That would all seem to be true."

"What we heard was, the driver's dead and the paramedics took away the two deputies, one of whom had unlocked the van and the prisoners to try to save them before he collapsed from smoke inhalation?"

"So far so good."

"One of the prisoners escaped, and one burned up in the van, right?"

"Again, your facts are impeccable, Detective Garvey."

"Mick, stop playing games. Where's the crime scene?"

Kendrick pointed to the ground, where something still vaguely recognizable as a human body lay, covered with a cloth tarpaulin.

"It would seem this is one Lydia Montgomery."

"I heard about her," Dan said.

"We all have," Jilly replied. The case, broken by their colleague Marlon Morrison, who notoriously never broke anything, had already become semi-legendary on their unit. He had, by his own account, single-handedly (actually, with the help of some well-armed backup) arrested no less than five armed gangsters, including the leaders of their city's infamously dreaded drug syndicate. One of those involved had been Lydia, referred to as "femme fatale" and "lieutenant's girlfriend" in some breathlessly lurid news stories.

Kendrick bent over the blackened remains and lifted the cloth. He reached into it with a gloved hand, gingerly pulling something out a few inches.

"And it would seem this is a blade."

Jilly took a few steps towards the body and squatted down, trying to stay sufficiently far from the body as to not touch anything. She looked at the length of slim metal coming out of the victim's chest.

"This is going to be one memorable hell of an autopsy but I'm pretty sure that she was dead before the fire got to her. Certainly she was circling the drain already. That explains why the other woman got out and she didn't."

"Any idea who this other woman was?"

"Yeah." Mickey pointed to a clipboard lying on the ground a few feet away. "Already got the IDs on everyone. Her name was Yvette St. Cloud, and I'd venture she's your prime suspect now."

"So, just what do we have to go on here?"

"Not much, I'm afraid. It is, after all, also an accident site. All kinds of responders crawling around here since it happened. If your girl Yvette left any footprints they've been trampled and plowed under. Maybe you might find something further away; the ground's still soft going up and down those hills. And I don't know what I'm going to be able to get for you from this hunk of barbecue."

Jilly suppressed a hard smile. When you see the stuff someone like Mickey sees every day, you develop a pretty harsh sense of humor. For that matter, it held true for her, Dan, and the rest of their unit as well.

"I might have something for you from the weapon. I'll send it to SID. Probably no prints but, maybe something."

"How can you be sure this is Lydia and not Yvette?" asked Dan, who had crouched down next to them and was inspecting what was left of the body.

Mickey delicately slid a long stylus under a blackened disc of metal somewhere around where the victim's throat had once been. "A silver religious medallion with the initials LM."

Jilly stood up, looking around. "Anybody here who might be able to tell us something about this Yvette?"

"I'm sure. There's gotta be a dozen different agencies around here. Try that guy there."

The serious, stocky guy in a windbreaker and goggles carrying a touch-pad turned out to be just the right guy indeed. His name was Tad Rasula, and he was an investigator with the Costa County Sheriff's Department. After quick introductions, Jilly jumped right in.

"Just why was Yvette St. Cloud being transported to your jurisdiction?"

"She's actually from down our way, a town called Santa Sangre."

"The name sounds vaguely familiar."

"It started as a farming town, took its name from a small mission. Like just about any town big or small these days, it's got its crime problems. There's a local gang called the SanSans that she ran with. She's twenty years old and already a hard case. Been in and out of juvie since she was about fifteen and when she reached majority she didn't stop. We don't know the specifics, but she drove up your way with a stolen car full of crystal meth and weapons, maybe establishing a connection here. She was apprehended for transporting with intent to sell. Some discussions between the two jurisdictions over who'd get her. We won the lottery."

"Any idea who she was contacting here?"

"My understanding is she got picked up here on an undercover burn. I also heard that Interrogations apparently got nowhere with her; she's a regular Sphinx. You might have more info from the arresting detectives on your side."

"How about any thoughts on where she might be headed?"

"Who knows? We just don't know that much about her. She may or may not have actual friends up here. She very well might be scared to return home. She could be going anywhere. All I can suggest is, let's trade contact info. I'll send you everything I got on her. And we'll be starting our own searches." Rasula sighed deeply. "Hope you find her first. Honestly, I sure don't want her." They thanked him and he excused himself to return to his tasks at hand.

Dan sighed heavily and stared unhappily at Jilly. "So I guess we can't put off looking for tracks any longer."

"Didn't like these shoes anyway. Which way do you want, partner: up or down?"

TWELVE

Had there been any actual witnesses around the mid-size automobile parked at the curb, they likely might have observed the very large man crammed into the front seat did not look in the least comfortable, despite having it jammed back as far as it would go. But since it was pre-dawn morning and he had deliberately parked far from the nearest streetlight, there was little chance anyone was going to notice him, much less remark on his apparent discomfort.

Next to him on the seat was a crumpled bag with the remains of two double cheeseburgers, an empty extra-large soda cup, and a screw-topped large-mouth container that had once held a half gallon of apple juice and now held something of a similar color. He'd only been there two or three hours, maybe, but it felt like forever.

How do those detectives do those stake outs, anyway?

He'd been sitting in the darkened car, peering up at the apartment building across the street until his eyes had started to burn. The late-night delivery dropped off at the front door earlier had convinced him he was at the right place. He was pretty sure he was focusing on the right unit, not one hundred percent sure but maybe ninety. He hoped for some further sign to remove all doubt.

Felix Sykes couldn't sit still in the "borrowed" car. It wasn't just that it was too small for a man as big as he was, and he wasn't really concerned that anyone was going to come looking for it. What he'd gotten himself into just didn't sit right with him. But there was nothing he could do. The past twelve hours had assured him of that.

Bored to death out here, there was little to distract him from the thoughts that plagued him. He kept going over in his mind just how he'd wound up out here, in this situation.

When his lawyer informed him that he was getting released from the detention center, it had come as good news indeed. His situation there was dicey at best. There was nobody he could trust. He'd kept to himself in custody, avoiding his old crew, big and nasty enough that the rest of the population obligingly left him alone as well. He even suspiciously avoided the crew lawyers that had been sent around. The public defender he'd requested was the only one with whom he'd been talking. The reason they'd been holding him along with the others, he was originally told, was because that treacherous shrew Lydia was singing a mile a minute about the entire organization and they'd figured they could stick him with something. Then, Felix learned, she'd suddenly retracted the entire operatic performance. There was no longer all that much on which to hold him, so they were letting him go.

He wasn't sure what he was going to do, but he needed to get far away from his old crew and stay there. His closest friend, T.C., the leader of the crew, had tripped out majorly. Felix thought back to the last hours the two had spent together before being arrested. The man had been seriously paranoid, raving on about some major conspiracy involving a shady mastermind who'd stolen their boss's money and set him up to take the fall. Felix's theory was that T.C. had started partaking of his own product and gone off the rails big time. On the other hand, Yancey himself was firmly convinced that the scheme to steal his money had originated with T.C. and his immediate crew, including Felix himself. The real truth might never get figured out, where the money had actually gone and to whom, but it no longer mattered. The world he knew was unsafe. Yancey was an enemy and T.C. was a dangerous person to be around.

He needed to get as far away from the people and the life he knew, as fast as he could.

Not an easy choice to make, considering the crew and the life—and his oldest homeboy T.C.—were pretty much all he'd known for many years now. But he'd have to reinvent himself somehow if he wanted to continue to live.

All this was going through his head crazily as he walked out the doors of the detention center, once again a free man. That was when the big surprise hit him between the eyes.

A Jeep Cherokee was waiting engine idling. Behind the wheel, with a smile, sat young Nate, a more recent member of T.C.'s crew.

Felix didn't like that smile. In his world, smiles were anything but reassuring. He hesitated at the door of the car.

Nate waved him in, calling out through the open passenger window, "It's okay, Felix. Everything's cool."

It took Felix a minute to weigh everything, but he needed to get far away from the jail. He decided to get in, warily. He kept the door unlocked, his hand on the handle, and his seat belt unlatched. His eyes stayed on Nate's hands as the kid put the Jeep in gear and pulled away.

"I know this is weird, man, but believe me, you and I are both good with Yancey."

"Just exactly why are you here?" Felix asked in a low voice.

""I gotta take you somewhere."

"Take me somewhere? You little fuck. Who you trying to play? What you *gotta* do is pull over. Right now."

Nate seemed a weird choice to send to take him out. Nate was no match for him, and they both knew that. If Nate pulled a piece, he could easily reach across, break his wrist and take the gun, or even just dive out of the Jeep.

"Okay, okay, okay." Nate braked hard at the curb. He raised his hands in the air. "He just wants to talk to you. In a safe place, public, with lots of people."

"Who's *he*? I'm supposed to trust Yancey?"

"Not Yancey."

"I don't like any of this."

"This is no setup, Felix, I swear. No shit. Come on, man, I was part of T.C.'s crew too. If he'd wanted us gone, I'd be gone too, right?"

"Nate, you're a straight dude and all, but, no offense, you're still green as shit. Lots of things you don't even *know* you don't know yet."

"This is what he told me to tell you: I let you out on the open street, in public. You check out where he's waiting to meet you, alone, and if it don't look right, you walk away. After that, you're on your own. But he said you're likely gonna like what he's got to say."

So Felix had found himself sitting at a corner table, back to the wall, in a popular coffee house across from Barclay Vickers. All around them were yuppies and millennials talking animatedly, all absorbed in themselves, their phones, their caramel lattes, and their own conversations. It was a totally laughable scene.

Barclay was speaking gravely, in hushed tones, keeping an eye out around them for listeners. "So that's the situation. You were T.C.'s right hand man but I know you had nothing to do with the shit he pulled. You're a valuable man. I'm offering you the same position with me. Plus, I know you're not afraid of being on the muscle side of things and Yancey's gonna need a reliable top enforcer. There's a lot of money and a lot of perks."

"But what you're asking me to do to get all that, that doesn't sit well, Barclay. Him and I, we go way back."

"I know, I know, I know." Barclay lowered his head and peered up at Felix. "Do you have any doubt that he's got Yancey's money?"

"I was there when he left the drop-off. I was there when we followed the dude who made the pickup."

"But did you see the money dropped off? Did you see it picked up? Were you *there*?"

Felix didn't answer, just sighed.

"Didn't think so. That Brick character, did anyone ever see him with the money? Did he ever admit to having it?"

"No."

"When you guys found him, T.C. was supposed to bring the dude to Yancey, wasn't he? And instead, the way I heard it, he disposed of him after first sending all the rest of you away, do I have that right? No witnesses? Convenient, wouldn't you say?"

Felix didn't say anything.

"Just tell me one thing. Those last couple days, was T.C. acting normal?"

Felix still didn't reply, but it was clear: no, he hadn't been.

Barclay leaned in even closer. "You got to face it, Felix. The guy's gone rogue. Making up all kinda shit about somebody impersonating somebody. Something's fucked up with him. He almost got you and the rest of your crew killed, and he might still do it if you don't do something about it."

"Man, I just want out of all this."

"You just wanta walk away, just like that. You *know* that can't happen. You're in the life. Only one way out. That what you want? 'Cause that's exactly what'll happen if you don't make all this right now."

Felix just stared at Barclay.

"You know stuff about your boy T.C. that the rest of us don't. All I need you to do is go find him for us, that's all, and your life gets instantly better."

Felix didn't want Tiny's old job. Not that he hadn't done enough "disposal" himself. That part didn't faze him. But it had always been a last resort, not the goal in itself. He didn't want it to be a major part of every day. He'd always thought that Tiny was majorly broken for doing that. But he could handle being "number two's number two" like he'd done with T.C.

He'd been handed a really big upside and a really bad downside.

He made his decision. He and Barclay cemented the agreement.

Once Felix had made that decision, he had a good idea where to begin. T.C. didn't think anyone knew about his secret crib. But he was wrong.

And now, some hours later, he found himself sitting in the dark in the car that Barclay had provided him, staring up at the window covered with shades. He could swear there was some light leaking out through those blinds, but there was no sign of life. He'd keep watching as long as he could.

There. A small crack of light between the blinds. Someone was up there.

That was all he needed. He was in the right place.

Sorry. T.C. This is some fucked up shit, but, business is business. It's you or me.

THIRTEEN

Leon got to his desk Tuesday morning to find Art already busy at his computer. You could always tell when Art was on a roll.

"This woman was a real piece of work!" Art exclaimed by way of greeting, never looking away from his screen, two-finger typing furiously. "I lucked out on a few calls to some insurance people this morning and there's a pattern that's forming."

"Fine, thanks," Leon replied, booting up his own computer.

Art finally looked over at him. "What's fine?"

"My evening. It was fine. Thanks for asking. And how was yours?"

Art ignored the question. "I got to talk to a couple obsessive-compulsives and learned a little more about our gal Halley. Enough to give me some ideas about a few things. She was quite the student of the hustle. About six months ago she pulled a liability scam—maybe her first, I'm not sure yet—on a small hardware store down in Sycamore. Claimed she cut herself on some tools that had been left out unsafely. The store's insurance company made her an offer and she settled. Then maybe a month later she tried another one, this time on a day care center. A trip and fall thing. Again, their insurance made a quick offer, and she took it."

Leon nodded. "The company just wants it to go away, whatever it takes as long as it's easy. Perfect scenario for an opportunist."

"But apparently she figured out it was what you'd call small potatoes."

"You would, Arthur. I hate that expression."

"Well, excuse me. Anyway, Halley seems to have figured out there were higher stakes to be gained. So here's the scenario. Three months ago, she walks into a big Food Extravaganza, clandestinely rips up a floor mat and spills a jar of pickle juice on the floor and does a dive. A real acting gem. But this time she's not ready to accept the insurance company's offer. She's made the acquaintance of our pal Applegate and she's been educated about going to court for a bigger prize. She shows up at the deposition decked out as if she'd fallen out of an airplane, moaning and groaning, their lawyers panic and make a bigger settlement to make her go away."

"Interesting. What kind of settlement are we talking?"

"I'm not sure but it's a new league from where she's been playing up to now. And it gets better. Now she's got fever for the game. You know what comes next."

"The swoop and squat?"

"Exactly. A major step up. She's got a partner. It's an active crime conspiracy. The idea is to cow innocent victims out of cash, scare them into running to the ATM to pay for the damages out of pocket. Only it doesn't go well. She rear-ends Moira Legge, who doesn't get intimidated and doesn't play along. Instead, she sounds the alarm and Halley gets picked up."

"While her mysterious accomplice beats it."

"So Halley's left to hold the bag, with the accomplished support of her lawyer Marshal Applegate. She's facing a felony charge. But something happens to convince Ms. Legge to not show up to testify."

"You might say Ms. Legge legs it."

"You might, Leon. I wouldn't."

"Touché, Arthur."

"The point is, Halley dodges a bullet and skates. But she's still furthered her education. Likely she decides the odds aren't good in that business. So now she's back to taking pratfalls, this time in front of a private home. I'm guessing she's learned to cruise the streets looking for the right setup, some potential liability that she can exploit. This time she finds an older neighborhood, lined with big beautiful old growth trees, where the sidewalks are being pushed up by the root systems. She takes one hell of a spill and comes up with her face covered with blood, screaming in agony. Once again, she and Applegate refuse the offered settlement and threaten to head to court. Another deposition with Halley in medical drag, and apparently with a doctor's note, and once again the insurance company caves and gives them a big payout."

"It'll be interesting," Leon mused, "when we can access any of her bank records to see what kind of deposits she made and how they tally up with these incidents."

"All of this is leading up to her final big score: the Mercers. I'm not sure how much she figured she was going to get out of them. She somehow pulled off a totally bizarre scheme. The part where she appeared out of nowhere just in time to get hit by Abigail as she backed out of her driveway, that was probably planned, but then getting bit by a monkey as well? Potential jackpot! Remember, Jack and Halley were about to be evicted by those delightful grandkids who inherited the property on Mockingbird Lane? The Mercers, they've got a nice house, not extravagant but nice. She was going to go for the house!"

"Oh yeah. The monkey."

"What I'm trying to figure out is, how does any of this translate into someone with big enough grudge to kill Halley and her husband as well? And so far, what I'm coming up with is, Halley had a Fagin."

"Come again, Arthur?"

"Come on, you read *Oliver Twist*, didn't you? A criminal mentor. Somebody taught Halley how to do this shit. Somebody tutored her, introduced her to different levels of scam. Somebody drove the other car in the swoop scheme. And somebody convinced Ms. Legge not to testify. I get the feeling Legge's no shrinking violet, as my maiden aunt would have said, so whoever got to her did a good job of intimidation."

"You're presuming a lot, but for the moment let's assume you're onto something. You're thinking this Fagin might have had reason to kill her and Jack as well?"

Art shrugged. "I'm just freestyling. Maybe when I get to talk to Abigail Pendleton and Moira Legge it might clear up some… um, you're spacing, Leon. What?"

"I was just thinking. There's a bar in their neighborhood that Jack and Halley sometimes frequented. I stopped in there last night. They were seen with someone the barmaid thought was a gangster, and someone else she thought might be a cop. If you needed to intimidate a witness, those would be two pretty good pools to choose from." Suddenly Leon shook his head and chuckled.

"Now what?"

"*Oliver Twist?* Really?"

Art raised his eyebrows.

"I like Dickens. So sue me. Are you telling me you never read it?"

"Back in high school, sure. You're clearly more literate than I am."

"So, anything else on Jack Donner?"

Leon shook his head. "Not so far. He's slippery. Seems like he was involved in as much sketchy stuff as she was, but I'm still looking to find anything solid. Makes me wonder about why Radley wanted to push me in his direction and brought up this Barnfeather character. I think another conversation with him is in order."

Leon's phone buzzed.

"Simpkins."

"Leon! Gene Gehm here. I got something for you on Barnfeather, but it's not much. One of our undercovers has seen him around. He's some low-level member of the Rybus crew. Picked up a couple times but never charged."

"Any connection with Jack Donner?"

"That name isn't ringing any bells around here."

"Anything else you can tell me about Barnfeather?"

"Seems to be involved in the selling side of things, not the muscle. He's only popped up recently."

"With all the current instability, maybe he's been trying to move up in the organization?"

"You know these knuckleheads, they were all probably jockeying for position as soon as Yancey and his boys got picked up. So, who knows? I've got nothing specific on him."

"What's this Barnfeather look like?"

"Kind of a skinny dude, not one of those monsters Rybus prefers. My guy said he had some attitude, maybe the only way he got noticed at all."

"Any chance he shaves his head?"

"No idea. A lot of those guys are doing that."

"How do I find Barnfeather?"

"Don't know what to tell you, Leon. Nobody seems to have seen him the last few days. But, let me ask you something: how exactly did he come up in connection with the Donner murders?"

"One of the uniforms mentioned him in connection with Jack Donner. I guess they were seen together at some point."

"This may sound like a strange question, but was there a dog at the property when you were there?"

"Yeah, the Donners had a big dog of some kind fenced in their yard. Animal Control took it. Why?"

"My guy did happen to mention, Barnfeather had a dog with him when he saw him. That's kind of unusual. The dog might connect to something else we're working on. Now you tell me he might have known this Donner guy. Just a shot in the dark, you know, for both of us?"

"Okay, I'll keep that in mind. We'll talk further on this. Keep me up to date."

"And you do the same. Especially let me know if you can find out anything on the dog, like what might have happened to it, okay? It might be important."

Leon hung up, rubbing his chin. Something strange about all this. Gene was holding back on something, but what? And why? And what was up with all this stuff about a dog? He idly looked over at Art, now on his own phone, jotting down notes as he spoke.

Art had reached Abigail Pendleton in Duluth.

She was immediately suspicious when Art introduced himself.

"What's this about, Detective Gowdy?"

"That's Dowdy, Ma'am. Arthur Dowdy. I'm calling in regard to the recent litigation you're involved in with Halley Donner."

"Oh my God, what now? What's that awful woman coming up with this time? What's she claiming we did this time—"

"Nothing like that, Mrs. Mercer. I just wanted to get some information about the lawsuit."

"Did she put you up to this? You can reach my lawyer if you need to ask any further questions."

Art rubbed his nose between thumb and forefinger. "I'm afraid that Mrs. Donner has died."

"What? What happened?"

"She was murdered Sunday."

Silence on the line. Finally, "Who killed her?"

"We're looking into that. I'm hoping you might be able to help me."

"How can I help you? I don't even *know* the woman! All I know is she set us up for a gigantic lawsuit and we could lose our house because of it!" She took a long pause. "That must sound terrible. I'm sorry she's dead, but all I can think of now is, won't that make the lawsuit go away?"

"What exactly happened?"

"I was backing our car out of our driveway one day when suddenly I heard this ear-piercing scream. I hadn't seen anyone around when I looked before starting up and it scared the daylights out of me. I got out of the car to see what had happened, and there she was, lying on the ground screeching at the top of her lungs that I'd run her over. And then Gummy Bear got out."

Art played dumb. "Gummy Bear?"

"He's a monkey. We had him in a cage. We were taking him to the vet for a checkup. My father—oh, it's a long story, but he gave our daughter Amelia the monkey. But Amelia hadn't fastened the cage completely and when I slammed on the brakes, between the screaming and the jolt, he got agitated and pushed open the door to the cage and jumped out. Before I could do anything, he skittered out behind the car and I swear, that witch *hit* him. She smacked him across the face. So I guess he bit her, which I really couldn't blame him for. Now she *really* started wailing."

"What did you do?"

"At first, I was worried she was really hurt. It was all so confusing. I ran back to see if I could help her. Gummy was going totally nuts with all the commotion. I somehow got him calmed down, back into the car and into his cage without getting myself bitten as well and went back to see if I could help the woman. Next thing I know, she's demanding all kinds of information from me: our insurance company and so forth. I asked if I could do anything to help her, bring her inside or take her to the hospital. She did this act where she struggled to her feet and coughed that I'd done enough damage, she could help herself. I gave her the name of our insurance agent and the next thing I knew, she'd disappeared again. Once I had the chance to calm down and think about it, I figured she probably had a car parked nearby. I began suspecting that she was faking the whole thing.

"But that wasn't the end. Shortly thereafter, our insurance agent called to tell us that she and her lawyer were demanding a huge sum for damages. Our policy didn't cover anywhere near what they were asking. And then the next thing I knew I got notice that they were suing us. On top of that, they made a complaint to Animal Control, and someone was sent over to take Gummy Bear."

"I'm sorry. Was the monkey, um, destroyed?"

"Is that what this is really about, you want to find him?"

"No, no, Mrs. Pendleton. I'm with Personal Crimes. I have nothing to do with animals. I swear, if somehow you kept them from getting your monkey, I'm not interested in that."

"Gummy's been nothing but problems, but Amelia loves him. I couldn't let them put him to sleep, so I told them he'd escaped. I gave him back to my father. I wish he'd never given her the damn creature to begin with. We might not have gotten into the situation we're in if it hadn't been for Gummy."

"Is Gummy generally dangerous?"

"Not really. He's a capuchin monkey. They're generally very tame. Do you remember that television show that was on some years back, the one about all the twentysomethings living together, and one of them had a monkey? That was a capuchin, and it set off a popularity thing about them."

"If I'm not mistaken, it's pretty much illegal to sell or own them in this state."

Abigail exhaled with exasperation. "Yes, I found that out from the vet for the first time. That didn't stop Craig—that's my father—from getting hold of one and gifting it to Amelia. He thought it would get him back on her good side, and through her, on mine. It just made it worse."

"Just curious, any idea how he got it?"

"Who the hell knows, Detective? I don't have much to do with Craig these days. It could have been just about anything. He's out of his mind."

So when Animal Control came for an illegal monkey that had demonstrated itself to be dangerous, she of course scooted it out the back door. Art was beginning to wish they'd never gotten this case.

"When did all this happen?"

"Around two weeks ago."

"And you've retained an attorney yourself."

"We've been talking to one, yes. Everything has been on hold until the suit was actually filed."

"Have you had any subsequent contact with Halley Donner since the incident?"

"God, no. Neither I nor anybody else in our family. I want nothing to do with that woman."

"And you've been out of town for a while now, is that my understanding?"

"I needed to get away from all this crap, so Wayne and I packed up Amelia and came here to spend time with my mother. We've been here since last Thursday." She paused for a minute before continuing. "Wait a minute, you don't think I had anything to do with that woman's death, do you?"

"Just trying to get some facts, Mrs. Mercer."

"That's crazy. I've got witnesses. We've been here since Thursday. None of us have been anywhere near the city."

"I'm sure that's the case, ma'am. As I said, I'm just trying to get as much information as I can on Halley Donner."

"You can ask my father about what happened. Craig Mercer, on Wyandotte Street. And if you want to confiscate the damned monkey, he's there too."

Art breathed with relief as he finally hung up, looking across his desk dejectedly to his partner, who was just finishing still another phone conversation.

Leon's call to Mickey Kendrick about possible developments in the autopsy had been futile. He said he wouldn't be able to turn his attention to the Donners until later today, at best. As he hung up, he looked over to see Art chewing on his pencil and staring at the pad on his lap. Leon felt as frustrated as his partner.

"What have we got on either of them?" Art finally said. "Clean, cold hit. They were hooked up with somebody serious, involved in something that got them in trouble, but how can we get an insight into any of this? No friends or family that we can find. They had a chest of powder, but we can't find any drug connections. They had a rack of guns but as far as we know so far, they were legit and nobody took any of them. Jack was a shady character and a thief, but with not much of an arrest record. No known associates, just the uni's throwaway mention of that Barnfeather character."

"We've got a bunch of people that Halley pissed off."

"Which so far aren't looking promising. Anything else?"

"Maybe when the lab and Mickey come through there'll be something. In the meantime, everything about this is just, I don't know, strange. I'm going to have another conversation with Radley. He knows more than he was saying. And then there's the Donners' dog."

"The *dog*? What about the dog?"

"When I spoke with Gene Gehm in Narcotics, he asked me about their dog."

"How did he even know about the dog? I mean, we hardly knew about it. Why would he care?"

"I don't know, Art, it's like we're in the dark here."

"Well, I guess we have to keep throwing shit against the wall until something sticks. I'd rather stay in motion anyway. I'm going to go look for Moira Legge and maybe stop and talk to this Craig Mercer guy. Not sure what else to do at this point until we get something from the lab or from Mickey or from somewhere." Art tossed the gnawed pencil onto his desk and rose from his chair.

Leon picked up the phone receiver one more time. "I'm thinking another conversation with Marshall Applegate might be in order. After which I'll hunt down Officer Radley."

Leon figured the odds of catching Applegate in his office were fifty-fifty; he might be at court or out chasing ambulances. He lucked out and caught him in.

"How about I come right over, Mr. Applegate, would that be convenient?"

"By all means. I'm afraid my office is, um, still being painted but we can talk in my conference room again. And Sigrid just made a new pot of coffee."

Leon found himself wishing that the guy could just come out and admit he didn't *have* a private office in his storefront. Well, as he knew from experience, truth didn't come easy to a lot of people. He hung up the phone and called to his partner, who was also on his way out. "Hey Art, hold the elevator!"

FOURTEEN

Elsewhere in the squad room, Jilly and Dan were involved in their own conversation, trying to make sense out of the events of the previous evening.

They'd been quite a sight when they'd returned to the unit late Monday, clumps of mud and dirt still clinging to their pants and shoes and had been immediately summoned into the office of their Lieutenant, Hank Castillo.

The Lou always had the remarkable ability to maintain unruffled decorum, no matter how much weight was being dropped on him by virtue of his position. He sat behind his desk, judgelike, with his salt and pepper hair and mustache, in two-thirds of a sharp three-piece suit, crisp white shirt and striped tie. Jilly couldn't help but cast an eye at the suit coat on a hanger in the far corner. She wasn't sure she'd ever seen the Lou in dark green before, but it was certainly a nice shade of green.

The news of the death of Lydia Montgomery and the escape of Yvette St. Cloud had preceded their return. In a rare moment of vulgarity, the Lou had proclaimed that the shit storm was in full explosion. Photos released by the Department of Corrections were already all over the various news media, portending a frenzy: escaped convict, brutal murderer, do not approach under any circumstances, the whole bit. Given little choice, the Police Department had to issue its own statements. Spokespersons were already assuring the public that all manner of alerts, BOLOs, and all-points bulletins were being issued and that "every available person" was being put on the high priority case.

Jilly privately marveled at not one but two crudities in a row uttered by their Lieutenant, an unaccustomed concession to the high level of stress under which he currently found himself. He correctly pointed out to them that the current mass of departmental shit ran in one direction, downhill, and that while he was somewhat down the slope, they were even lower down. Then he leveled his penetrating gaze at each of them and asked what they had for him.

Unfortunately, that wasn't much. There were footprints all around the scene, way too many of them. Over a dozen people had scoured the muddy hillside. St. Cloud could have escaped back up the hill to the arterial road or worked her way down to the rocky coast nearby. She'd have to find someplace to shed her shackles and prison scrubs and lay low, but they had no idea where to start looking into those possibilities. They were waiting on whatever personal info Tad Rasula would provide them on the suspect and hadn't yet had the opportunity to start their own inquiries.

None of this, as might be expected, appeased the Lou. He simply said, "I hope I don't have to tell you this case needs forward motion on it immediately," and returned to the paperwork before him. Castillo did not stand on ceremony; when he no longer paid attention to you, it meant you were dismissed.

There wasn't much they could do any further that evening before signing out, but they did look up the record of St. Cloud's bust in their city. As Rasula had suggested, it had been an undercover setup from two detectives in Narcotics, Gene Gehm and Olivia Venuto. Jilly knew Gene from his Personal Crimes days, but Olivia was a new name. In any case, neither one would be available on their unit until tomorrow. That was the note on which Monday evening had ended.

They'd returned Tuesday morning and now they found themselves still searching for something on which to proceed. One lead had come through the previous night: Rasula's email with the information on Yvette St. Cloud. Dan had it open on his desktop monitor. Jilly peered over Dan's shoulder as they went through the material.

Obviously, the case held some urgency in Costa County as well. Rasula wrote they were on the watch for local places and people they could connect with St. Cloud, and he was sending everything he had about her. There was a fair amount of material to go through.

"If you don't mind," Jilly said, patting Dan on the shoulder, "I'm going to let you start going through that while I give Narcotics a call to see what I can find out about St. Cloud's bust. Maybe she had a contact here in the city they can afford us a lead on."

"No problem," Dan said, never looking away from his screen as he tapped on his keyboard. "Anyway, I've met Gene a couple times and that's plenty. I'm okay with you dealing with him."

"He's not my favorite either, Dan, but this still beats what comes next."

Dan sighed. "Covering the roads and streets near the crash to see if there are any witnesses or cameras that might have caught her. I can't wait. Let's pray for a break. Do you believe in miracles?"

Jilly was about to pick up the desk phone to call Gene when it started buzzing and she answered it, "Garvey."

"Detective Garvey, Tad Rasula here. Are you guys going to be around for a while?"

"We could be, Detective Rasula. What's up?"

"I've just been contacted by an attorney regarding the St. Cloud case, and they'd like to bring someone over to talk to you. That work for you?"

"You make it sound mysterious. Who's this person?"

"The guy that was in the car with her when she was arrested. They'll ask for you and your partner."

"What's that all about?" Dan asked, continuing to type as Jilly hung up the call.

"I guess we're going to have to wait and find out," she replied as she tapped in Gene Gehm's number at Narcotics. "Dare we hope it's your miracle?"

* * * *

Gene, having just ended his conversation with Leon Simpkins, sat back in his chair, arms folded, in deep thought, accompanied by the usual cacophony of the Narco squad around him. As he'd hung up, something began to occur to him from their conversation.

There might be a ray of hope to get out of the dark, scary situation he'd now found himself in this horrific morning.

He'd still been in the parking lot when his cell phone buzzed with an incoming text message that looked at first like a piece of spam. He'd been about to delete it when he looked at it more closely.

U MAY BE ELIGIBLE FOR A GIFT CARD OF YOUR CHOICE, BE SURE TO CHECK UR PHONE ENDING IN 69. DO IT NOW! OFFER EXPIRES SOON!

Gene quickly erased the text, but he'd caught the meaning. His heart sank.

Oh shit.

Double shit.

What I was afraid might happen. And here I hoped I was out from under.

He rummaged in his glove compartment until he found the phone that he hadn't had reason to use in some time now. He looked around to make sure nobody was watching and turned it on, then dialed in the one number he'd ever dialed on it.

It was picked up almost immediately. An all too familiar voice, one he'd prayed he'd never hear again, said silkily, "Aren't you going to welcome me back?"

"What do you want?"

"Why, information, of course. Important information. As soon as you can get it for me. Probably need to get it from someone in homicide, but you, lucky soul, you're the closest I've got to them right now."

The call was brief and to the point. Gene jammed the burner back under the pile of papers in his glove compartment, locked up his car, and headed into work. The minute he'd gotten to his desk he was dialing Leon Simpkins in Personal Crimes.

Leon, he figured, was his best shot at someone who'd talk to him. He'd had to be careful, couldn't push him too much, finding out what he could from him. He might have overdone it; he hoped he hadn't.

But the important thing was that out of that conversation grew the germ of a plan how to get out from under the thumb of Yancey Rybus. That dog, that damned mutt, was the key.

He was still muddling that over when his desk phone rang.

"Gene, this is Jilly Garvey in Personal Crimes."

"Jilly, long time, how are things? What can I do for you?"

"I was helping you might be able to help us out on a case we pulled."

"Are you working on the Donner case as well? I just talked with Leon and told him everything I knew, which wasn't much."

"The Donner case? No. I don't know anything about what Leon and Art are working on. This is about Yvette St. Cloud."

It only took him a moment to place the name. It had been all over the news, and the moment he'd walked into the unit he'd seen the notices posted prominently. "The chick that's been on the news, the escaped convict? What about her?"

He could almost see Jilly's eyeballs rolling and he could hear the slight hitch in her voice before she answered. "The *young woman,* yes, that's the one. I need to get whatever you might be able to give me on her."

Give me a break, he thought to himself. "Why would I have anything on her?"

Another pause and then she cleared her throat, trying to keep her patience. "Because you and your partner, Olivia Venuto, were the ones who picked her up to begin with. Some kind of undercover bust."

Gene pinched the bridge of his nose, closed his eyes, and thought. It finally came to him, where he'd heard the name before. "Oh yeah. Yeah. Her. Dumbass gang kid from out of town. We were following an anonymous tip."

Gene decided not to mention that the anonymous tip had come directly to him personally at Narcotics, through unorthodox channels.

"She thought she was making a deal, selling meth and weapons to someone in the local organization. Imagine her surprise when her customers turned out to be us. She had quite a treasure trove in the trunk of her car, which also turned out to be hot. And she's the killer that got loose yesterday?"

"One and the same. It's a high priority over here and my partner and I landed it."

"Just your lucky day, Jilly."

"Do you remember anything else about the bust? Any known associates, anybody with her at the time?"

"Damn, it's a blur. Let me think. Wait, yeah. There was somebody else in the car with her. Young guy as I recall. He bolted."

Now it came back to him: he'd stayed with the girl while Venuto took off after the guy. Gene had just gotten too old these days to attempt any unnecessary legwork. Olivia had returned a while later, out of breath, angry, and empty handed.

"Any idea who that guy was? At least what he looked like, anything?"

"Neither of us even got a good look at him, just that he was young and could run like a rabbit. He was in a hoodie, the hood was up, and that's all I remember. We've got notes on the bust. I'd have to refresh my memory and talk to my partner. I'll send you over copies of whatever I've got."

"Thanks, Gene, the sooner the better."

Something else occurred to him, now that he thought about the news reports. "She killed that gal picked up in the Rybus thing, right? The one that Marlon arrested?"

"Lydia Montgomery, right. St. Cloud is a desperate one. I'm surprised you don't remember more about her."

Now that Gene thought about it, Yvette had given them both a fair amount of attitude and resistance. She'd made the mistake of thinking Olivia was going to be the easier of the two of them and went off on her. That was a lesson learned hard.

Yvette ended up taking the entire rap and wouldn't say a word about who had been in the car with her, who was supposed to meet up with her, or anything. Tough kid. She kind of scared Gene, in fact. Gene actually admired that, even though it made his own job that much harder.

"She didn't talk much," Gene finally replied. "So she didn't leave much of an impression. I guess she must have been a little intimidated by me and Olivia. What can I say?"

* * * *

"Before we start, I want it absolutely clear that Mr. Litotes has come forth voluntarily and is willing to tell you what he knows as long as it's understood he has not participated in any crime and there will be no attempt to hold or charge him with any."

Jilly and Dan gave no indication of what they were thinking but Jilly was privately impressed that Yolanda Lerner was ready to defend her client tooth and nail. Pretty interesting for a young guy in khakis and a flannel shirt who professed to be totally innocent. Well, Ms. Lerner was also young, full of fire and idealistic.

Jilly nodded. "It's not our intent to detain or charge your client, Ms. Lerner. What we're interested in is what he can tell us about Yvette St. Cloud, and I assume that's why you've come here today, to do just that."

"So, what can you tell us?" Dan asked the young man sitting across the grey table. They were in one of the less grotty of the unit's interview rooms, but none of them were exactly showcases of interior decor. This one had at least been repainted in the last year and the color was a reasonable beige instead of the more common dingy greenish grey. Lonnie Litotes was tall, thin and nervous, scowling and shifting his gaze back and forth between the detectives. He looked to be in his very early twenties, with wisps of hair around his chin and upper lip.

"I was with her," he said hesitantly, glancing over at his lawyer. Lerner nodded to him in encouragement. "The night she was arrested."

"Are you from here, or from Costa County?"

"No, I drove up with her. We both live down there, in Santa Sangre."

"Why did you come up here to begin with?" Jilly asked.

"Evie needed money. She figured if she grabbed a bunch of stuff to sell, she'd do better up here."

"By 'stuff' do you mean guns and drugs?"

Litotes looked at Lerner for several seconds before answering. "It was something she thought she could make some money on, whatever. I didn't know what she had in the trunk. I was just along for the ride."

"Why?" asked Dan. "If you didn't know what she was carrying, why did you ride with her?"

"She asked me to come along, just for company, you know? Maybe for support?"

"What kind of support? I mean, you did run away when she was arrested, right?"

"She was worried about, you know, having to deal with hard guys. They don't always respect a woman. I was just show. Shit, Evie could hold her own. She could kick my ass seven ways to Sunday. Cops, that was a different matter. I knew I couldn't help her."

"So, you two are like, friends?" Dan continued.

"Not like, you know, romantic? We've just been good friends for a long time."

"You both in the SanSans?" asked Jilly.

"I'm not in that anymore. Used to be. I got out a couple years ago. Evie was ready to leave. But it's not that simple. You don't just shake hands with your homies and say bye-bye, keep in touch, you know?"

Dan nodded. "So, what did you both have to do to get out?"

"Me, I was jumped out, you know what that means? They put me in the hospital for a couple days."

"And Yvette?"

"They treat the girls different. Evie had to pay tribute. A lot."

"So she needed money, a lot of it, fast."

Litotes nodded.

"Where'd she find the weap—" Jilly looked at Lerner, who was following this line of questioning very carefully and had her hand poised to drop onto Litotes' arm. "Where'd she find whatever it was she was going to sell?"

Litotes, trading looks with Lerner, shrugged. "Didn't ask. Don't know."

"So, this *merchandise,* she stuck it in the trunk of her car and decided to bring it up here to sell and asked you come along with her as backup."

"Yeah. That's about right."

"And let me guess, you also had no idea the car itself was stolen."

"Really? No. This is the first I heard anything about that."

"And she contacted someone here to arrange a buy?"

"I got no idea. I mean, I guess she must have, but I had no idea who."

"But she knew where she was going when she got here, right? Did you drive right up here directly to the meeting place?"

"Yeah. I don't know this city at all. I don't think she does either, so she maybe was following directions. We got right off the freeway, and she took us right there."

"So, you pulled up on some street for what was supposed to be a prearranged meet."

"I guess so. It was starting to get dark. She said she was supposed to meet this, um, person or people or whatever, around eight or eight thirty or like that, I forget. We sat in the car for a while and she was getting nervous. Then this car pulls up behind us, flashes its lights and then kills them. We both get out, Evie asks me to stand by the car, look tough, hands in my jacket like I'm strapped, keep an eye on her, all for show, and she starts to walk back. She's bent down talking to the guy in the driver's seat for a minute, all of a sudden, he and his partner are getting out of the car and I hear one of them say 'Police.' I guess I panicked and took off. One of the cops, the woman, lit out after me. I don't remember much until I realized I'd been running as fast as I could, jumping over fences and shit, scooting through yards, and I was out of breath in some strange neighborhood. I had no idea how far I'd gone, but nobody was after me anymore. I was near a railroad track with a lot of trees and bushes so I found a place I could hide and stayed there until morning."

"How'd you get back home?"

"Found my way to the bus station. I had enough cash on me for a ticket."

"And you've been back in Santa Sangre since then?"

Litotes nodded vigorously, looking down at his hands on the table. "I was scared they'd come after me. And, well, I, well, I felt bad I'd left Evie behind. I was afraid the word would get out that I'd bailed on her."

"Why did you come forward now?"

"I guess I finally felt worse about Evie than I felt scared. I was still afraid to just go to the cops, so I took the bus up here and looked in the phone book for a lawyer and found Ms. Lerner."

"And I agreed to act on his behalf," Lerner added.

Jilly leaned forward towards him. "You heard the whole story about what happened Monday, right?"

"Yeah. Sure. That's kinda why I'm here."

"Do you think she headed back to Santa Sangre after she escaped?"

Litotes shook his head emphatically. "No. No, I don't think so. She's got nothing back there but trouble." He looked up at Jilly. "But she didn't do this thing you said she did. She's tough and she can be mean, she can take a beating as well as she can give one, but she's never killed nobody."

Jilly sighed. "Lonnie, there's no doubt about what happened. She and another woman were being transported in that van when the accident occurred, and it caught fire. The other woman was stabbed to death and left to burn up, and Yvette St. Cloud escaped."

"I don't believe it," Litotes said sadly. "She didn't do it. She didn't kill anybody. She couldn't. I know people—" he looked over at his attorney— "some people who, you know, could maybe have killed other people. There's something about them, you can feel it. Evie's not like that. She couldn't be one of them. It was why she wanted out of the SanSans."

"What do you mean, she couldn't be one of them?"

"Look, Evie comes from the same place I do. Her parents weren't worth shit, school was a waste of time, she ran with the same people I did all her life. Most of us in Santa Sangre are never going to be worth all that much. But Evie, she's smart. She was hoping to go back to school, get her GED, and maybe learn a trade or something. She's actually pretty good with cars and thought she could be a mechanic. She was sick and tired of fighting all the time and doing all the shit you have to do in a group like the SanSans."

"You had already dropped out. Did you encourage her to do the same?"

"I guess I did, yeah. I got the same idea. I want to go back to school, maybe be a chef someday, something like that. One thing I'm totally sure about in any case. You want to make something of yourself, you first gotta get away from that group of losers."

"So if Yvette felt the same, then where would she go when she escaped?"

Litotes shrugged. "She sure wouldn't want to go back to Costa County. Nothing and nobody there for her. Plus, they're looking for her now. She didn't know anywhere else. She'd be running blind. Who knows, maybe she'd stay put and hide out here? This is a big city. Well, especially to someone like her or me who spent our whole life in a little town. This city seems like it's got a million hiding places."

"Do you really think she'd have stayed here?" Dan asked.

"Either that, or head out as far from Santa Sangre as possible. I dunno. But if you find her, you gotta realize, she's no killer. I don't care what the evidence looks like. Evie didn't do this."

Jilly eyed him carefully. "And you haven't seen or communicated with her since you got out of her car and ran that night?"

"No, swear to God, I haven't."

"And there's nobody you can think of who she might try to get in touch with?"

"I told you, no. I figure I'm the only friend she's got, else why would she have asked me to ride with her that night? I don't think she liked or trusted anybody else around her. Certainly not the SanSans. They're a bunch of losers."

Lerner cleared her throat. "I think we're covering old ground now. So, unless you have any further questions, Detectives?"

And that was that.

After seeing Litotes and Lerner to the elevator, Jilly and Dan returned to their desks. Jilly simply sat on the edge of hers while Dan dropped himself loudly into his swivel chair, exhaling like he had just run a 10K.

"What do you think, Jilly, is this guy on the level?"

"In general, I can buy his story, though I don't think he was as innocent of the whole thing as he makes himself out to be."

"Why was he willing to come out of hiding? Just to help us find Yvette?"

"I think he's worried she's in bigger danger if we don't find her, for whatever reason. Maybe she crossed the gang and stole the contraband she was trying to sell. And maybe he's closer to her than he's letting on, but I don't see how that matters to us anyhow. What does matter is if he may have given us something of value." Jilly stared up at the ceiling as she let her brain run. "So Evie gets free of the van and what are her immediate concerns? She's in a totally strange environment, doesn't know her way around, knows nobody that can help her. She stands out like a sore thumb in her prison gear." Jilly began to tick off items on her fingers. "She has to find a place to hide. She has to break her shackles and change out of her prison scrubs. She's got to eat and have a place to sleep."

"It seems she's good with tools," Dan said. "And once she gets herself out of the shackles and the prison garb, it wouldn't hurt if she could get some fast work for a few quick bucks that would allow her to move on. If she could find some work with a small car repair guy who doesn't ask too many questions, pays in cash, maybe even gives her a back room to sleep in...."

"I see what you're getting at."

There were easily several hundred independent mechanics and service stations scattered around the city.

Jilly threw her hands up. "Okay, partner, at least it's some kind of direction. The question is how far away from the crime scene are we going to have to scour?"

Dan slowly rose from his chair, feeling much wearier than a man his age should. "We won't know until we do it, will we?"

"Well, the day is still young. Hopefully we can get the Lou to pull some unis to help us cast further. "

"Jilly, have I ever told you how much I love this part of our work, scuttling around aimlessly, walking a thousand streets and knocking on a thousand doors?"

"Not really."

"And I never will."

FIFTEEN

Karlotta Fields was aptly named; her title was Field Manager for the city's Department of Parks, Recreation and Wildlife, a job she'd ably held for several years now. She was conscientiously reading through a new sheaf of forms from the city when her phone rang.

"Good morning." The voice was deep, full and precise. "This is Gaines Murrough from the law firm of Martin, Martin and Murrough. I wonder if you might be able to help me. I'm trying to locate Webster Musgrave. It's my understanding he might have worked for your department recently?"

Had he ever.

Karlotta rubbed her temples. She'd liked the guy immensely, but she was still dealing with the fallout from Webster's encounters with the public that had led to his dismissal. "Yes, he did, up until last month. How may I help you, Mr. Murrough?"

"We are acting as executor for the estate of someone who recently passed away and we have a disbursement for Mr. Musgrave, but unfortunately, he's no longer at the address we had been given for him. I was hoping you might be able to provide us with a more recent whereabouts so we can contact him to arrange for him to receive what he has coming?"

That certainly sounded like good news for Webster. He'd contacted her with a new forwarding address for his severance check, and it sounded as if he'd found a new job, but she had a feeling any kind of windfall would mean a lot to him. Web, she decided, was never going to be a guy without money problems.

"As a matter of fact, I do have an address where he can be reached. He recently moved downstate to a town called Crystalline. I've got a post office box address."

"Crystalline! Where is that, exactly?"

"I wasn't familiar with it either, Mr. Murrough. It's a small town out in the desert down there. I'm afraid that's all I've got for you."

"That might be fine. My firm can likely trace him with that to start. Thank you. This is a big help."

Karlotta dug through her papers for the letter Webster had sent and read off the mail address over the phone. The man thanked her once again and rang off.

Despite all the trouble he'd caused for her, she had a fondness for Web Musgrave, and she felt bad for what he'd had to go through recently, what with her having to fire him and all. She hoped that phone call had been a harbinger of good things to come for him.

* * * *

Theo put down his burner phone and looked at the paper where he'd jotted down the PO box address. Against all odds, he'd lucked out almost right away. He would have figured that, once the brilliant masquerade was no longer necessary, the mastermind who had been leading a second life as park ranger (or whatever he was) Webster Musgrave would have just left his identity behind and vanished into thin air. It was a million to one shot that Theo would be able to pick up a lead, but here the guy had, for some reason, left a trail behind. He wasn't sure what that meant, but there was a reason. This was a sharp, cunning operator who *always* had a reason. Theo knew he was going to have to proceed cautiously.

But now, he had something to go on, a destination.

He hadn't been able to sleep well all night, his mind racing as he formulated a plan of action. He'd put on the television at a quiet volume just for something to do and saw the news flash about the bizarre death of Lydia and the search for her killer, Yvette St. Cloud. They ran a mug photo of her with the standard "extremely dangerous, do not approach."

Damn, she was just a kid. Looked like she was still a teenager.

He hoped she got away and wasn't going to be found. If Rybus's people had put her up to the kill, they'd see her as an unnecessary liability. Better they didn't find her. And if it had just been a freak accident and she'd killed Lydia to escape, oh well. He might feel bad for Lydia despite everything that had gone down, but this was all for the better. Either way he was rooting for Yvette St. Cloud.

"You go, girl," he muttered.

Just a bit earlier, he'd had a telephone conversation with his attorney, Winston Montrose. Everything seemed to be going as he'd figured there. Montrose had eluded his pursuers and was going about his everyday activities. He reported seeing a couple of cars that were obviously Yancey's men keeping an eye on him, but everybody was keeping their distance. Theo had figured it was too dangerous for them to come after a high-profile lawyer like Montrose, that he'd serve as a distraction without being in any danger himself. But he had to admire the guy for having the nerve to put himself in this position to begin with.

And at least Theo had eaten well. He'd had no trouble late-night ordering a few cartons of groceries. They'd been left inside the front entrance where he could slip down and get them without being seen. It was a quiet building; he'd seen nobody and, he was confident, nobody had seen him. So far he was in the clear, and now he wouldn't need to stay here much longer. He could begin to make his plans to go after the man who had his money, the man who'd led a double life as Webster Musgrave.

The dude had to have the money there with him, of that Theo was positive. It was just a gut feeling and his gut never steered him wrong.

Crystalline. Where in hell was that? He'd have to look it up.

He'd be ready very soon.

SIXTEEN

Leon decided Marshall Applegate's coffee really wasn't all that bad as he sipped from a Styrofoam cup and regarded him across the conference table.

"This whole case seems curious to me, Mr. Applegate. Why wouldn't Halley accept the insurance company's offer?"

"I always counsel my clients to reject the first offer. These companies are notorious at trying to lowball an injured person."

"And in this case, what amount would have been considered reasonable?"

"The exact amount we were asking is confidential."

"More than the Pendleton's actual coverage? I happen to have an idea of the kind of amount you and she were demanding, and it would seem the only way they could have done that, had you won, was to hand over their house."

"She and I arrived at a figure based on the circumstances of her injury. She was attacked by an aggressive wild animal—an *illegal* wild animal, I might add—allowed to run free on their property. It was entirely possible the animal was a health risk, carrying rabies or Lord only knows what other communicable diseases. And in the act of trying to get away from said attacking animal, she was hit by their vehicle, which was being driven in a totally unsafe manner."

Leon shook his head and raised his eyebrows. "That's not the timeline as I understand it. Your client stepped out from hiding and jumped behind the car, and then when Abigail stopped to investigate, the monkey got out of the car. It's not clear exactly how she wound up getting bitten by the monkey but there's a question about whether she in fact provoked it."

"That's definitely not the way my client reported it, Detective. The truth would have come out in court."

"It didn't strike you as unusual how many cases Halley came to you with? You didn't suspect she might be initiating these incidents herself to capitalize on them?"

"Clients come to me to settle their liability issues. I know nothing until they do so, and I do not unnecessarily judge them. Each case is handled on its own merits."

"And you felt all three of Halley's cases had merit?"

"The insurance companies settled the first two; obviously they felt her claims held water. As I said, they'd tried to lowball her. She had legitimate medical expenses and legitimate pain and suffering."

"Did you know Jack Donner, her husband?"

"I knew of him, of course. As I believe I mentioned last time, I never met him."

"Did you happen to know that they would likely have been evicted before very long from the house they rented for a number of years, and might soon need a new place to live?"

"I never heard such a thing. What are you getting at, Detective Simpkins?"

"I'm getting at the fact that Halley Donner caused a lot of people a lot of trouble trying to profit at their expense, and now she's dead, Mr. Applegate. Possibly those things are related."

"People sue each other all the time. They don't go killing each other over it!"

"Actually, sometimes, yes. Yes, they do. Take my word for it."

"So, what, are you asking if I knew of anybody who made threats against her during the lawsuits? No!"

"Was anyone else involved in these incidents? Was anyone with her when they occurred, or was anyone else involved in your discussions of the cases?"

"To the best of my knowledge, Halley Donner was alone when all three incidents occurred. My standard operating procedure is to gather all the information from the client and then they leave it to me. The only other person who even sees any of it is my assistant, Sigrid, who does all my clerical work, transcriptions and billing and such. She's worked for me for many years, and I can guarantee you, she never talks to anyone about her work. Aside from her, nobody else knew anything about the cases."

"What about the swoop and squat?"

"That was *alleged*. No court found Halley Donner guilty of anything whatsoever. She retained me to defend her when she was arrested."

"Just her?"

"Yes."

"Nobody else was involved in the scam?"

"Please stop referring to it as her 'scam.' Nothing was ever proven or determined that she committed a crime."

"Because the other person involved in the collision declined to testify as a witness, and there was nobody else to come forth, correct?"

"Detective, do I need to remind you that we are innocent until proven guilty in this country?"

"Why did the witness suddenly refuse to testify?"

"I have no idea. Perhaps her conscience got the better of her."

"You don't think there could have been any coercion, for example?"

"Detective, what are you implying? Are you accusing me of—"

Leon raised his hands placatingly. "No, no, Mr. Applegate, not at all. But is it possible that someone else could have gotten to her, a friend of Halley's, or someone with an interest in preventing the case from proceeding?"

"I know of nothing to suggest that."

"What about the other participant in the swoop?"

"What other person is that?"

"Reportedly the collision happened when another car pulled in front of Halley's car, and she braked. Then the car drove away."

"I don't see how that car had to have anything to do with Halley Donner."

"Oh, come on, Mr Applegate. Don't insult my intelligence."

"I know there are such schemes as the one you mention. There was nothing to indicate that that other car had anything to do with Halley Donner whatsoever. The other driver failed to stop in time and plowed into the back of her car, exacerbating old injuries and causing new ones. According to my client, the other driver then came up with the whole story about an alleged scam to get out of being held responsible."

Leon sighed. *Exacerbating?*

"One thing I don't understand though, sir. Once she was no longer being accused of felony fraud, it seems Halley didn't persist in going after the other driver in court, despite her claims of serious injury. Am I correct?"

"That's correct, Detective."

"Why not?"

Applegate exhaled a deep, exasperated sigh. "In fact, I did bring it up to her. She seemed reluctant to continue. She said the arrest had deeply unsettled her and she'd rather just forget the whole thing. And there was one other bothersome fact."

"Which was?"

"The other driver, the one who had accused Halley of fraud, couldn't be located. I took some time, believe me, to try to keep tabs on her after the dismissal. I couldn't find her."

"Are you saying she doesn't have any local listing?"

"Oh no, she's in the book, as they say, although who's got an actual phone book anymore? But I tried calling multiple times and nobody ever picked up at the number, and nobody seemed to be at the address. It appeared to be vacant. She clearly didn't want to be found, at least not by me." Applegate sat back on his chair and laced his fingers, staring at Leon.

"A shady witness, pissed off at the deceased and off the radar. Now that I think about it, isn't that just the kind of thing you came to me looking for?"

Leon nodded thoughtfully. "Thank you for your time, Mr. Applegate. And for the coffee."

In his car, Leon texted Art quickly to let him know he was going to look into one more angle on the staged accident before he chased down Radley. Then he made a couple more quick phone calls and headed off to the Criminal Courts building.

* * * *

"I've only got about ten minutes, Detective, but I'll try to help you."

Assistant D.A. Stacey Wong was young, serious, and clearly over-worked. The very fact that she'd nevertheless been receptive to meeting Leon in her office was a good sign. More than once he'd been blown off by a prosecutor who just didn't have the time.

She opened a legal folder on the desk and spoke rapidly as she paged through it.

"We've gotten a lot of this kind of thing. Collision fraud. A staged ac-cident. I'm sure you're familiar with it."

Leon nodded. He'd certainly heard of it but hoped it might be helpful to be walked through it in detail by someone who dealt with it regularly and said so.

"The way the scam usually works, two cars are working together. They might keep in touch by phone or radio. They look for the right configura-tion, where cars are in traffic the right distance apart at the right speed. Con One, let's call them, is in front of the intended victim and slows to close the gap with them. Con Two pulls in directly in front of Con One. That's the swoop. Before the victim can slow down and open up the space, Con Two hits their brakes, as does Con One, who knew it was coming. The victim has no time to brake in time and plows into Con One. Con Two takes off, as if they have no connection to anyone or anything, but the victim and Con One stop, get out and have a conversation. Con One claims they had to brake in a hurry because of the jerk in front of them, the one who drove off, and the victim shouldn't have been following so close, been more alert to stop in time, something along that line. Sometimes it's a straight insurance fraud: another confederate will appear off the street as an 'objective' wit-ness in support of what the scammer claims happened. Sometimes Con One just starts wailing about injuries and damages. The idea's to keep things moving fast, extort quick cash money on the spot from the victim while they're still flustered, not really thinking things through, and just want to avoid an insurance hike. There's usually an ATM close by. It might be one reason the scammers picked the area they did."

Leon nodded again. "Interesting."

"It would seem that's what the intent was in this case," she continued. "The perpetrator got out of her vehicle and started screaming about her injuries and the damage to her car—which was a piece of junk she had no intention of putting a single cent into repairing."

Leon decided he liked ADA Wong.

"What she *didn't* expect was that the victim wasn't having any part of it. She called it in before she was even out of the car and began making phone videos of everything going on."

"That would be Moira Legge," Leon said.

"Yes, that's right. The police arrived pretty promptly and the perp—"

"Halley Donner."

"Yes. Ms. Donner tried to leave, but Ms. Legge prevented her from doing so until the officers could be on the scene. She was fairly aggressive."

"Were there any other witnesses?"

"One pedestrian, who described the event, sufficient corroboration to fraud. He later declined to testify. Said he didn't want to get involved."

"Apparently there were sufficient grounds to bring charges against Halley Donner."

"Ms. Legge was adamant, and the circumstances warranted it. It was hardly a high-profile case, but this kind of scam really burns me and my boss felt the same way. I've prosecuted a few of these and I welcomed it."

"But Halley Donner was the only one charged. Did she or anybody else ever identify the accomplice?"

"Unfortunately, no. Identification of Con Two, person or vehicle, was spotty at best. Ms. Donner denied there *was* an accomplice. She never admitted to it being anything but a bona fide accident. We still had a decent case against her. Ms. Legge was a good, believable witness, and with some effort we thought we might be able to locate one of the pedestrians to corroborate."

"What contact information did you have for Legge?"

"She left me a cell phone number."

"Do you think it might still be good?"

"Last I tried it, I got through to her no problem, but that was a while ago."

"Please, can I have it?"

Wong shrugged, rustled through the papers, and turned it around for Leon to copy. Leon noticed another sheet in the stack.

"Is that the on-site report of the staged accident?"

"That's right."

"May I take a quick look at that as well?"

She turned the other sheet around. Leon scanned and made quick notes. As had been mentioned, Halley was not driving her Blazer but a seventeen-year-old domestic compact. Moira Legge, on the other hand, was driving a late model Mini Cooper. It seemed like she was a clear pick for a setup.

"Was Halley in custody at that point?"

"She made bail right away. Her lawyer posted it." Wong looked quickly at her watch. "Only got another minute."

"And then the case fell apart."

"Ms. Legge all of a sudden informed us she didn't want to testify and wished to retract her entire statement already made to us."

"For what reason?"

Wong shuffled through the papers. "She'd decided she was unclear on what might have actually happened." She looked up at Leon.

"You look like you think something else was going on."

"I'm probably not supposed to say this, but that seldom stops me. Up to then she had been unequivocal about what she saw happen. Just between you and me, Detective, it smelled to me like she was either coerced or bribed. Or maybe both."

"By whom? Halley Donner?"

Wong shrugged. "No idea. At that point, I knew I had to drop it and move on to the next battle. I didn't have the luxury of reflecting on it. And now, I'm afraid, I gotta go."

They both rose and shook hands. Leon thanked her for her time. Privately, he wished her well. She was clearly sharp and still sufficiently young to have ideals and to speak out for them, even in the small battles. He wondered how long it would be before that all started getting worn down.

* * * *

Wyandotte Street had, to put it nicely, seen better days.

It had once been a tree-lined street of well-kept homes and small apartment houses. The buildings were still there but they showed wear, age and neglect. The trees were huge and untamed, their roots pushing the sidewalks into an up-and-down obstacle course for pedestrians. Halley Donner could have set up five or six pratfall cases along it, no problem.

The neighborhood was what realtors would call "promising." Art figured, as he locked up his car and walked up the street, that the street was already probably in the sights of the developers, contractors and flippers. Maybe this was another one of those areas where rezoning was being negotiated between big-buck builders and the city fathers. Big-ass apartments or condos would mean a windfall for someone with its subsequent trickle-down to those on board.

Art Dowdy, ever the cynic, was no fan of redevelopment.

2038B was the address he was looking for. The "B" tipped him off that he was looking for something in the back, like a "mother-in-law" building that was common in the city, often no more than a converted garage that provided extra income from a boarder for the owner of the house. He made his way down a driveway at 2038, past a badly oxidizing old Chevy Camaro. He needn't have worried about not finding the place; he could have followed his ears back.

Three older guys were sitting on folding lawn chairs on a small patch of lawn in front of the unit that was 2038B. They had a boombox blaring 1970s style hard rock. Art recognized the band, a popular one in its day.

They were all oblivious to anything going on around them but their jokes, the music, and the cans of beer they were hammering back. One of the guys idly tossed his can over his shoulder, where it clanked onto the top of a pile of empties in a plastic trash can, and reached over to the cooler that sat diplomatically equidistant from all three of them. They all had huge guts sticking out from under their shirts, balding pates, ruddy complexions, and noses that could pass for asteroids. There was laughter that resembled wheezing and hoarse conversation trying to be heard above the music.

And yes, there was a monkey. He was sitting, a leash attached to his collar, on the shoulder of one of the guys, who was feeding him peanuts from a bag on his lap.

The Three Wise Men, mused Art as he advanced. One of them, the guy in the black T shirt, finally looked up and noticed Art, who smiled half-heartedly and waved, opening his sportscoat to show the detective badge on his belt.

Black T reached over and patted the knee of the guy with the monkey and pointed. All three of them turned to Art. Monkey guy—who Art assumed was Craig Mercer—reached down and turned down the music.

"Help ya?" he asked.

"Craig Mercer?" Art asked.

"Could be. And you are—?" he peered at the badge as if he was missing his glasses.

"Detective Dowdy, Personal Crimes. Mind if I ask you a few questions?"

"What's this about? You're not gonna bust some guys for having a few beers on a nice day, are you? Somebody complain about the noise? What?"

"No, nothing like that. I've got some questions about the person who was suing your daughter." He looked at the other two characters, who appeared to be trying to figure out exactly where they were. "If you'd prefer to talk in private—"

Mercer put down his beer and waved a hand. "Anything you can say to me, you can say to Roy and Duane here." He started laughing. "Shit, couple hours from now, they're not gonna remember anything that went on here anyway, right?" Roy and Duane started giggling and snorting. The monkey started making noises at them. Mercer reached up to pat him to calm him down.

"May I assume that's Gummy Bear, the monkey you gave your grand-daughter?"

"You know about that, huh? I originally called him just Gummy, you know, like weed gummies?"

His Greek chorus of buddies started snickering again.

"Gummies. Uh huh, yeah, I get it."

"But I didn't think that was, you know, appropriate for a little kid, so he became Gummy Bear. So what's this about? Is that she-devil making even more trouble for Abigail now?"

"Mr. Mercer, I'm a homicide detective. The woman who was suing your daughter is dead."

The comment may not have sobered them up but it did shut them up for a long moment. They all stared silently at Art.

"You're shitting me."

"No, sir."

"What happened?"

"She was murdered. That's what I'm looking into."

"And, and what, you think Abby had something to do with it? She's not even here. They went out of town last week."

"I'm just looking into everything, gathering whatever facts I can. I was hoping you could tell me a little bit about the trouble between the victim and your daughter."

"Shit, I don't know hardly anything. One day Abby calls me and says she needs to bring Gummy back to me. She sounds all crazy. So, I say sure, and she shows up here with him and tells me there's this crazy-ass woman suing her claiming she got run over by Abby's car and then bit by the mon-key, and then she found out you're not supposed to have a monkey and they're going to try to take him away and maybe charge her, so she needs to get rid of him. That's it, that's all I know. And that Abby was worried because the shrew suing her was insane and crooked and had an ambulance chaser lawyer and they were coming after everything she had. It sounded like the world was coming down on her. I offered to help but, well, Abby and I are sort of on the outs. Last thing in the world she wants is my help. We don't talk all that much." Mercer took a swig from his can and under-handed it into the trash can. "I'd kinda hoped that Gummy would be a kind of peace offering, maybe we could start talking again, but it turns out he made things even worse."

"If you don't mind my asking, Mr. Mercer, how long have you and your daughter been, um, estranged?"

He waved a hand as he reached into the cooler. "Oh geez, since she was a kid, like a young teenager. Hard enough to get along with a daughter at that age if you're a *great* father, you know? Which I wasn't. I gotta admit, I was a shitty father. Truth be told, never had all that much interest. Abby's mom Ruthie and I broke up a long time ago, and she moved to, I don't know, somewhere in Minnesota or Wisconsin? She got a job as a teacher or something."

"Nurse," offered Black T. "Isn't she a nurse of some kind?"

The third guy, in a faded plaid flannel, finally opened his mouth. "Nurses can get jobs most anywhere." He belched. "'Scuse me."

"That's right. She was a nurse, and she moved away."

Art needed to get this back on track.

"So how long had it been since you and your daughter had communicated before you got the monkey?"

"Oh God, years. I'd had time to develop some regrets, you know? I really wanted to be able to see my granddaughter Amelia, maybe have, like, some kind of relationship again. So when this friend of mine had a monkey and offered it to me, I figured it might be a way to get my foot back in the door, you know?"

Art rubbed his temples, looking down at the ground. "Mr. Mercer, forgive me for asking this, but, do you have a job?"

"I'm on a pension. Used to work for the city, got injured. "

"Sorry, but I'm just, you know, wondering. A monkey like that, what is he, a capuchin?"

"That's what I'm told. Right, Gummy?" The monkey looked like he was trying to groom what was left of Mercer's hair, picking little things out of it and smoothing it down with his fingers.

"He had to be expensive."

"Oh, you're wondering how I paid for him? He was supposed to be five big ones. But the friend, well—"

"He had to leave town in a hurry," Plaid Shirt offered. "Personal business."

"Yeah. He gave Gummy to me for two. I could swing that. I had some money saved up."

"So, your daughter and her entire family were out of town this weekend, you said?"

"Yep. Since Thursday."

"And how about you, Mr. Mercer? What were you doing on, oh, say, Sunday evening?"

"Me? I was over at Duane's."

I can vouch for that. He was with us all Sunday afternoon and night." Black T, who Art assumed was Duane, nodded vigorously.

"Doing what?"

"Gettin' shitfaced. We party every Sunday."

"Shitfaced Sunday!" laughed Roy.

"Damn straight. Bring out the good stuff. Good music, good old movies or a good game on the TV, good booze, a little good weed." He winked at Art. "Hey, that's legal now."

"Not to mention good friends," Mercer laughed, reaching out to high-five Duane.

"Yep. We bring in a few pizzas and other snacks, usually start around, oh, three or so and go on until the night."

The neighbors must love these guys, Art figured.

"Just you three?"

"Sometimes one or two other guys. This last Sunday it was just us three though."

"And you say you got started around three?"

They all looked at one another and nodded. It apparently took the hive memory to affirm that. Clearly there wasn't enough brain power here to be trying to get their stories straight.

"And nobody left all night?"

"Left? Damn, none of us can usually move after a few hours! We just woke up Monday morning, cleaned up, and moseyed on back to our lives."

"Cleaned up is right," Duane roared. "Damn, Craig, you got sick all over yourself, son."

"Aw, come on, Duane, no need to tell that to anyone. That was kinda embarrassing. Think it was the hot dogs."

Duane slapped Mercer on the back. "Shit, could happen to anybody." He looked at Art. "After he technicolor yawned all over himself, know what this bastard did? Didn't want to bother us so he just jumped into my shower tub, clothes and all, and washed himself down. You know, whatever works after partying hearty, am I right? Happy to be of service. Everything you need to have a good time, including cleanup."

Roy laughed again. "Don't forget the Tylenol. Duane's always got a lot of that for the hangovers." The others found this hysterically funny and joined him in guffaws.

Art sighed deeply. "I take it none of you have a job to go to Monday morning."

"We're all retired. I used to be a security guard. Duane there, he was a carpenter. Now we just relax and enjoy a life of leisure."

Enjoy, thought Art, was putting it mildly.

If there was anything else in terms of coherent fact to be gleaned, it went undetected.

Art trudged back to his car, thoroughly exhausted by his encounter with Craig Mercer and his two drinking buddies and frustrated that he had gone through all that for nothing. He pulled out his phone and called Leon.

Leon answered saying, "Hey partner, what's up? Any luck?"

"Negative on that. The Monkey Man is a drunk stoner who couldn't tell me the time of day."

"How about the monkey, was he at least cute?"

"Adorable. Simply adorable. Smart as a whip. Easily the smartest one in the crowd. We might be able to get him work as a detective. He probably wouldn't do any worse than I'm doing. You?"

"Applegate, that man would slide off a level table. I got a better look at the bigger picture talking with him. Halley was really honing her swindle chops by trial and error. I don't know; maybe there's something there, maybe not. I want to run it all by you later, after I talk with Radley."

"Sure. Hopefully we'll have some answers from Mickey or the lab. I'll meet you back at the ranch, but first I'm going to try to run down Moira Legge. That'll probably be a total bust as well. Who knows where she's hiding?"

"Yeah, about that," Leon said slyly. "I got something you might try."

SEVENTEEN

Radley and Ochida had just pulled into the parking lot of the station and were removing their gear from the back of their vehicle. They turned at the sound of Leon's voice.

"Officers, just getting off?"

"Yeah," Radley replied wearily as he closed the tailgate. "Early shift today. We get to go home while there's still daylight now and then. What's up, Detective?"

"I wanted to thank you for your help securing the crime scene yesterday. That was a hell of a day." He turned to Ochida. "I appreciate your holding the kid's hand. He was totally messed up."

Ochida still looked a little shaken recalling the experience. "That's not something you want to walk in on unprepared."

"What happened with the dog in the yard? It's okay? Any idea what's going to happen to it?"

"The dog?" She looked momentarily puzzled. "Oh yeah. It took them a while, but Animal Control came. They'll likely pass it on to a shelter. Call them and inquire. Ask for Arlene."

"You interested in adopting it?" Radley asked. "Looking for a dog?"

"Just curious. I might know somebody who is."

Radley handed a canvas bag to Ochida and asked her to go on, he'd join her in a minute. When she was out of earshot, he turned to Leon.

"We need to talk," Leon said.

Radley nodded. "I had a feeling. But not here. The Park. Half an hour?"

It gave Leon pause but he agreed.

Sunset Park was its formal name but nobody in the city ever called it that. It was simply the Park, a four-block respite from urban sprawl, with rolling hills and wooden benches, not that far from the station. Leon, sitting on one of those benches, decided to try a call to Arlene, the person in Animal Control. He was informed Arlene was indeed the person with whom he should speak, but she was out of the office and would not be available for another hour or so. He pocketed his phone just as Radley, now in street clothes, approached up the walk. The officer sat down on the other end of the bench and folded his arms.

"I only got a few minutes."

"Appreciate your coming."

"Any luck finding Barnfeather?"

"Nothing so far, and I mean nothing. Nobody's heard of him. There's no record, no mention of him. Who is this guy and why do you think he's relevant?"

"Druggie Barnfeather." Radley shook his head in disgust. "He's a low-level guy in the crews. Deluded knucklehead that thinks he's hot shit. Jack Donner believed his rap and got himself mixed up with him. Did some drug deals, hot merchandise. Petty, stupid shit. With all the disruptions recently, some of those characters are pulling some especially stupid and desperate moves. I think that's how Jack got himself killed, and his wife as well."

"And you know all this how, exactly?"

"You hear things. You know."

Leon sighed deeply. "All we can find so far seems to point to Halley, not to Jack, being the likely target. Was she involved with this Barnfeather guy as well?"

"Halley had nothing to do with whatever was going on. Nothing."

"I can't help but think you know a lot more that you're not telling me. What's your connection to Halley Donner, anyway?"

"God damn it." Radley stared down at the ground for a long time. Leon let it play out. It took a while.

"Okay. Halley was in trouble. She came to me for help. That's how I know."

"Why you?"

"We met a couple times in a bar. She knew I was a cop. She said she had nowhere else she could turn."

"What about Jack?"

"Oh, fuck Jack! He was almost always stoned out of his gourd. He wasn't worth shit. He was either getting wrecked or working on that piece of shit car of his or coming up with some dumb ass get-rich scheme. Or all three."

"What kind of trouble are we talking?"

Radley didn't answer, just continued to stare down at the ground.

"Come on, I need to know this."

"I just wanted to keep her out of it. Away from all this shit."

Damned if it didn't sound like he was trying not to get choked up.

"Go on. Tell me the rest."

"Jack was getting involved deeper and deeper with Dougie. And Dougie started trying to move in on the things Halley was into. Okay, she was running some insurance scams, I know that. But they were small level. He wanted her to get into some deeper stuff. He called them 'capers,' like they were something out of a movie."

"The staged accident?"

"That was the first thing he worked out. It was his idea. And he really pushed her to go along. Stupid idea to begin with and it just got worse."

"Not only didn't come off but she got arrested and charged."

Radley nodded. "Dougie told her that if his name came up, it wouldn't go well for her, but she wasn't the type to rat on anyone to begin with."

"There was a witness, the intended victim of the swoop. She withdrew, then disappeared, and the case fell apart. Was that Barnfeather's doing as well?"

"That would make the most sense."

A comment Leon found curiously evasive.

Leon considered the box of powder on the Donners' living room table. "A couple times now you called him 'Druggie' Barnfeather."

"That was Halley's nickname for him, yeah."

"I'm guessing he was Jack's dealer as well?"

"Yeah, I'm sure he was. Jack loved his snow."

"And you're telling me Halley never, um, partook of any of that?"

"No, I can't really say that. I'm sure she did. But just occasionally, not like Jack."

"Any chance Jack was planning on doing some dealing on his own, maybe opening up a side business with or without Barnfeather?"

"I never heard anything like that, but those guys were both insane morons, so it's not out of the question."

It didn't need to be said: in Rybus's city, that kind of freelancing could be a death sentence.

"Did you ever actually meet Doug Barnfeather?"

"Just kinda bumped into him, once or twice. I tried to warn him off her. I told him not to try to pull her into any more of his 'capers.' Problem was, Jack was still interested in doing business with him, so it was almost impossible to keep him away from the house. In recent times, Dougie had some new enterprise he was wheedling Jack into, something Halley wanted no part of. So she was pretty pissed at his popping in regularly and thought something might be coming to a head."

"Sorry to be blunt, but it sounds to me like you and Halley had gotten pretty close for you to be so protective."

Another long, agonized silence followed. Finally, Radley spoke, quietly.

"I lost my wife this past year."

"I'm sorry."

"She had a long bout with her cancer. She fought like the devil, but it was a hellacious time for her before she finally got taken."

"Must have been pretty rough for you as well."

"I guess I was just, I don't know, looking for something. Somehow, I ended up drinking with Halley one night. I liked her. She was tough, no nonsense, had a wicked dark sense of humor. I swear, she would have made one hell of a cop. I was sick of the people telling me shit they thought I wanted to hear, the kid glove treatment, you know? I didn't want anybody feeling sorry for me. Still don't. I was avoiding a lot of people. But with Halley, I could just laugh and forget things." Radley looked up at Leon. "I don't know, maybe she was just using me because she needed help. Didn't matter. Maybe we were both using each other to get something we couldn't get any other way. I've got nothing to hide on that score. There was nothing I did that crossed the line, not ever."

Nothing to hide. The things we make ourselves believe, that we need to make ourselves believe.

"Did Jack find out?"

"We only met up a couple times, but he wasn't very friendly, so I figure, yeah. He at least didn't like that I was standing between Barnfeather and them, that I was so interested to begin with."

"Were you ever in the Short End with Jack or Halley?"

"You did do your homework, didn't you?"

"I'm a detective, Radley."

He laughed. "Yeah, once or twice. It was convenient for them, being close to home, but that was exactly why I didn't like to go in there. Had a little face-off with Jack in there one night in fact, just some words."

"This Barnfeather, what's he look like?"

"Lanky dude. Shaves his head, has a mustache. Your stereotypical wannabe gangster. A showboat. Big mouth. Likes to talk himself up. Kind of guy who isn't going to end up well."

"Why can't I find any trace of this guy anywhere? Where is he? Nobody seems to know him."

"I don't know what to tell you. I don't know who he might know or hang with. I never saw him with anybody else. He was always alone."

"Did he ever have a dog with him?"

"A dog? No. That's a strange question. No dog. Why?"

"Long story. Probably not important. You said he was up to something new with Jack in recent days?"

"That's what Halley said. Something that was going to bring him up in the world. That's how she said Jack put it."

* * * *

Art was nowhere to be seen when Leon returned to his own desk and wasn't picking up his phone or answering texts. What *was* waiting for Leon was an emailed overview of the autopsies from Mickey. Wonder of wonders.

But before Leon could open the email attachments he'd been sent, he heard Castillo's voice booming out from the doorway of his office.

"Detective Simpkins, would you please pick up on line three and speak with the woman? She's insisting on taking to Detective Morrison."

"Marlon's on vacation, Lou."

"Yes, thank you, Leon, I do know that. I don't know what the lady wants but maybe you can help her or refer her, I don't know, somewhere."

Leon sighed, picked up the receiver, hit 3. "This is Detective Simpkins speaking, how may I help you?"

"I need to speak to Detective Morrison."

"I'm sorry, Detective Morrison is not here, can I be of assistance?"

"I have to talk to Morrison. When's he going to be back?"

"He's taking some vacation days. What is this regarding?"

She exhaled in frustration. "My dog! They stole my dog!"

"Miss..."

"Wambsgans. *Ms.* Myra Wambsgans."

"Ms. Wambsgans, this is Personal Crimes. We don't deal with animal thefts. You want Property Crimes. I can transfer you—"

"Don't you dare! I've been through all this for a couple of days now! I've talked with people in Property Crimes and God knows who else I've been transferred to. Nothing's being done. I need to talk to Morrison."

"I'm not sure I understand. Why Detective Morrison?"

"Because he'll understand. He's the one who arrested the guy to begin with."

"Wait, what guy is that?"

"The guy who owned Beatrice! The gangster!"

Leon felt a headache coming on. He had a feeling the Lou was sitting in his office chuckling.

"Who's Beatrice? Who's a gangster?"

"No, no, no! Beatrice isn't the gangster! Beatrice is the dog! My dog! Well, I don't know what she used to be called. It's what I named her. I'm fostering her."

"I'm sorry, can you start over and tell me the whole story?"

Myra Wambsgans heaved a sigh of frustration.

"I volunteered to foster her, and the shelter told me they'd gotten her from the police, that she'd been confiscated when some criminal was arrested. She needed a home, and I love pit bulls. At first, I was a little hesitant, but she was such a nice dog, I found it hard to believe she'd been owned by some, some gangster. It was clear she'd been treated very well. I named her Beatrice."

"How long ago was this?"

"Only a couple of weeks ago. She was still settling in. Then last Saturday evening, I came home to discover someone had broken into my yard and taken her!"

"Last Saturday, you say."

"That's right. I called the police and got shuttled around to various people who took down my information and said they'd get back to me. It's been three days now and nothing's happened. I don't know if the gangsters came and took her or some other thieves got her, but I'm sick with worry. She's a sensitive dog who's been through several changes of home and people and she was just starting to feel at home again, and now who knows what's happening to her? I did some research in the news and saw that Detective Morrison had been involved in a major arrest a few weeks ago and a dog was involved. So I looked him up. If this *gang* is involved in this, it might help him to know this, and maybe he knows something that can help me get Beatrice back."

"Ms. Wambsgans, suppose you let me look into this for you. I know the case you're talking about, but I can't be sure your Beatrice was the dog involved in that. Let me get your contact information and I'll let you know what I can find out. If this hasn't been resolved by the time Detective Morrison returns, I'll make sure he knows about it as well."

This did not totally placate Myra Wambsgans but it was the best results she'd gotten so far. She gave Leon her phone number and said she would check back with him if she hadn't heard from him in a day or two. Leon hung up, two thoughts running through his head. One was: *Thanks a bunch, Lou.*

The second was: *What's with all these dogs, and are they connected?*

That reminded him to try calling the Animal Control officer, Arlene, again since she should be back by now. At least he could get an answer about the whereabouts of the dog taken from the Donner residence.

As it turned out, it it took more than he'd expected. Arlene said that they had not been informed what had happened after they'd brought in the dog and referred him to another number. Three calls and several transfers later, just as he was about to give up and return to more important matters, he was put through to someone who knew exactly the case to which he referred. Apparently, procedure had not been followed and confusion had reigned. It was a classic case of a dumb bureaucratic snafu.

The line from a classic song by one of his favorite singers came to mind: *we never do anything nice and easy.*

Leon wasn't sure it had been worth the time and effort, but at least he had gotten the information as to where the Donners' dog had been taken, a shelter on Vaughan Street. He hoped that when he found the time to try to trace down the confiscated "gangster dog" adopted by (and stolen from) Myra Wambsgans, it would go easier. He'd get back to that when he could. He did stop to consider the coincidence that the Donners' dog, if his memory served, was some kind of pit bull or mix also. Well, it was a very popular breed. It would be quite a stretch of coincidence, he mused, if the two were connected.

All these dogs. What's up with all these dogs?

On to other matters.

Leon opened his computer and noted he had an email from the ME's office. Mickey Kendrick promised a more detailed report to come but gave a general outline of what he'd found. The slugs he'd found in the bodies were from a .22; he'd sent them on to SID for further examination. The range of the shots were consistent with being shot in the chest from across the table, then in the head at closer range. Time of death looked to be about 7:00 P.M. Sunday evening.

Just as he was closing the email, Leon's desk phone rang again.

"Leon, Gene here. I got something on Douglas Barnfeather for you. Not much, but something."

"At this point, I'll take whatever you've got."

"The name was familiar to a confidential informer. They saw him hanging out a few times with a Rybus associate named Barclay Vickers."

"I've heard the name. That fits with what little I know about him as well."

"Vickers seems to be the guy picking up the slack while Rybus is away. The prevailing sentiment is he's the new number two. If this Barnfeather guy is anything, he's just one of the soldier ants, another aspiring crew member of some sort, but he's latched on to a rising star if so. He's got a lot of company trying to cozy up to Vickers these days."

"Any chance Barnfeather's been freelancing, working his own private enterprises while the organization is in flux?"

"Your guess on that is as good as mine. Anything's possible. Sorry, I told you it wasn't much."

"Any photos?"

"Not sure. I'll see what I can do for you."

"Anything you can get on the guy would be a help, Gene, thanks."

"So, any word on the dog?"

"Actually, yeah. For some reason the Donners' dog got lost in the system briefly after being picked up by Animal Control but wound up getting sent to the Vaughan Street shelter. I assume the dog's there now."

"Do you know what kind of dog it is?"

"Some kind of pit, white, female. No collar, no tag. They hadn't checked for a microchip yet."

"Vaughan Street. I know where that is. Thanks. Gotta run. Let's keep in touch."

After ringing off, Leon sat for a moment, still wondering what in hell was up with Gene and that dog.

And still no sign of Art. He shot off another text and started wondering what had happened to his partner.

EIGHTEEN

Art Dowdy was not what you'd call a "glass is half full" kind of guy. When people referred to you as "The Mortician," it generally wasn't due to your rosy optimism. So naturally Art continued to debate if it wasn't a total waste of his time driving over a half hour out of the city, as he was doing now. He couldn't even be sure that when he got to his destination, the person he was seeking would even be there.

Leon would have looked at this as an adventure. Art just wanted to get it over with and get back to the unit.

As he'd expected, the phone numbers he had for Moira Legge had been a dead end. But he'd called in a trace on the license number of the Mini Cooper that Leon had given him and it came up still registered, not to Moira Legge, but to Wanda Lantana, in the town of Washburn, a good forty minute drive away.

If there had just been anything else at all to go after, he might have decided to let it wait. But they had nothing solid at this point except the various people to whom Halley had done dirt, and this one seemed to have gone to some effort to disappear.

Maybe Moira had sold the car to this Wanda Lantana and Art would have driven almost two hours back and forth for nothing. But everyone he'd ever met who owned a Mini Cooper had developed an attachment to it. That's why they bought then to begin with. Maybe Moira was still connected with her car somehow.

Art instinctively realized he couldn't just look up this Wanda Lantana and call her. He was sure that if Moira were still connected with her and got word, she'd bolt. There was clearly either some big carrot or stick that had motivated her off the case to begin with. There was only one way to handle this, so he'd dumped himself back into the driver's seat of the car, hit his GPS for a route to the address, and headed out, muttering to himself.

The address was on a nice shady suburban street, a small split-level home with a carport in which sat a burnt orange Mini Cooper. The plate number checked out. Art parked across the street, debating with himself how to play this. Should he go up and ring the doorbell, or should he wait?

His phone was buzzing again; Leon had been trying to reach him. But before he could read the texts and bring his partner up to date, the front door opened, and a woman emerged. By the time she'd locked her door, Art was halfway up the walk.

She turned and said, "Can I help you?" She was a tall, very athletic looking woman, in exercise attire and big sunglasses, her dark hair pulled back in a ponytail. She husked the big canvas bag she carried higher up on her shoulder and placed her hands on her hips, flexing an impressive set of arm muscles.

No shrinking violet, this one, Art mused. He had his badge at the ready to show as he approached.

"Oh shit," she nearly spat. "Now what the fuck do you guys want? How in hell did you find me anyway? Can't you just leave me alone?" She looked partly frightened, as if she would bolt, and partly righteously pissed off, as if she was about to launch into Art. Neither prospect was what he'd come all this way for. He raised his hands placatingly, still holding the badge.

"Look, Ms. Lantana—you are Ms. Lantana, right? I don't know about anybody who might have been bothering you. I'm a homicide detective, investigating a case. You're not in any kind of trouble. I just need to talk to someone I think you might know. I'm looking for the prior owner of your car, Moira Legge. It's very important I speak with her. Can you help me?"

It was like she'd touched a live electrical cord. She stood there, frozen, for a long time, her mouth open. Finally, she raised her hands in disbelief. Even through the dark glasses Art could feel the glare.

"Know her? You're looking at her!"

It took Art considerably more time to convince her that he presented no threat to her and to get her to agree to sit down and talk with him for a few minutes. She protested that she had a gym appointment, but Art played the sympathy card of an overworked public servant who'd just spent the better part of an hour dragging himself across the state to find her. His normal glum hangdog expression for once helped his cause. Finally deciding Art was at least innocuous if not totally okay, she made a quick call to postpone her appointment and invited him in.

"So how did you find me?" she started. She hadn't offered him coffee or a glass of water or anything and Art didn't ask. She had just indicated for him to sit at the counter in her kitchen and sat down across from him.

"The Mini. It would seem you're trying not to be found, Miss—is it Lantana or Legge?"

"Moira Legge is my real name. Well, it was. Wanda Lantana is my professional name and what I go by around here."

"Professional name?" Art looked puzzled.

"Ever hear of OWWWL?"

"Who?"

"No, the other kind. OWWWL. Three W's. Out of this World Women's Wrestling League. OWWWL. On television?"

Art stared blankly. "Not my thing, I guess."

"Well, I'm a professional wrestler. If you ever watch the show, you'd see me. Wanda 'Leggy' Lantana. Took the last name from my former husband. About all I ever got from him. The league is based in Washburn, so this seemed a good place to move. But now let me ask you a question before you go on. You said you're a homicide detective?"

"That's right."

"Who died?"

"Halley Donner and her husband Jack."

"Wow! No shit? What happened?"

"They were shot in their home."

"Where's that?"

"In the city." Art stared at her placidly.

"Okay, you want to play it that way, huh? Sounds like you're here to, how do they put it on the TV shows, eliminate me as a suspect? Can you tell me *when* this happened within a better time frame than say, a month?"

"Sunday evening."

"Well, it just so happens that I was in the ring in tag team matches and one-on-ones at the Washburn Arena in front of something like twenty thousand fans and a bunch of TV cameras Sunday afternoon and evening."

"Seriously?"

"This is big shit, Detective. Popular as hell. I've got quite a fan club myself."

"But you remember who Halley Donner was?"

"Oh shit, how could I forget. The collision scam. Forgive me if I don't seem particularly broken up, I know every woman's death diminishes me and all that, but that one was quite a piece of work."

"Did you know her husband, Jack Donner?"

"Nope. Didn't know she even had a husband. I guess it must be true, there really is somebody for everybody. Knew nothing about her and didn't want to. Never saw her again after that day."

"What do you remember about the accident?"

She hesitated, looking wary.

"Miss Legge, if somebody's threatened you not to talk about this, I've got nothing to do with it."

She stared up and down at him. "Yeah. I can tell. You're not like the other guy. Not at all."

"Whoever the other guy is, I've got nothing to do with him. I just want to know about the accident."

"The *staged* accident, you mean. My God, that was about as blatant as you could get, pure unadulterated attempted theft! The whole thing, her jockeying for position in that beater of a car, the other guy pulling in ahead of her. I could see it coming and tried to slow down and open the space between me and her, but they moved fast and boom, it happened."

"You seem to know a lot about this kind of thing."

"My world is an interesting one, Detective. Kind of like being on a pirate ship sometimes. Lots of characters from all over. I've heard about all kinds of things. And I'm suspicious by nature. I learned early on not to let people think they can take advantage."

"So, you saw it coming but there was nothing you could do to prevent it."

"That piece of trash jammed on the brakes almost immediately, before her pal even finished moving in ahead of her. It wasn't just obviously criminal, it was incompetent. She was like instantly out of the car, holding her head, screaming about her car and her back and her legs and her neck. I'm surprised she wasn't claiming a miscarriage. The henchman floored it and disappeared. They count on the victim to get all convulsed in a situation like this and panic. I don't play that. I stayed cool, tried to take in as much as I could of what was going on around me. I got out my phone and hit 911 and reported being in a scam. She kept squawking at me to get out of the car. Finally, I did. I let her holler at me and piss and moan about every place her body was broken and hurt, and how much it was going to cost to fix her rolling trash bin. Shit, her rear was dented. The whole piece of crap probably wasn't worth as much as the front bumper of my Cooper, you know? And I doubt she'd been injured in the least."

"Then what?"

"I said something about trading insurance information, just as a stall. Everything I was doing was to keep her there and distracted as long as possible. Meanwhile I was making videos of everything with my phone. and taking in all our surroundings. I noticed that there was a branch of a very widespread bank right across the street, with an ATM conveniently handy. I didn't think that was a coincidence. And I was right. She went right into her spiel, how this was going to totally fuck me up in regards the law and my insurance company, and *maybe* it would be better for us to just settle right on the spot."

"Did she specify a sum she wanted from you?"

"She hadn't gotten down to haggling but she was talking thousands. There was no way I was going to go for that, but I kept her talking, hoping the cops were on their way, and they were. A cruiser turned the corner. I interrupted her Academy Award winning performance and waved them down. Suddenly she was saying, 'Oh forget it then' and tried to get back in her car but I told her she wasn't going anywhere. She wanted to settle this, so let's settle it. I didn't, like, physically restrain her or anything like that, but I can be kind of an intimidating presence when I need to be."

"That's pretty clear."

"It was clear to the officers that it was all a bad act too. After they sorted things out, they carted her off."

"Were there any other witnesses to what happened?"

"That surprised me. My understanding is there's usually another scumbag accomplice who turns up, playing the role of a supposedly random witness supporting the scam. That didn't happen; just one more way they were incompetents, thank heaven. There were a couple people on the street and one of them gave the cops a statement, but that was the last I heard about him. I'm guessing he, you know, didn't want to *get involved*." She made air quotations to stress the last expression.

"So, there was just you and her. But you apparently were ready to go after her, enough to convince the prosecutor to pursue the case."

"You better believe it. I was insistent. I don't like assholes like her."

"But then, you changed your mind and declined to cooperate with the prosecution suddenly. What happened?"

She got that wary look again, right through the sunglasses.

"Someone threatened you. Or alternatively, they offered you something."

She still just stared at Art. He could almost feel the argument going back and forth inside of her.

"If somebody pressured you to drop out of the case, I promise you, I'm not going to get you in any trouble. That's not why I'm here."

"He just showed up one night at my door. Like around midnight."

"Who did?"

"The guy. He made it clear things would be better for me if I changed my mind about being involved in the case. He started to lay out how he could make things difficult for me. Look, I'm a performer and I don't want to jeopardize my career. I've got a good life, and I do pretty well. He said I should go somewhere and keep a low profile for a while. So, I called the prosecutor and told her I'd changed my mind, and moved out of my apartment in the city. Luckily, I've always compartmentalized my private and public lives. I'd bought this house near OWWWL headquarters a few years back as an investment, though I prefer the city, so I moved in here permanently. I miss the excitement and fun in the city, but nobody knows me as Moira Legge and nobody fucks with me here as Wanda Lantana."

"Were there physical threats, on your life?"

"Not specifically. I got the feeling he wasn't intending me bodily harm, at least not at this point. It would have been hard to frighten me on that score. This was more, as he put it, making things difficult for me."

Art rubbed his temple. "What kind of difficult? Was this guy, like, a gangster? Do you know who he was?"

"The stuff he was talking about, well, I've got fans and an image, and the league cares a lot about that kind of thing. Professional difficulties. And one thing was pretty clear. He wasn't a gangster. He was a cop."

NINETEEN

"Dumpster diving, detectives?"

The duty sergeant, clipboard in hand, just happened to be passing the elevator as it opened. He stared up and down at the two bedraggled figures emerging from the car.

"Actually," laughed Jilly, "we were."

Without breaking step, as he passed, the sergeant muttered, "Hope it was good pickings."

As the elevator closed, Jilly and Dan stared back and forth at each other and simultaneously erupted in laughter. Several other people in the unit turned to look at them. A few choice wisecracks sailed their way.

"God, will you look at us," Jilly said. "We both need a bath."

"So do our clothes," Dan said, sweeping his jacket with the backs of his hands. "I'm thinking when I get home, I'll just leave them on and jump into the shower."

All things considered, it hadn't been great, but it wasn't a total wash. They were exhausted and glad to see the end of the day, but it hadn't been a futile pursuit.

They'd begun by consulting a map and plotting out a course in a widening circle around the crash site. The immediate area was largely open space. The adjoining neighborhoods were long in the tooth, largely industrial and commercial, with some older residential buildings mixed in. There weren't even much in the way of stores or restaurants, just an occasional small market or food stand. The two detectives, and four uniformed officers, weren't sure what they hoped to find, but set out in earnest search hoping for *something*. The one thing in their minds was that St. Cloud's immediate objective would be to rid herself of her shackles and her prison garb, and to avoid notice. That meant looking for out of the way hiding places such as stores she could break into where she might find a change of clothes and something to break her shackles. They kept their eyes out for any possible security cameras that might have captured her passing through. It seemed an overwhelming task. They pushed through overgrowths of foliage and behind buildings, especially mechanic shops and other places that might have tools. The immediate neighborhoods were sparse, without many people, but they did have a lot of car repair garages, mostly small, with five or six vehicles jammed onto the property awaiting attention to the backdrop soundtrack of pneumatic wrenches.

It was in their third hour of trudging back and forth that they encountered an older guy in a dark blue coverall with a push broom, sweeping up broken glass from the front of his two-stall garage, under a weathered hand-painted sign that read *Brakes • Transmissions • Alinement*. The glass pane to the door to the office had been shattered. One of the stalls had an oxidizing Mercury Cougar. The other was empty.

It turned out the guy, who was about ready to give up the ghost on his business after multiple decades, had decided to skip work yesterday in favor of some doctor appointments. As he crankily observed, his own body was in more need of attention than his few customers' cars at the moment. Then he'd decided to come in late today, to be greeted by—he emphasized it with a grand sweep of his hand—this. The glass front door had been smashed in, his cash register had been broken open and emptied of several hundred dollars, and the keys to the stalls and the dark green Mustang in the second berth had been lifted, along with the car itself, which was unfortunately all too ready to be driven away. On top of that, the burglars had swiped a set of his coveralls, one of his hats, and a bunch of his tools. He could understand the money and the Mustang (which, he allowed, was pretty cherry and the owner was going to be *righteously* pissed) but why the clothes and only a handful of tools?

The detectives inquired what tools had been taken. He said, as far as he could so far figure, a hacksaw, hammer, chisel, and his battery powered Dremel. They'd also used his electric angle grinder and left it, still plugged in, on the garage floor.

The guy was totally amazed when Jilly and Dan donned nitrile gloves and asked if they could dig through his trash cans and the greasy dumpster in the back. Some time and a lot of dust and detritus later, they came back and asked if he had any kind of security cameras anywhere in or around the property. Unfortunately, he didn't.

In their dumpster dive, they'd come up with a set of olive drab scrubs and some lengths of chain. The guy couldn't figure why that seemed to make them seem happy, as they dug plastic zip-lock containers out of the trunk of their car and bagged their newfound treasures. They decided it was worth calling in SID, so they asked him to stop cleaning up, leave everything, and wait for the lab techs to come. The guy at this point no doubt had arrived at the conclusion that he was definitely getting too old for this shit. They took down his information and everything he could provide on the stolen car, instructed him to file a theft report right away, then called Castillo with the description and plate of the stolen Mustang. They informed him that St. Cloud would now likely be wearing mechanic's coverall and cap so a bulletin could be sent out immediately.

They left the guy their business cards, and waited for the SID van to show up, which, mercifully, it did promptly. They handed off the bagged material and moved on.

Another hour trekking back and forth along the sparse street turned up no security cameras that might have been trained on the garage. They remarked to one another how St. Cloud had lucked out, so quickly finding just the right locale so close to her escape point, given she knew nothing about the area.

They finally called in the unis, none of whom had come up with anything in the nearby areas and declared it a day. Now that their perp had a car and close to a day's head start, it was highly unlikely she would still be anywhere in the area.

They made quite a sight, trudging off the elevator into Personal Crimes, looking the very definition of bedraggled and wondering how bad they might smell at this moment.

Art and Leon paused in their own earnest discussion to smile wide-eyed at Jilly and Dan as they paraded by. Jilly just murmured, "Don't ask."

When they knocked on Castillo's door to bring him up to date, it was all he could do to keep from holding his nose. Observing propriety, he did invite them in, but did not invite them to sit down. They filled him in in detail, at which point he sighed deeply and said, "So you're telling me there's nothing else to go on at this point."

Jilly folded her arms and shook her head. "She's got a car and as far as we know there's nobody who knows her and no particular place she'd go. If she's smart, she's getting as far away from here as possible. We've got nothing."

The only action available, to put out notices far and wide, did not brighten the Lou's disposition one bit. Being dismissed, Jilly and Dan repaired to their desks to close up and call it quits for the aggravating day.

Leon watched them wearily moving and remarked to Art, "Looks like they had some fun."

"Hopefully," Art observed wryly, "they did better than us."

Art had given his partner the story about his encounter with Moira Legge, a.k.a. Wanda "Leggy" Lantana. The part about her harasser being a cop particularly bothered Leon.

"That son of a bitch," Leon muttered.

"You're thinking it's Radley?"

"It has to be. And that means he was even more involved with Halley than he let on to me. And maybe that means he was willing to go to further lengths for her than he wanted me to think."

"And how did Jack fit into Halley's schemes at that point?"

"That," Leon said thoughtfully, "is one more thing we're going to have to find out."

TWENTY

Barclay strained to keep from yawning and to keep himself at least *looking* alert.

As far as he could determine, Yancey seemed happy to be back on his throne in his fiefdom, the comfortable chair at the carved walnut table in his office above the club that served as the front for the headquarters of his operation. He only appeared slightly peeved at the minor disarray that still existed in the room. Well, it couldn't be helped. A seemingly endless series of search warrants had been served and the various authorities who'd tromped through the place like they owned it had hardly been respectful, and it had been some job to clean up after them. But Barclay and his crew had risen to the occasion. They'd quickly removed anything that could have been considered incriminating beforehand, and they'd swept back in to reasonably straighten everything up after the invasion had subsided.

Yancey had credited Barclay for his efforts and his timely decisions, and that was all to the good.

But Yancey prized a certain fastidiousness, and he wouldn't be totally satisfied until everything, including his physical space, was sufficiently tidy. There was a matter of the man's pride as well; his life had been unceremoniously uprooted, and he demanded that it all be returned to the rightful order. To those matters, the Ice Man had been devoting his attentions nonstop since he'd walked through the door and seated himself at his table. Before he'd be satisfied, every single lieutenant at every level would sit across from him, reaffirm their loyalty to the chief, deliver detailed updates, and receive further instructions.

Since early in the day, Barclay had sat at that table with him, absorbing orders and discussing issues, sitting in on updates from the various crew leaders as they came and went, occasionally taking leave to tend to necessary matters they had discussed but always returning promptly. A third person had been a constant presence in the headquarters as well: Yancey's new hand-picked bodyguard and enforcer, a particularly ugly and mean-tempered individual who went by the handle Mace.

This guy, Barclay had already decided, was going to be trouble.

There were already stories about him and his sheer nastiness that were approaching folklore. One day somebody asked him why he was called Mace; the answer he got was "On accounta it's my name, asshole." So, the questioner had replied, "Is that your first or your last name?" and Mace replied, "Both."

"So, your name is Mace Mace?" the wiseass laughed. To which Mace had near cracked the guy's skull open with a pool cue.

Nobody had ever asked him his real name again. Nobody except Yancey Rybus.

Barclay had never liked the guy to begin with and never felt comfortable around him. He was unpredictable—a wild card. Barclay was looking for every way to maneuver his own inner circle of people into position, and Mace was clearly not one of them. To his way of thinking, Felix would be a much better fit in his own plans. If only things worked out with Felix as he hoped.

The day had rolled on. By early evening Barclay was privately hoping for a respite so he could grab some dinner and maybe catch an hour's shut-eye. He struggled to suppress yawns and not to let his body language show fatigue. It looked as if they'd be going late into the evening taking care of business. But the indefatigable Ice Man was showing no signs of slowing up or even wanting a break, and Barclay knew he couldn't let his attention lapse or show the slightest sign of weakness. It was just part of the price of ascending in the ranks of the organization. Mace, for his part, might as well have been a statue in the corner—a particular ugly statue, for sure, unmoving and surveying the scene for hour after hour.

There'd been no letup for Barclay for the past 24 hours. In between tending to business for Yancey, he'd been slipping out to make phone calls, trying to take care of his own private affairs, primarily trying to track down Dougie Barnfeather.

Now, *there* was a problem.

He'd been able to mollify Yancey with answers about how his beloved Vanessa had turned up at the Donner household without bringing Dougie's name into it. He'd pieced together enough of the story of the murder of the Donners that it seemed an unfortunate but unrelated fluke of fate, but the boss still had lots of questions. Sooner or later, he'd get back to them as an item in his lengthy agenda. Barclay had better be ready with some good answers.

Whatever had happened at that house had clearly spooked Dougie sufficiently that he'd gone to ground. Barclay had talked with every crew member he could find; nobody had seen nor heard of him since Sunday.

From what Barclay knew about the fool, it made no sense in hell that Dougie could have killed the Donners. He didn't have it in him to kill, not in that cold and clean a fashion. But Dougie was scared, majorly scared, of something. He was a piece of the puzzle. Until he could be located, Barclay couldn't perform his own damage control on the current situation.

Barclay had to admit he owed the dude. Dougie had provided him a great opportunity that he couldn't turn down, one that had cemented his present role as Yancey's second in command. On the other hand, he was clearly a liability: too flash, too mouthy. If there was one thing Barclay had learned from T.C.'s time as number two, it was the value of a low profile. You didn't make yourself too obvious in your choice of clothes, hair style, facial hair or demeanor. The less you called attention to yourself, the better.

From the moment Dougie showed up, he'd stood out, all right, and not for good reasons. In the criminal field, where there's usually someplace where everyone can find a niche, Dougie was just a monstrous incompetent. He was eager enough to go wherever he was sent, plugging holes as needed. He was scrappy, but he was too small and not sufficiently ruthless or intimidating to fit in as a muscle guy. He seemed a better fit on the product end of things but showed some sloppiness there as well. His business sense, his ability to size up people, it all sucked. He looked like one of those rare guys who couldn't do *anything* well. But then something changed.

It was when he'd come to Barclay with some inside information, and a proposition, that he'd first made any kind of favorable impression. Dougie came from Costa County downstate and had some connections with a set there called the SanSans. He was setting up a deal with a woman he knew there who wanted to find a buyer in the city for a large quantity of crystal, and a number of weapons thrown into the deal. But he'd also made some quiet calls to some very unhappy higher-ups in the SanSans from whom the merchandise, it turned out, had been stolen.

He'd hatched a surprisingly intelligent and devious plan: lure his friend up, set her up to get busted, and use her as a bargaining chip. Dougie knew about Lydia being a potential state's witness against Rybus and that she was wanted for murder in the same Costa County. What if Rybus could use his assets in the system to get both women sent back there for trial, to a system where the SanSans notoriously held some serious sway? Both groups' concerns could be taken care of at the same time. It couldn't be all that difficult for that to be arranged. County detention, after all, could be a violent and dangerous place, especially in Costa County. Shit happened to people, as often as not never resolved as to who or why.

Barclay had to hand it to Dougie: it solved the problem of Lydia, with no connection back to the Ice Man. He liked the idea, and he discreetly passed it on to Yancey via his attorney, as if it were his own brainstorm. Yancey had liked it too.

Dougie received the nod to tell his "friend" the deal was set and give her directions where and when to come up for the meet. Meanwhile a particular Narcotics detective received an anonymous tip. The hapless young woman arrived only to find herself caught in a sting. The wheels were in motion.

That did the trick. The Ice Man had been thrilled at the initiative shown by Barclay, who by now felt confident in assuming the mantle once held by Theo Charles.

And it only got better. By a wicked stroke of luck (and some paperwork manipulation), both those problematic women had found themselves being transported together down to Costa County in the same transport, neither one suspecting that certain SanSans associates planned a warm welcome. That would have been good enough. Then fate intervened in the form of a gasoline truck. The news media blared the gruesome details: one of the duo, Lydia Montgomery, was dead. The other, Yvette St. Cloud, had escaped.

The fate of St. Cloud didn't matter to Yancey, whose only concern had been removing Lydia from the picture. In fact, despite his usual reserved manner, he seemed to take serene pleasure in the news of Lydia's gruesome fate. The SanSans might not be as happy, but that was of little concern to him. He'd kept his part of the deal. The rest was, as he referred to it sardonically, "An act of God, Barclay; an act of God, and all to the good."

Dougie's name had never once been uttered by Barclay. Assuming the credit for an obscure subordinate's achievement is a long-honored tradition in any business organization and this one was no different. He was simply a useful resource. But there was the downside: Dougie was still a constant potential liability because of his impulsiveness and lack of sense. He tried to keep him at a distance and kept putting him off, no matter how insistent he got.

Barclay's worst fears came true when Dougie called him Saturday evening, proudly announcing he'd "liberated" Vanessa from foster care and would be transferring her to a "safe haven" just in time to be a welcome home present for Yancey on his release. This time, Dougie insisted, Barclay would *have* to mention his name to the boss. He had some other brilliant enterprises coming down the pipe that Yancey was going to love. Moreover, his promising new friend in this scheme, Jack Donner, would be a great addition to the organization.

Another problem.

This Donner, an unknown, sounded like an even bigger flake than Dougie. The very prospect of the two of them filled Barclay with dread, and he privately swore that none of this fantasy of Dougie's was going to happen. Dougie, however, was convinced that once Yancey had been tearfully reunited with his beloved Vanessa, the Ice Man would be in a grateful mood to hear out some of his brilliant proposals and find a place for them both.

The tearful reunion plan, of course, had gone off the rails. Jack Donner was the subject of a murder investigation. Dougie Barnfeather was probably no longer looking forward to a personal introduction to the boss. And Barclay was feverishly working out ways to discreetly erase the affliction that was Barnfeather from the picture, completely and permanently.

There would be other obstacles to deal with soon enough. Barclay had his own grand plans, and a couple possible rivals were not going to be offering any other interference to them.

"Any new word on T.C. yet?"

Yancey's sudden words yanked him out of his reverie. Had the boss noticed he had been drifting? He shook his head.

"He hasn't emerged yet. Sykes is still convinced he's in that apartment house. He's got to come out at some point."

Once Felix had contacted him that morning, Barclay had dispatched more of the crew to the area. He'd relieved Felix briefly with a second shift and made sure he had a wingman when he returned to his post. More eyes were always good. And just to be sure, he'd sent a second car to the area without letting Felix know they were there to help keep an eye on the apartment house—and on Felix, just in case.

Belt and suspenders, as his grandmother used to say. Hedge your bets.

If Felix was right, T.C. didn't think anybody knew about his secret safe house and he'd figure he could hole up to prepare and make a break unobserved, but he couldn't take long to do so. It stood to reason that T.C. wouldn't be so stupid as to keep Yancey's money there in the apartment with him. He was on his own right now, without friends he could trust or hardly anything in the way of resources. He'd have it stashed somewhere safe and he'd have to gather it and make a run for it, soon.

All they needed to do was keep their eyes open and wait. At least Barclay hoped that was how it would work out.

Yancey sat back and laced his fingers. "Let's fervently hope that Sykes is correct. I'd prefer not to go in after him, so we'll wait for now. If T.C. sticks his head out of there, I want people on him, judiciously, but not observed. Nobody comes too close. Right up to the minute he lets on where the money is. Then, well...."

An unfamiliar ring tone started sounding, not the one Barclay had heard several times already. Yancey dug into a pocket and pulled out a phone Barclay hadn't seen before, listening and then speaking quietly and tersely into it.

"You're sure of this? And it has to be me personally? Why? I see. I'll get back to you and let you know when." He tapped the phone and replaced it in his pocket. "Something else to deal with first thing tomorrow. Now, where were we?"

TWENTY-ONE

Felix still couldn't figure why they'd sent Nate, of all people, to sit watch with him. The kid was okay, and he liked him, but he wasn't anywhere near the sharpest or most observant member of the crew. Still, having any second person in the car made things easier. They could take turns watching and resting, and a pit stop didn't involve a juice jar but rather a quick step out of the car into the nearby bushes. And the other two-man relief shift had been welcome as well, when they'd spelled him long enough to grab some sleep and pick up a bag of burgers, fries and drinks along with Nate for the next shift.

He checked his watch: two fifteen in the morning. Wednesday morning? The days were all running together crazily for him. The street, a peaceful neighborhood at the edge of a park, was deathly still.

"Keep an eye out," he told Nate, opening the car door. "I'm gonna take a whiz." He strolled to the nearby bushes at the perimeter of the park and stepped back behind a thicket, casually looking around. He still had a clear view of the apartment house.

He heard the unmistakable sound of an automatic gate opening.

"Damn!" Felix hissed, zipping himself up and running back to the car.

A dark Toyota slid out onto the street. Felix crammed himself into the driver's seat. He'd moved so quickly that he startled Nate.

"Is that him?"

"Gotta be," muttered Felix as he hit the ignition.

The Toyota turned in the opposite direction from them. Felix pulled the car out, not turning on his lights. "He's on the move. Call it in. Quick."

The Toyota was just taking the corner and disappearing as he pulled a U turn and floored the gas. At the corner, he stopped and checked before proceeding. He was going to have to play this cautiously. He couldn't let T.C. know someone was behind him but he couldn't lose him either. Hopefully Yancey had other cars in the vicinity ready to pick up the pursuit.

Felix had no idea just how close. With all his attention on what was going on in front of him, he didn't notice the black Charger half a block back that also pulled out, its lights also off.

The driver and any occupants in the Charger were also paying no attention to what might be behind them; consequently, nobody happened to notice the green Mustang still further down the block that suddenly pulled out and fell into the line behind the others. Quite the pre-dawn parade, all in all, and none of the participants apparently aware of anyone behind them.

* * * *

Barclay had finally been able to grab some precious sleep for about an hour before his phone pulled him back to consciousness. He looked at the time: 2:20.

"It's Nate. T.C. is on the move. We're following."

"Where's he going?"

"We got no idea yet. He just pulled out of his crib."

"All right, stay on him but be careful. I want constant updates. And just so you know, I've got somebody backing you up, right behind you. Don't let it trip you out."

Barclay broke the connection and immediately tapped in the number for Alex, in the Charger with Antoine. Alex picked up instantly.

"We're on top of the situation. We're about a half block behind Felix. Traffic's light. We can keep the tail without getting too close."

"All right. Stay on them. Keep me informed." He ended the call and sat back. There wasn't going to be any more sleep tonight.

Barclay hoped wherever T.C. was going, it wasn't far, and this could all be over tonight. But as he continued to follow the rapid reports coming in from Nate and Alex, it became pretty clear that wasn't happening. T.C. had taken a circuitous route to the freeway and headed south. He may or may not have been aware that he was being followed, but both of Barclay's pursuit cars were keeping him in view. As the updates continued and over an hour had passed, the outlook didn't change. T.C. was heading way *way* out of town.

He cursed his luck. He had people on 24-hour alert all over the city, including keeping track of that lawyer of T.C.'s. Anywhere that T.C. was spotted, he could have lots of them converging in the area in no time. But there was nothing he could do about someone speeding away from town and getting farther away every minute.

Barclay decided he'd better appreciate the short nap he'd gotten. There likely wasn't going to be much opportunity for more in the foreseeable future.

* * * *

The realization began to dawn in both pursuit cars that, if this major road trip kept up, they'd need to refuel at some point. Their hope was that T.C.'s Camry would need gas before their own somewhat larger cars did. If he pulled off the freeway into a service station, that presented its own set of problems in following and not being detected, but they for sure preferred to take that chance than to run out of fuel in the middle of nowhere.

Somewhere around four, in rural country, they lucked out. Felix was several hundred feet behind T.C. on the dark, sparsely traveled freeway, with one lone car between them, and saw him pull into the right lane without signaling as they approached an exit ramp.

"Let Barclay know," he told a drowsing Nate as he pulled into the right lane as well. "We're getting off."

Sometimes, luck holds. The exit had a motel and a couple of restaurants, and two service stations across the road from each other. T.C. pulled into one of stations all the way to the front. There were two other vehicles gassing up. The station was large enough to have several rows of self-serve pumps so Felix could pull into a different row a distance behind him.

The Charger likewise followed suit, pulling into the other, smaller station across the road. This one was deserted but their car was partially obscured by the pump to which they pulled up. Alex jumped out, jammed the gas nozzle into the car, and told the driver, Antoine, "Damn. Gotta make a quick pitstop. If he looks like he's finishing, toot the horn and be ready to roll."

Antoine, looking weary, nodded. He sat in the car, arm out the open window, staring across the street at the other station. He heard a sound and looked in his side view mirror. There was someone not far from the car, in coveralls and a cap. Well, he figured, there was usually somebody on site 24-7 just in case something went wrong. Maybe the attendant was checking on some problem on the pump behind him.

He yawned, stretched in the seat, and looked back over across the street. T.C. was extracting the nozzle from his own car. Antoine turned to see if Alex was returning yet, ready to hit his horn.

He didn't see what was coming.

A minute later, Alex ran out from behind the station, still zipping himself up, priding himself on how fast he'd taken care of business. He looked across the street in time to see T.C. pulling out of the station, and Felix's car following suit a distance behind. Both cars turned onto the nearby onramp of the southbound freeway.

"What the fuck!" he shouted. "Antoine! What is the—"

He swiveled his head to look at the Charger.

"Oh shit!" he spat.

The driver's side door was open, and Antoine was sprawled halfway out onto the ground. Alex saw blood.

He heard the growl of an engine and the sound of screeching tires. A dark green Mustang peeled out from the side of the station onto the road and roared towards the onramp.

He ran to Antoine, who was gasping for breath, a gush of blood from his neck area staining his blue shirt collar deep purple. He'd been stabbed deep, down between his throat and collarbone.

All Alex could say was "Oh shit, oh shit," over and over and over.

* * * *

Barclay got the panicked call from Alex at 4:20, trying his best to lay out what had happened.

"Antoine got cut bad! Paramedics are here, cops are coming. This is fucked!"

"Who was it?" was Barclay's first question.

"I got no idea. It was so fast it was crazy! The station looked empty. I started the pump and went to take a quick piss. I was gone less than a minute while Antoine kept an eye on T.C. across the street. When I got back, they'd done him. Looks like they got his piece too. All I saw was a Mustang leaving rubber."

"How's Antoine?"

"I don't know. They say they're not sure, he might make it, he might not."

"Okay, look, you're gonna have to answer a lot of questions. You got a story straight?"

Alex was clearly shaken but he was maintaining his focus and his cool. Okay, he was young, he was freaked out. But he'd be okay under pressure. Barclay had been limited in his choices, but he decided he'd chosen his men well.

"Yeah. We worked out some stuff on the drive in case we got pulled over. We were on a trip to visit friends of Antoine's downstate. We had to be back by late tonight for work tomorrow at the warehouse, so we didn't have any bags or shit with us." The organization had business owners on their payroll to provide job covers to crew members. The story would be okay in that area if it came to it.

"If he pulls through this and they ask him questions," Alex continued, "his story will match. The Charger belongs to him and the tags are up to date. As far as the story of what happened to him, we pulled into the station to get gas and some fuckin' maniac came out of nowhere and attacked him. Which is what did happen."

"Anything else you got that you shouldn't? Weapons, anything?"

"That's been taken care of before anybody showed up."

"All right, stay with Antoine. Any news, let me know right away. I'll get someone down there to cover you with the cops and get you out of there."

He closed off the call, cursing quietly in the darkness of his apartment. He didn't believe for a moment that it had been a random psycho who'd attacked Antoine. Someone had been following them. But who?

His mind raced furiously; there wasn't much time. He hadn't thought T.C. had anybody left he could count on for backup. Maybe he was wrong.

He ran through the crew members who'd been closest to T.C., who might have fallen back in with him, and he could account for them all. The one who stood out was his lifetime homie Felix. If anybody in the crew had turned back into T.C.'s camp, it would be the big man. But Felix was in the other tail car, with Nate. Still, it stirred Barclay's suspicious nature. Had he made a mistake in recruiting that one?

The only other possibility was that somehow T.C. had bought himself some new allies with some of that stolen money. He wasn't sure how he could confirm that.

The big question now was how, and what, to tell Yancey. Maybe the better question: how long to hold off telling him anything?

While he frantically made plans for damage control, he tapped in Nate's number to apprise him and Felix of the situation and to doubly stress for them to stay on T.C.—and to be careful.

A minute later, further down the road, Nate uttered a few terse words and hung up his phone.

"We've lost our backup."

Felix was peering into the darkness beyond his low-beam headlights, just barely keeping T.C.'s red taillights in view.

"What do you mean?"

"Alex and Antoine, who were tailing us. Barclay says something happened to them and we should be careful. Somebody else is following us, and they're not our people."

"What happened?"

"He didn't say. But he did say, we're on our own now."

"Fuck," muttered Felix. He began to wonder, in earnest, whether he'd made the right choices after all.

* * * *

Maybe it was the lack of sleep over the past couple days, but Barclay wasn't sure he was thinking straight or paying attention, and he needed to be right now. Too much was going wrong that he had no control over, and there would be no excuses acceptable to Yancey.

There was that important thing he had to do, if he could just find Dougie. But the dude wasn't picking up his phone and nobody had seen or heard from him. For whatever reason, he was running and hiding like a scared rabbit.

Maybe he could talk him down. It couldn't hurt.

Barclay tapped in Dougie's number and, just as every other time, he got shifted to voice mail. Luckily the mailbox wasn't full yet and he could leave a message. He modulated his voice to sound calm and casual.

"Dougie. It's Barclay. Listen, man, everything's cool here. Yancey's cool with you. He understands that you had nothing to do with what went down at the Donners' house. He told me that it was a genius move to bring his dog there. Who knew they were gonna go and get themselves whacked in a home invasion robbery? Maybe you're nervous, but everything's cool. I repeat, everything is cool. Yancey's talking to me about moving you up. The window is open. The opportunity's knocking for you, right now. But you have to come see me, man. Come see me, and I mean *right away*. Call me back soon's you get this."

He finished the call and took a deep breath. Maybe it would work, maybe it wouldn't. There wasn't much else he could do.

* * * *

Felix yawned and rubbed his right eye with a knuckle. He was starting to lose it. The sun was up and it was getting warm. They were flying down the freeway through the long central valley of the state. Most of the other traffic around them consisted of trucks, which he figured worked in his favor to stay unseen. About sixty feet ahead of them, he could see Theo's grey Toyota. Felix hoped that he'd be pulling off soon, for gas, food, a bathroom break, anything. His own gas was still pretty good, but he really needed to switch off and let Nate take over the driving while he just closed his eyes for a few minutes. He hoped the kid could continue the pursuit as well as he'd been doing, but at least they were on a stretch of limited access highway, nothing but farmland for miles, where you couldn't lose somebody all that easily. If his memory was right, maybe another hundred miles or so down the road, some other major routes joined this one and they'd have to be ready for whatever direction the Toyota took, but he figured Nate could handle this part for long enough for him to catch his second wind. Now if only he'd pull off.

They passed a blue sign that read REST AREA AHEAD CLOSED TEMPORARILY. As they approached the exit, the Toyota suddenly pulled across two lanes into the far right and took the offramp.

"What in hell?" Felix muttered, pulling their car into the exit lane as well. He slowed, pulled over to the shoulder, and stopped, watching as the Toyota swerved around a couple of orange barriers and continued into the shut-down rest area. It pulled into one of the herring-bone parking slots at the far end of the area, near the rest rooms.

A pitstop.

Felix gave it a minute and then hit the gas, pulling around the barriers and parking at the back end of the deserted area, where he could see the Camry, which now appeared unoccupied. It was risky but there were enough trees and bushes around that possibly Theo wouldn't notice them. He waited another minute and decided Theo had run into the men's room.

The sequence of events next came all at once.

Felix took his gun off the seat next to him, moved it to the console, and opened his car door, starting to say to Nate, "Quick switch."

Nate exclaimed, "What the fuck!" and swiveled in his seat to look somewhere behind Felix.

There was a sudden explosion of glass as the rear left window shattered and Nate was hurled against the passenger door.

There might have been two or three shots. Felix wasn't sure.

Pure reflex took over. Felix rolled himself out the driver's side door with amazing speed for a big guy crammed into a not so big car. He fell to his knees on the pavement, facing the rear.

Felix found himself staring up into the barrel of a Bereta M9.

"Don't fucking move," hissed Theo, standing over him.

Then, a moment later, "Felix? What the fuck! What the *fuck!*"

Felix glared up at his old friend, otherwise remaining motionless.

"Put your hands behind your head and don't move!"

Felix complied.

"And who's that in the car?"

"Nate."

"Nate? *Nate?* Of all the people—aw, *fuck!*"

"You know how this works. I had no choice. This is business. Staying alive business."

"You do know you're pretty shitty at following without getting noticed, right? I know you've been on me since the beginning. That move in the gas station, you might as well have waved a flag. How come you haven't tried to take me out yet?"

"Orders. Yancey wants his money first. He figures you'd lead us to it."

"Jesus Christ, you asshole, you *know* I don't have his money! That guy Musgrave, Lydia's partner, has it and he's taken off with it!"

Felix rolled his eyes. "Still running that shit, T.C.? Come on, it's me. Nobody's buying that bullshit story."

"So that's how it is. This is what it's come to."

"That's how it is, T.C."

"So when Yancey gave the word, you were gonna, what, take me out? You?"

"You know how the game is played." Felix looked up into Theo's eyes. "Only one of us gets out alive."

"Damn, Felix, you and I came up together! We go back as kids together! Why you?"

"It's the life. We all made our choices. You and I both know how this has got to end. It's you or me. So let's get it over with."

He had to hand it to Felix, full blooded gangster to the end, true to the code. He always was a straight up dude.

Theo held the gun steady in two-handed stance. It wasn't the first time he'd had to do this. This one was just the hardest. He squeezed the trigger twice.

* * * *

It had all been cloudy; Felix had no coherent memories of anything except pain, until he felt something clamp down over his face and saw some guy up close and personal, staring down at him.

It was an oxygen mask. He felt the cold pavement underneath him.

"Can you hear me?" the guy was saying. "Can you tell me your name?"

Felix turned his head as far as he was able right and left. There were flashing lights and several people standing around over him. The guy talking to him seemed to be an EMT or something like that.

"What's going on?" he tried to say. He got the first word out.

"We found you here, you and the other guy. Someone driving by called 911 when they saw the burning car. You were both lying a few feet away from it. You've both been shot and lost a good deal of blood. You're lucky we got here when we did."

He was joined by another guy in a uniform.

He recognized it. State Police.

"Sir, can you tell me who did this? And what you were doing in this closed area to begin with?"

The EMT interrupted him. "We've got to get him in the ambulance. You can talk to him at the hospital." Felix felt himself being moved onto some kind of stretcher and then onto a gurney and rolled toward some vehicle he couldn't see.

"Nate," he coughed.

"Is that your friend's name?" the EMT said. "He's alive. We're going to do what we can to keep you both that way. Now don't try to talk any more. Just hang on."

TWENTY-TWO

"It wasn't Barnfeather that threatened Moira Legge to drop her testimony. It was you!"

When Radley and Ochida had approached their black and white at the start of their Wednesday early shift, they'd found Leon and Art waiting for them. Radley had told them they didn't have time to talk right then but the grave expressions on the detectives' faces told him that they weren't taking no for an answer. So he'd told his partner to wait for him and he'd walked over to the far end of the parking lot with them. The conversation wasn't friendly.

"What do you mean it was me? Oh fuck, you found her, didn't you? How—"

"That's not important," spat Leon. "What's important is that you are in a pile of shit, and the pile is only going to get bigger if you keep lying to me."

"I just wanted to scare her off, I wasn't intending to actually do anything."

"So this is why Halley originally approached you to begin with, to frighten off the witness."

"No. She was scared of Dougie. Like, really scared. He'd rung her into the accident scam and she realized it was a mistake. It was bad enough that Jack was getting in deeper with the guy. She hoped I could get her out of the mess that the whole thing had turned into, and maybe chase Dougie off from Jack as well. The first thing I had to do was get her off the hook for the criminal charge. I knew that if that went away, Dougie would no longer be concerned and wouldn't be a threat. So I went to visit the Legge woman and just made some vague threats."

"You told her you were a detective," Art said. "You suggested some kind of evidence could appear implicating her in some drug thing."

"No, no, *no!* I never told her I was a detective. She might have taken that impression, you know? But I never misrepresented myself. I never threatened outright to do anything like plant evidence, if that's what you're suggesting." He looked back and forth at Leon and Art almost pleadingly. "It was all show. I never planned to do anything like that, just impress on her the importance of her dropping out. I told her if she just disappeared for a while everything would be all right."

"You scared the ever-loving shit out of her," Art said gruffly. "She still thinks someone's coming after her. And believe me, that's not a woman who scares easily."

"Look, all I wanted was to get Halley off the hook. Then I could deal with Dougie, tell him to keep away from her."

"So she could just run her own insurance scams from then on," Leon replied.

"I was trying to get her out of all that, away from that shyster lawyer who was enabling her. Get her into something legitimate. She had this, this thing on some kind of online store with accessories and jewelry and stuff, that I figured I could help her get more business on it, or maybe help her open an actual boutique store somewhere. I told her this had to be the last insurance scam."

Art and Leon just stared at him with undisguised contempt.

"Hey, you guys, you can't hang me up on this, come on! You gotta give me a break!"

Leon ignored the plea. "There's more to this than you've told me, like how this fits with Halley and Jack getting killed."

"I don't know! I don't know! I don't know anything about the stuff Dougie was getting Jack into. Jack wanted nothing to do with me. And he'd stopped telling Halley about most of it as well because he knew she'd tell me."

"You, Halley and Jack," Leon said quietly. "Sounds like it turned into quite the triangle."

"And quite the mess you'd made for yourself," Art added. Both detectives stood, arms folded, glaring at the officer.

"You're thinking I had something to do with their deaths? Oh, man, come on!"

They let that sit in the air for a long, awkward moment.

"I've got nothing more to say to you," Radley finally said. "Maybe I should get my union rep before I answer any further questions."

"That's up to you. *If* you think you need to do that."

"Dougie's the one with the answers! You find him, you find the answers!"

"Well, that's the thing. Nobody knows where Dougie has disappeared to. You don't seem to know either."

"Fuckin' A, you guys, what kind of detectives are you? You want me to find him for you? All right, I will. But this is bullshit. I had nothing to do with this." The anger flared in his eyes and his voice, but Leon was sure he could see the slight suggestion of a tear in the corner of one eye. "Maybe the one person who gave a shit for Halley was me. I might be the only one who'll actually show up at the grave to mourn her, for fuck's sake. Now, anything else, or can I get to work?"

"Sure," said Leon as they turned to walk away. "Go on out and serve and protect."

Radley heaved a deep sigh and began his own trudge back across the lot. He opened the door to the cruiser, got in, and slammed the door heavily.

"What was that all about?" Ochida asked as Radley started up the engine.

"Just some bullshit," Radley muttered. "Hey, look. There's something we must take care of this morning. I'll explain later."

* * * *

"What's that you say, Olivia?"

Olivia Venuto looked up at the fellow Narcotics detective passing her desk and shook her head.

"Sorry, just talking to myself."

She re-read the text on her phone, still quietly cursing at her partner, and not for the first time.

Will be late this AM, taking care of personal biz.

This was bullshit.

She didn't know what had been up with Gene recently but she'd had enough. There was something serious going on that he wouldn't open up about, which in itself she could have handled. They all knew the stresses of the job and they all dealt with it in their own ways. But lately, it was more like they were each working solo rather than covering their cases as partners. The guy had just gone rogue on her. Whatever was up, he needed to either confide in her or take care of it on his own time. He'd left her high and dry way too often of late.

Then there was that whole thing yesterday where he'd had her ask around about some guy named Barnfeather that nobody seemed to have heard of. He made up some elusive story about an inquiry by one of his old Personal Crimes colleagues, but the story didn't ring true. It was just her gut feeling that he hadn't been leveling with her lately. Whatever the real story, he wasn't being straight with her about it.

She closed the messages on her phone, still muttering a quiet, desperate litany of obscenities. It was time to confront him about everything. Or maybe, she considered, it was time to go request a change of partners.

* * * *

Jilly and Dan had both just reached their desks when they heard Castillo call out "Garvey! Lee!" from his doorway. He didn't even bother to sit down, just greeted them at the door.

"I just got a call from the coroner's office, from Medical Examiner Kendrick, about your case."

"He called you?" Jilly replied, trading a baffled look with Dan. "How come?"

"Dental records positively identified your vic."

"Okay, but I still don't understand why Mickey—"

"It's not Lydia Montgomery."

"Wait, what—"

"The victim. It's not Lydia Montgomery. It's Yvette St. Cloud."

Before either of them could recover sufficiently to reply, Castillo turned back to his desk, saying over his shoulder, "Montgomery is now the fugitive we're seeking. Get me any info you've got on her right away so I can get it out through the Department. And then I'm leaving it to you to notify any family about St. Cloud's death.

"Oh," and Castillo added as they turned to leave, "and don't forget to notify Detective Rasula down in Costa about this new development. I'm sure he's going to love it as much as we do."

TWENTY-THREE

"Barclay! That you?"

Barclay had taken the call on the first ring. He could hear the strain in the voice.

"Dougie! Aw, thank God, man! Where are you?" He hoped he didn't sound too solicitous. The last thing he needed to do was spook the dude any further than he already sounded.

"It's all fucked, man! Everything's fucked! I totally fucked up!"

"Take it easy. Calm down. What's all fucked?"

"I went over there Sunday! I fucked up major! Now everyone's looking for me."

"You went over where? You mean where you brought the dog?"

"Yeah! I went back there Sunday and, oh shit oh shit oh *shit!* Some detectives been asking all around about me. The po-lice are probably all over lookin' for me. I'm seeing Yancey's guys everywhere too, I mean *everywhere!* I'm fucking dead meat!"

What the hell was he talking about? Was Dougie caught up in those two deaths at the house? If he'd been there, or done it, or just knew who did, oh hell, it was better not to know, not to pursue it.

In any case, he couldn't let Dougie get picked up by the police now. Too much dangerous out of control information. He had to plug this, fast. He kept his voice cool, soothing.

"No, it's gonna be all right. Damn, I am so glad you called me, Dougie. You did the right thing. It's all gonna be all right. Yancey's okay with you. I told him all about you, how you were the one who handled things with the SanSans and with the dog. He told me himself, he's cool with everything."

"Man, there's crew everywhere with their eyes out, lookin' nasty! I can't step out on the street without a couple of those dudes rolling by."

"None of that's for you, Dougie. They want this other guy, T.C., the one that stole the money. There's an all-eyes out for him. You're cool. Trust me. I'm in tight with Yancey now and I know the story."

"But what about the heat?"

"Okay, now the police, they could be a problem, but nothing we can't work around. First thing is, we have to bring you in out of the cold."

"Out of the cold, huh? Yeah. Yeah, but how we gonna do that?"

"You gotta get to me so I can get you under wraps and maybe move you somewhere safe until we work this other shit out. You know about Yancey, right? He's a master arranger. You got the whole machine on your side, bro, and you know what that means. Everything's gonna get ironed out and then you've got a solid place with the organization. Just what you've been working towards."

"Okay." Dougie, still out of breath, was starting to come down. Alone in a corner as he was, the promise of family, powerful family, watching his back was irresistible. "Yeah. Yeah. Sounds good."

"How fast can you meet up with me?"

"I don't like the idea of going out in daylight. Can we wait 'til night at least?"

"No, it's gotta be soon. The sooner the better. Like, now. And this is prime time. It's early, cop shifts will be changing, nobody paying attention. We got a window. Can you get to someplace remote where nobody will be looking?" Barclay had to play this carefully. He had a specific place in mind but couldn't make it sound like he was pushing it. "Cops don't go out of the city, just to the north where the bay comes in. You know any of that area?"

"I'm not from here, you know that. I'm from Costa. Isn't there like some kind of big park up there?"

Open the door, Dougie, and let me drive right in.

"Yeah! yeah! The Point, they call it. Right on the bay. It's wide open, hardly anybody up there, especially early in the morning. That's a great idea."

"Tell me where."

Barclay paused a long moment, as if he had to think about it. Then he gave Dougie the directions.

Just be careful, Barclay thought as he tapped out of the call. *I only need you to stay alive and free for a little while longer.*

His ring tone blared again.

"Barclay, my boy, I trust I did not waken you."

Did the guy never sleep?

"No, Yancey, I've been up for a long time. Getting ready to go on some unannounced early rounds, check up on how the supply is going down and everybody's setting up."

"I'm pleased to hear this. Always good to keep the crew off balance. I'll be heading over to pick up Vanessa as soon as the Vaughan Street shelter opens this morning."

"Why not let me send someone over to get her?"

Yancey sighed. "She's got a chip implant and apparently, they will only release her to someone who can prove they are her registered owner, which of course is me. Which is highly responsible of them, and of which I approve. Luckily, they don't know about that unfortunate foster person who was stuck in the middle of this, only that Vanessa was rescued from a crime scene. It would make sense that the faster I extract her from this situation, before it gets any more complicated, the better."

The most bad-ass gangster in the city, the guy everybody's terrified to shit of, has a doggie he adores. A gangster doggie. With a fucking computer chip, like some kind of Yuppie pet. Barclay shook his head silently.

"Aren't you worried this could be some kind of set-up?"

"Barclay, I appreciate your solicitous attitude on my behalf, but I'm confident in my information."

"Do you need me to send a couple of the guys over to go with you?"

"No need. I've got Mace. Why don't you come by the club around ten thirty, would that work?"

He well knew, Yancey's pointed politeness still conveyed a command. A couple other dudes he'd known had learned that the hard way. *Be here at ten thirty. Period.*

"Of course."

"Stay in touch in the meantime." Yancey rang off.

And Mace. That guy, Barclay knew, was ultimately going to be a problem.

One solution at a time. There'd be time to deal with Mace.

No time to shower or grab breakfast. He snatched up his car keys from the table and headed for the door. He figured he had time to arrive ahead of Dougie. He knew the shortest way to the park at the Point. But he still had to hurry.

As Barclay figured, the big, extended parking lot was almost empty at this time of the morning. It was opened early to accommodate the locals who went to fish off the pier. There were several of their cars already parked, at the far end of the lot by the trail that led to the pier. There were no cars at the other end, adjoining a wooded area with a rustic path that led to a different part of the bay. That was where he'd told Dougie to meet him. He pulled all the way to the edge of the lot and waited.

The minutes went by slowly. His impatience was driving him nuts. He was beginning to wonder if Dougie had gotten lost or had just lost his nerve. Finally, he saw another car pull into the lot and turn towards him. He'd only seen Dougie's car once before, but it was hard to mistake it: a gold decades-old showboat Pontiac Firebird that had seen better days but was still his pride and joy. It sputtered and roared as he hit the gas coming into the lot. Thank God Yancey had never seen the damned thing: not exactly the low profile he preferred his crews to be taking. No wonder Dougie was worried about being spotted.

So much for making a quiet entrance. This could be a problem. Luckily Dougie was at least sensible enough to park some distance away from him. Barclay got out of his car, pointed to the path, and began to walk that way. Hopefully the fool caught the idea.

Hidden by the trees, Barclay stopped to look back. There didn't seem to be any other cars entering the lot after Dougie, who was getting out of his Firebird and giving the area a once-over. Maybe he'd lucked out and hadn't attracted any untoward notice. *Not like there aren't lots of car guys driving around,* he mused, *even early in the morning, lots of guys like mechanics and construction workers. Maybe he just got lost in the noise of the city.*

Barclay resumed walking down the path towards the bay, not too rushed but fast enough to keep Dougie a ways behind him. When he got about halfway to the water, he stopped, turned, reached into his belt for his .32, and waited, holding it behind his back.

He didn't have to wait long. He heard the crunch of quick footsteps behind him and Dougie's heavy breathing. He came into sight around a bend from behind the bushes, in a pair of jeans and a white T shirt, and stopped to catch his breath, head down, hands on hips.

"Man, what is up with this?" he huffed. "We couldn't just meet in the lot?"

"With that fucking beater you showed up in? You could hear that coming a mile away! Why not blast your speakers while you're at it? I told you not to attract attention to us so we weren't seen together."

"Well, how else was I supposed to get here? That's my ride!"

"All right, all right. But now we better wait and see if anybody else shows up and that nobody's around before we go back to my car."

"You mean I gotta leave my Bird here?"

"Well, what the fuck did you think was gonna happen? I'm afraid so. We can always come back and get it later. It'll be safe here. I can send one of the crew back to pick it up later today."

Dougie nodded, his brain slowly grasping the idea. "I guess I didn't think this through. You're right. Okay. So, what's the plan?"

"Like I said: we wait. When it seems safe, we head back."

"Look, I'm telling you, nobody followed me. Nobody came into the lot after me. In fact I didn't see anybody once I took the exit road down to the park."

"No cops around?"

"Sure, I saw a couple black and whites. But they didn't pay me no mind. Just doing their patrol shit. Like you said, just going off their shifts."

"You sure now?"

"I'm sure." Dougie suddenly stared at Barclay. "How come you got your hand behind your back?"

Barclay brought it out, with his .32 pointed at Dougie.

"Aw fuck, man. Come on!"

"Sorry, Dougie. You're a liability."

Dougie held his left hand up, fingers splayed, as if to ward off what was coming. It was enough of a distraction that Barclay didn't notice his other hand reaching behind him. "Wait. Wait. Hear me out before you do that."

That momentary hesitation was enough. Dougie's right hand reappeared from behind his own back with a gun of his own that had been tucked into his belt. It looked like some kind of cheap .22. Barclay was sufficiently taken aback that he had to laugh. He started to say, "What in hell is that toy, a starter's pistol?" But he only got the first four words out before Dougie started firing, and kept doing it until all he heard was a click.

Barclay, in shock and pain, never got a shot of his own off. His own weapon slipped from his hand and fell to the ground. His last fading thought was, *I didn't think he had it in him.*

Dougie stood frozen for several moments, watching Barclay tumble to the ground. Somehow every single round had landed in dead center body mass. He jammed the empty handgun into his belt behind his back and pulled his shirt down over it, then wheeled around and began to run back down the path. He hadn't gotten more than a few steps before he heard a car braking and a door opening out in the parking lot. Suddenly there was a figure at the head of the path, a hazy shadow against the morning sun behind it. Dougie, through a confused haze, saw a uniform. And he saw the figure had a weapon of its own, pointed in a two-hand stance directly at him. He staggered to a halt.

"Hold it right there, Dougie," he heard a familiar voice hollering. "Don't move. Don't fucking move an inch further."

He'd thought, just a moment earlier, that he was as scared as he could ever be. He'd thought it couldn't have gotten any worse. He'd been wrong.

What in hell was Radley doing here, now?

* * * *

The Lexus took the turn off the access road called Vaughan Street onto the blacktop driveway, traveled about twenty feet, and came to a stop. Mace, behind the wheel, peered through the windshield at the wooden barricades that had been drawn across the road and what looked like a hastily hand-lettered sign that read PARKING LOT TEMPORARILY CLOSED FOR REPAIR, SORRY 4 THE INCONVENIENCE.

"Looks like we have to park out here and walk in, Mr. Rybus," Mace said in his hoarse voice. Yancey, from the back seat, allowed himself the slightest of sighs, about as demonstrative as he ever became.

"Then I suppose you'll have to pull over to the side and we'll walk in."

As they exited the vehicle, Mace cast his gaze around in every direction. They had passed a deserted parked car right at the turn-off but besides that, they'd encountered no other vehicles. Past the wooden horses and across the deserted parking lot, beyond more trees and bushes, he could see the walk-up entrance to the Vaughan Street Animal Shelter. He could vaguely hear some dogs barking from way back in the building, and the morning traffic of the nearby freeway could be heard through the trees, but otherwise all was early morning stillness in the deserted area.

Mace noticed there were actually three cars parked at the end of the lot, nearest the building. Strange in a lot that was supposed to be closed. He saw no construction vehicles or pickup trucks. There didn't seem to be any kind of construction or repair in progress. Maybe it just hadn't begun yet. Maybe it was all on the up and up. But he was being paid to be suspicious.

"I don't like this, Mr. Rybus. Something's not right. Are you sure you want to do this?"

"Your caution is appreciated, Mace. Stay alert. But I do want my Vanessa back."

"All right, sir. Let me go ahead of you." He pulled his automatic out of a shoulder holster and held it down at his side, hidden by the folds of his coat. "Stay close, please."

Yancey had withdrawn his own weapon and was likewise holding it low at his side. If need be, they could both holster their pieces quickly when they got within view of the people in the shelter. But paranoia was never a bad thing in the world of the Ice Man.

They were just a few feet past the wooden horses when they heard the sound, not much but enough to set off both of their instincts. It was the slightest scraping of feet on the blacktop pavement behind them.

Both men wheeled around.

And all hell broke loose.

TWENTY-FOUR

The call that Leon got from Radley was brief and mysterious. He simply said that "Druggie Barnfeather" could be found at a specific county holding facility, and he'd follow up later when he could. Thirty minutes later, Art and Leon were ushered into an interview room where a thoroughly abashed Barnfeather already sat at a table.

"Hello, Douglas," said Leon as they pulled out chairs and sat. He introduced himself and Art.

"I didn't do anything," Dougie said glumly.

"Is that so. Looks like quite a job you pulled on that guy this morning."

"Hey, that was totally self-defense. He was gonna kill me. I had no choice."

"It would appear you emptied your weapon into him. The officer heard at least three or four shots. The other guy never got a chance to get a single shot off."

"It was a set up. He pulled on me first. I was lucky. I coulda been the dead guy and he coulda been the guy sitting here now."

Leon nodded. "Seems like there are a lot of people looking for you right now, including us. You've been a hard man to find the past few days."

"But I didn't do anything. Well, none of what you're all looking for me for."

"What is it you think we're all looking for you for?"

"The Donners. I had nothing to do with that."

Art and Leon just stared at him for a long time. Finally, he added, "The killings, I mean. Yancey's crews and the cops, everybody thinks I did, but I didn't."

"Kind of interesting, they were both shot with a .22."

"I didn't know that. So what?"

"Doug," Art said, with exaggerated patience, "you had a .22 when you got picked up. You do know we're going to compare the slugs to your gun, right?"

"I had nothing to do with that. That was somebody else with a .22. They're not exactly rare, you know? You can pick one up easy as buying a candy bar."

"So," continued Leon, "if you're so innocent, why were you so worried we'd find you?"

"Well, I was there that day. At the Donners'."

"And why were you there that day?" asked Art.

"It was about the dog."

"The dog?"

"Yeah. I brought them the dog."

"The dog we found there, the big white one? That wasn't their dog?"

"No. I brought it to them for safe keeping."

"You brought the dog to the Donners on Sunday when they were killed?" Leon considered that Helena Corkendale had said the dog had been barking the whole weekend.

"No, no. That was Saturday. I came back on Sunday to talk to them about the dog, make sure it was being well taken care of."

"Was this your dog?"

"No. It belongs to Yancey Rybus. I was getting it back for him and needed a safe place to leave it until he got out. That's why I came back on Sunday, to make sure they took good care of it. It was, like, raining, and I wanted to make sure the dog was out of the rain and the cold. They sometimes weren't, what you call it, attentive to shit like that."

Art sighed deeply, rubbing his forehead. "Maybe you better back up a bit and fill us in a little more on how you were connected to Jack and Halley Donner."

"How far back you want me to go?"

"How'd you meet them? Let's start with that."

"They were two of the first people I met when I first came up here late last year."

"Up from where, exactly?"

"I come from a town called Santa Sangre, ever heard of it?"

They both had.

"I figured it was a good time to try to get on board the organization up here, what with the stuff going on and all, there'd be people who could use some new talent like me. I had some connections from down there that I might be able to use."

"The SanSans?"

"You know about them, huh? Anyway, as soon as I got up here, I started trying to introduce myself around. That's when I met Barclay."

"Barclay Vickers? The guy you just shot?"

"Yeah. You might say things went sour between us."

"To say the least," said Art.

"But it was good at first. It was good for quite a while. He and I hit it off, you know? I started letting him know of all the shit I could do for him, and he was open to that. I could see he was in good position to be the new number two."

"We're still waiting for how Jack and Halley fit into this."

"I'm getting to that. I started looking around to see how I could make myself useful. I started making the rounds, hanging out, meeting people, keeping my ears open, asking questions, looking for angles. Overheard a lot of gossip and news. I tried to get to know some other people here and there, anybody I thought might help me get some things going."

"Things? Such as?"

"Well, I figured if I could be the go-between with the organization and the SanSans, I could get some supply pipelines running. I'd need my own network of locals on this end. That's when I ran into Jack. He struck me as a prime candidate. He was eager and willing, and he talked a good game. But I needed something to bring me and my network to the attention of Barclay and Yancey."

"Your network? How big a network did you have at this point?"

"Well, it was mostly promise still."

Art sighed. "Uh huh. I see."

"Jack was on board; he believed in me. Everybody else was what you'd call skeptical. I had to prove myself, and then all the pieces would fall into place, you know?"

"Just how were you going to do that?" Art asked.

"I hit on a nice stroke of luck. It was sheer genius on my part. I heard about this chick who was giving Yancey the fits. She'd been the girlfriend of his number two, knew all kinds of shit, and she was threatening to rat everybody out. She had to be the prime target on his list."

Leon nodded. "Lydia Montgomery."

"That's the one. They said she'd been charged with murder one down where I'm from and was going to be sent back there at some point. The problem Yancey had was, how to get to her and eliminate her as an issue, cleanly and safely."

"And this was a stroke of luck for you, how, exactly?"

"Well, I also happened to know this other gal from my hometown who asked me to help her find a buyer up here for some shit she had. I also happened to find out she'd ripped off the SanSans. They had no idea who'd done it but they were righteously pissed. The opportunity just sorta came to me: two organizations with major problem individuals, is there some way to broker a solution for them both and profit from it? I suggested to Barclay that if I told her I got her a buyer up here and then set her up so she got picked up, there might be some way to arrange for both of them to be sent back to Costa County where someone could be waiting to take care of both of them in custody. There'd be no way to trace anything back to Yancey, and I'd have my in with the organization."

"So, you sold out your friend," Leon nodded, not really surprised. "Sheer genius."

"Yeah! Yeah! That's what I'm sayin'!" The irony was apparently flying high above Dougie's head. "It went better than I could have imagined. Barclay passed on the proposal to Yancey who ate it up. Turns out Yancey's got all kinds of connections in the system. He got word to some detective what was going to go down, and when she showed up at the agreed place and time, they grabbed her with all her stuff. Then Yancey tweaked a few more things so that the two chicks would be taken back down to Costa. It was fucking brilliant."

"And your idea actually worked," Leon said. "Your friend was Yvette St. Cloud. She and Lydia were together in the prisoner van that was in the accident."

"This is all interesting," Art said, "and we can come back to it, but how does this connect to Jack and Halley Donner and last weekend?"

"Well, like I said, I'd started to get tight with Jack. Jack, he was different from most of the others. He could see the promise in my ideas."

Genius recognizing genius, Art thought to himself.

"And," Dougie continued, "he was interested in some things I could offer him right away."

"You mean you were dealing drugs to him?"

"Can we not get too specific here?"

"Just theoretically speaking. My point is, say you were dealing to anybody and weren't as yet officially connected to the Rybus crew, wouldn't that be kind of dangerous freelancing?"

"If we're just talking, like you say, theoretical, someone could be buying from outside the city and bringing it up, I suppose. Outside the established supply chain."

"Which would also account for your keeping in close touch with your old homies down south. Theoretically speaking. Still a perilous game."

Dougie shrugged. "Perilous life, know what I mean? They say fortune goes to the bold or something like that."

Art's eyebrows raised. "You read a book somewhere along the line, Douglas, I'm impressed. So that's how you and Jack first met up, when he came looking to buy?"

"Actually, it was over his 944. You know his car?"

"Matter of fact, we do."

"We were in a bar, and next thing you know, we were talking about our cars. We talked a lot about our cars. He dug my old Firebird, and he liked to talk about how he was going to fix up that Porsche. I liked to kid him about the piece of import trash he was wasting his time and money on, but he had a sense of humor about it, and he did love that ride, so I kinda respected him for it. Then he introduced me to Halley, which was a whole 'nother thing. But in the meantime, our conversations opened up to all kinds of new horizons. I tell you, I liked Jack. He had ambitions. He had balls. He was willing to listen to someone with imagination and try new shit."

"Like what kind of 'shit' are we talking?" Art asked.

"I'd rather not get too specific. Whatever would make a buck. He and I both needed a stake. He was willing to be, like, an entrepreneur, you know?"

"Looks like Jack got in over his head a few times. He got popped for possession of stolen goods and drugs a few times."

"Far as I know he skated every time too."

Art had to smile wryly. "Sounds like you were his Tom Sawyer in the background."

"Tom who? What are you talking about?"

Art waved his hand. "Never mind. One book seems the limit. You didn't happen to be the one getting him into all this aforementioned trouble, by any chance?"

"Hey, I was the best friend that guy had. He woulda been broke if it hadn't been for me."

Leon said, "Sounds like Halley didn't feel the same about you."

"Man, that chick. What a piece of work. I tried to help her too, get her involved in the program, but she was just this block of ice, you know? Not a trusting bone in her body."

"Like the accident scam. Your idea?"

"You know about the accident gig, huh? Yeah, I guess you would. That would have been a sweet gig. Pick up a couple of old beaters, crack 'em up a few times with one of those entitled yuppie types in nice cars who drive while they're on their phones or thinking about other shit and not paying attention and collect. Their own fault and they can spare the money. Shit, it even teaches 'em a valuable lesson about presence of mind, you know? It's kind of what you call a win-win! We coulda brought in a few thousand every couple weeks. I figured she was great for that, seeing as how she was doing so well on those insurance riffs of hers. You know about them, right?"

Art, looking very tired suddenly, closed his eyes and nodded, resting his chin on his hand.

"Way I see it," Dougie continued, "those companies and those rich people, they got the money to spare and they learn to be less careless in the future. She was a natural at those things, a real instinct for it. I was just introducing her to the big leagues."

"But that didn't go so well," Leon said. "Your intended vic didn't just roll up in a ball and head for the ATM for you."

"Damn the luck. Next one would've gone better. But Halley nixed it. Man, she got pissed at me."

Art remained silent, eyes shut, as if in meditation, so Leon kept up the conversation.

"Well, you did run out on her and leave her hanging with the officers who showed up."

"Aw, come on, that's how it works. If it had been the other way around, I'd have understood if she took off."

"You weren't worried about getting involved in the criminal charges?"

"That did get heavy for like a minute. I knew she wouldn't turn on me. That woman was hard core."

"So, you didn't threaten her?"

"Man, no way. I knew she'd find her way out of the situation."

"And you didn't contact the witness, the one you'd been trying to scam?"

"Never came near her. I tried to lay low for a while after that. I never figured it would come to much, but still, no harm in being cautious. I was relieved when the case got dropped. Got no idea who she even was."

Leon continued, still waiting for Art to open his eyes again. He suspected Art was hoping when he did, Dougie would have disappeared. "But you kept trying to get Halley interested in your 'projects,' anyway?"

"She would have been a definite plus. I mean, Jack was a game guy and all, ready and willing, but she was the brains of the household. She was a player! Jack was a little too interested in getting fucked up in one way or the other. He liked crystal and blow, and he loved getting drunk and stoned. Sometimes it got in the way of things. Then that cop, Radley, who was coming around, she kinda sicced him on me, telling me to stay away."

"The same guy who arrested you at the Point, you mean. He was around a lot?"

"That's the one. He clearly had a thing for Halley."

"Jack knew about that, I imagine? How'd that go down with him?"

"I got the impression, not well. He never talked about it, but I picked up the vibe. It wasn't good between them. More often than not she wouldn't be around when I was with Jack, so I didn't see them, you know, interact all that much."

"So, these business deals you were setting up with Jack. What kinds of things?"

"A little of this, a little of that. I was trying to teach him the ropes, establish his bona fides so I could introduce him to Barclay and the rest of the crew."

"Meaning you guys were stealing stuff?"

"Let's just say we were trying a lot of things and leave it at that."

"And you were also supplying him with his drugs, like coke and meth?"

Dougie raised his cuffed hands. "I never said that. You're puttin' words in my mouth."

"Okay, for the sake of argument, hypothetically, let's assume he was being supplied with stuff from someone. Can we assume he was also reselling?"

"Well, hypothetically, maybe."

"That could be a real problem, competing with the very people you were going to set him up with."

"Let's say that if he were going to do something like that, and I were to know about it, I would have strongly discouraged him, but it might not have stopped him."

"Another reason for Halley to disapprove of you hanging around."

"Yeah, she could be, like, protective of Jack, downright possessive. Which was kind of strange considering she was hanging with the cop."

"So you met this officer, in person, right?"

"Couple times. He def did not like me."

"Sounds like quite a foursome, all of you."

"Not exactly a love fest or the Brady Bunch, you got that right." He noticed Leon staring at him with some puzzlement. "What, you don't think I watch old TV shows on those cable networks? Gotta love them old sitcoms, man. Wish I could have grown up in a fam like one of them."

"How's the dog fit into this?" Art, apparently resigned to the fact this wasn't going away, was sitting upright, eyes open, and back in the conversation.

"Oh, that was my most genius move of all. Barclay told me Yancey loved my plan with the Sans, but I still sensed there was some concern that I was, like, this rogue outsider guy they couldn't trust. And I knew I couldn't bring Jack in with me without further establishing our cred. I kept hearing how Yancey loved that dog of his, the one they took away when he was arrested. The story was, he loved that damn animal more than anything else in the world. And it had been handed off to some strange lady and Yancey was really pissed. I did a little calling and checking around and found out who got the dog."

"Pretty efficient of you."

"I musta lucked out. I was surprised I was able to find her."

"Amazing," Art said dryly, "what you can do with the proper motivation."

"And then, it was easy enough to case her place for a day or two, find out she lived alone and went to some job or something on Saturdays. I waited until she left, let myself in, and took the dog. I was afraid it was going to be vicious, so I brought treats and hunks of meat that I'd spiked. That dog was suspicious at first and looked scary as shit but turned out to be a cream puff, go figure. Some gangster dog. Loved the goodies I'd brought and got a little bit sedated. It kinda staggered with me out to my car. I figured the safest place I could bring it was to Jack. Their house was real out of the way. Nobody knew about him, and no one was going to find him, certainly not before Yancey got out of jail. Then I called Barclay and told him."

Art exchanged a look with Leon. It all fit together.

"What'd Barclay think of that?" asked Leon.

"He wasn't as happy about it as I'd expected, which I didn't understand. It'd be a lot easier for Yancey to go get his dog back from Jack than from some strange old woman. Barclay just said that I'd better make damned sure that the dog was being treated right. That's why I went back to see Jack on Sunday."

"To impress upon him the importance of keeping the dog safe."

"Yeah, and to make sure he had food for the dog and was keeping it out of the rain. Turns out they were making hamburgers, and they made some for the dog as well. And they had it chained up in the yard but under an overhang where it could be out of the rain."

"What time did you go there and how long were you there?"

"I don't know, it was around dinner time. I do remember it was raining pretty hard. They didn't seem real happy to see me. They were eating the burgers and drinking beer. Never offered me any of either. It was kinda weird. Uncomfortable. I got the impression maybe they'd been having an argument before I got there. Anyway, the conversation was just, awkward, you know?"

"They were in the living room?"

"Yeah, sitting at their table."

"And you pulled up a chair and joined them?"

"No. They never invited me to sit down. I kinda stood there in the room, leaning against the wall. I did most of the talking. Finally, Halley told me, 'He'll take good fucking care of the fucking dog, okay? Are we done?' And Jack, who was sort of out of it, just shrugged. So I got the hint and got out of there."

"Very sharp of you to pick up on that. What time do you think that was?"

"I don't know, maybe six or seven? With all the rain, it was hard to tell. Everything was kinda dark."

"So you're saying they were alive when you left them."

"Yeah! Yeah! Absolutely. For sure."

"If that's the case, that would make you the last person to see them alive."

"Oh shit," Dougie said, looking pale.

Art chimed in again. "Where was your car parked?"

"Right in the little turnaround of their driveway. I ran out, trying to not get too wet, and drove off."

"Nobody else was with them when you were there, is that right?"

"Right. Just me and them."

"Happen to see or hear anybody when you left?"

"Man, nobody is ever in that area. It's always deserted. It always felt like out in the middle of nowhere."

Leon shook his head. "Douglas, you see how this looks bad for you, right?"

"See, this is why I was hiding from you guys. That's why I'm telling you all this now. I didn't do anything! Last I saw them, they were alive. You gotta believe me."

"Then help us out. Give us something. You didn't see or hear anybody, anywhere?"

"The only car I even passed was some hunk of junk rust bucket Camaro coming up Obrigato, probably one of the crazies who live there who don't take care of their cars. Made a lotta noise, musta had one of those big V8s in it. It was just, like, idling on the street. Whoever took out the Donners, they must have come later, after I was gone." He looked back and forth at Leon and Art. "My money woulda been on Radley. When I saw him at that park with his gun aimed at me, I figured I was done for, that he was gonna off me right then and there. There was no reason for him to be there. We weren't even in his, whattaya call it, jurisdiction."

"You really thought Radley wanted you dead?"

"That's all that made sense to me, that something had gone wrong between him and them. There weren't all that many people hanging out with Jack and Halley."

"Is there some kind of war going on in the Rybus organization, or something?"

"I don't think so. I mean, things have been kinda up and down with Yancey in lockup, and there's been some agitation, but Barclay seemed to be pretty much in control of things now."

"But could there have been some faction out to get Jack Donner? They were coming after you, maybe they were coming after him as well."

"Naw, that don't make any sense at all. Nobody *knew* Jack. Like I said, that's why I took the dog there. He was off the grid, you know? Whatever they got against me, it just don't make sense it had anything to do with Jack personally."

"If it's true that the organization has it out for you, then Officer Radley might have just saved your life."

"Now ain't that a kick in the head, if locked up in here with guys like you is the safest place I could be."

TWENTY-FIVE

They walked to their car in the station parking lot in silence until Art spoke up.

"Quarter for your thoughts, Leon."

"I'm not sure quite what to think right now. Maybe it is Dougie."

"I've got no doubt they'll match his prints all over the house, but that doesn't prove anything. Seems he spent a lot of time there."

"We'll know when the ballistics report comes back on his .22."

Art shook his head. "Pretty tangled relationship there, the Halleys and Dougie and Radley."

"That's for sure. What's with the expression?"

"Maybe it's nothing."

Leon stopped and stared at his partner. "I know that look. What's *it?*"

"Just thinking, what if the ballistics don't match? Then what direction do we go? There's something else he mentioned that's sticking in the back of my mind as well. I need to figure out what it is."

"Another one of your fugues, Arthur? Go for it. They've pulled us out a few times."

"Fugues, you're calling them now? I prefer freestyling, myself."

"Whatever. I'll take whatever we can come up with on this one." Leon pulled his phone out. "In the meantime, I better give Jilly a heads-up on Dougie. They're going to want to talk to him as well."

He one-fingered in the number. Jilly picked up on the third ring.

"Garvey."

"Jilly, it's Leon. I thought you'd like to know we just interviewed a guy who's got a connection to your St. Cloud case. Turns out he was the one who set her up to get busted to help out Yancey Rybus. Seems the plan was to eliminate both her and Lydia Montgomery."

"Funny you should mention Rybus," Jilly replied. "I happen to be look-ing at him right this minute."

* * * *

"Looks like someone was waiting for them and caught them in the open. Likely just one assailant."

Jilly and Dan were looking down at the two bodies on the pavement as two uniformed officers busily cordoned off the entire parking lot with yellow tape in anticipation of the SID arrival.

Dan nodded. "Shotgun at close range. But they weren't totally taken by surprise. They had their own weapons out. And they got their own shots off." He pointed to the casings on the ground near the bodies. "Four shots. I'm impressed." A few paces further away, he again pointed down. "Blood spatters." He swept his hand around to point at the shotgun shells on the blacktop near the wooden barricades. "The shooter took off, didn't even try to pick up the shells." He followed the blood drops back along the ground. "It was an ambush. They were caught in this closed-off lot."

"The manager of the shelter says she didn't understand why the lot was blocked off like that, with that sign and the sawhorses. When the staff arrived earlier, the lot was wide open." Jilly pointed at the three cars parked by the building. "It was a set-up."

"And she said she didn't see anything?"

"Everyone got here about an hour earlier and saw nothing. After that, they were all busy inside, setting up to open. There's apparently always a lot to be done after the night custodian leaves, and the morning staff arrives. They heard the gunshots and when they came running out, all they saw was these two on the ground. They were both already dead by the time they got to them."

"I didn't know the big ugly guy but that one's Yancey Rybus, isn't it?"

Jilly nodded. "Sure looks like him. Just got back on the street, too. Some kind of trouble was certainly waiting for him."

"What was he doing here? Everything I've ever heard about the guy, he was super cautious."

"The manager said they've got a pit bull that was rescued from the murder scene the other day, the case Leon and Art caught. Someone had called saying it was their dog and they were going to come over this morning to do whatever was needed to take her back home."

"So, they've got Rybus's infamous dog? That was his dog that was at that house?"

"Certainly looks that way."

"And somebody knew he was coming here this morning and was lying in wait. Set it up so they had to walk in from the street. That must be Yancey's Lexus we passed on the way in."

"Whoever the shooter was, they must have parked down the road and waited in the bushes along there. Let's take a look and see what we can find."

"We're going to need to keep the crime lab van out there too," Dan said, looking down as they walked. He noted more blood drops as they proceeded past the horses. "Gotta give it to our guy, he kept moving. I wonder how far he had to go to get back to his own car."

"Let's see what we can find out," muttered Jilly, hands in the pockets of her jacket as they slowly trudged along the road, past the deserted Lexus.

"Sure is quiet out here," Dan observed.

"He could have been lying in wait somewhere around there," Jilly said, gesturing to a crop of bushes and trees to their right. "Look at that path that's been cleared."

There were lots of fallen dead leaves on the ground, but a walkway had been pushed away, probably by foot, from over the dirt surrounding the thick foliage.

"Smart," said Dan. "So, they wouldn't hear him stepping on leaves and stuff when he came out after them."

They continued along the roadway, heads down, eyes sweeping the pavement in front of them. Every ten feet or so, they saw another dark stain of dried blood drops.

A blue van pulled off the freeway onto the Vaughan Street access ramp a few hundred feet ahead.

"Lab techs," said Jilly. "You keep following the trail. I'll fill them in and tell them what to avoid."

Dan simply raised a hand in acknowledgment, concentrating on the ground in front of him. Jilly waved to the van and set out to intercept them.

The trail, down the center of the road, got easier, as the stains got gradually larger and closer together as he continued. Dan began to wonder if the assailant could have gotten too far even in a car if he—funny how they'd both presumptively decided it was a *he*—had taken a slug or slugs and was losing blood. Dan was almost all the way back to the offramp, past the SID van where Jilly was still talking to the techs, when the blood trail veered off to the right and stopped at the unpaved shoulder. He could make out tire tracks on the dry loose dirt, and some skid marks where the car had peeled out heading back to the freeway. Maybe the lab could pick up something from the patterns on the ground.

* * * *

"Do me a favor and walk us through it. Just how did you happen where to find him, and outside the city no less?"

Dominic Radley, sitting across the table from Leon and Art, folded his arms and settled into his story.

"I didn't know, for sure, where Dougie might be. I had a vague idea of what part of the city he hung out in, and for sure I knew that old Firebird he drove. I've been keeping my eye out for it every day since the murders, all through our shifts. He's clearly been laying low and maybe keeping his car under wraps as well. This morning, I lucked out. I mean, I was particularly looking for him, like I told you earlier. I made a point of having us cruise around his known haunts. I told Ochida we had a BOLO and needed to keep an eye out."

"So, you just happened to see Barnfeather's car, where exactly?"

"Actually, she caught it first. One of those streets off lower San Pablo. Hard to miss that heap. The idiot's got it so souped up, you can hear it coming a block away."

"And you pursued the vehicle? Did you try to pull him over?"

"I had to pull a 180 and by that time he'd turned a corner and taken off. I closed in and was about to hit the lights when he got onto the freeway. I lost him for a moment, but I followed and then caught him as he was pulling off at the Point."

"So, you stayed on him, even though you were now leaving your jurisdiction."

"You wanted the guy, right? So, I followed him. By the time we caught up to him, he'd parked his car and was somewhere down one of the paths that go to the shore. Then I heard the gunshots. Apprehended him, notified the county sheriff and waited until they came to take over the scene. At that point, I called you guys. We had to get back on a call of our own." He spread his arms and smiled. "And now, here I am, filling you in. Told you I'd find him for you. Did he tell you anything helpful when you went to see him?"

"Remains to be seen," Leon sighed.

* * * *

"Three more people dead in one morning. Just what is going on here?"

Jilly was expressing the frustration and bewilderment of everyone sitting around the table in what was optimistically termed the conference room of the Personal Crimes Unit. The four detectives had come together to compare notes upon their return, but there seemed to be more questions generated by the events of the day than answers.

"Could there be a war starting up?" asked Dan. "A power struggle? Everything seems to go back to Yancey Rybus."

"It all relates to him one way or another," Leon replied, "but I don't think it's all specifically connected. Douglas Barnfeather knew the Donners, but as far as we can ascertain, he only knew Vickers in the crew. He never even met Rybus. In fact, I get the feeling Vickers was actively trying to keep the guy away from Rybus."

Jilly nodded. "We got the same impression when we went to talk to him as well. He's clearly a loose cannon that you'd want to keep at arm's length. But he knew Yvette St. Cloud, and he was instrumental, through his association with Vickers, in her being apprehended and ultimately being in that transport van with Lydia Montgomery."

"So who was the other guy killed with Rybus at the shelter?"

"His name was Maceo Mason. Seemed to have been Rybus's bodyguard. We're still trying to piece together more about him. No record to speak of. We figure someone at Narco might have more info on him."

"And no indication who the shooter might have been?"

"From what we've got, we figure a solo, with a pump shotgun, and no idea beyond that so far. The shooter picked an optimal spot. It's a deserted stretch, absolutely no cameras, no other witnesses. Our one hope is if the tire tracks offer anything, but that's a long shot. No real theory as to the motive yet. Rival organization, disgruntled crew member making a play, who knows? With everything upside down, it could be anything."

"And the Donner murders," Dan asked, looking at Leon and Art. "Is Barnfeather your guy?"

"That one's still up in the air," said Leon. "Some of it will come down to Ballistics' report on his weapon. If it's a match to the killings, we luck out. If not, that doesn't necessarily prove anything one way or the other. He could have had another gun or been involved in some other way. We're hoping to have a search warrant for his apartment soon to see if that turns up anything." He shook his head. "Or he could be totally innocent like he claims."

Art, finally opening his mouth, asked Jilly, "Any word on your escapee?"

"Lydia? Not a clue. Someone found the plates for the Mustang she stole in a dumpster a few blocks from the garage, which means she switched plates with some other vehicle somewhere and as yet we've got no idea who or where. She could be anywhere."

"And then there's the dog," said Leon.

"That's some story," Dan remarked. "So, as I understand it, Rybus's dog was confiscated when he was arrested, and sent to a shelter, where it got adopted as a rescue?"

"Vanessa," said Leon. "He named her Vanessa. Apparently, she was his one vulnerable spot. As I've heard the story numerous times from Marlon, Lydia kidnapped the dog for a big ransom. The dog got returned and the money vanished. Rybus suspected it was an inside job and it provoked a public confrontation within his ranks. That's when Marlon scooped them all up."

Jilly shook her head in amazement. "Too bad Marlon's on vacation. I'd sure love to talk to him about all this in further depth."

"And then," Dan continued, "Dougie stole the dog from the rescue lady and took her to the Donners?"

Leon nodded. "She—the rescue lady—had renamed the dog Beatrice."

"So, the Donners got killed and the dog, Vanessa or Beatrice or whatever, got taken into custody again, and this time wound up at the Vaughan Street shelter."

"And there," Jilly said, "she still remains. The shelter manager said someone had called inquiring about her but nobody ever showed up for her. That had to have been Rybus, who only got as far as the parking lot this morning."

Leon's gaze focused on something far away.

Jilly smiled. "Earth to Leon. I know that thoughtful look. What've you got?"

"It would seem Beatrice got lost in the system this time around. There was so much chaos around the process, what with the murder and all. Her foster lady couldn't locate her despite a lot of time and effort. She even talked to me in the process. I had to make several official calls on my own to find out where the dog had been taken. But somehow, Yancey Rybus found her, almost immediately."

"You're thinking he had an inside tip."

"Certainly, one that none of us had. Now here's the interesting thing: Gene Gehm was asking me a lot of strange questions about a dog the last few days. I hadn't been able to make sense out of that. Now it seems relevant."

"Gene was talking to you? Funny, we were just talking to him as well. He and his partner were the ones who busted Yvette St. Cloud to begin with, on some kind of anonymous tip."

"Is that so?"

"And Marlon had some dealings with Gene around his case as well. He found it strange, Gene suddenly getting all buddy-buddy with him and asking about all sorts of things. No great love between those two, going back to Gene's Personal Crimes days as Marlon's partner. Now I really wish we could get hold of Marlon."

"Yeah, well," Leon replied, "after all the hoopla with Rybus and his circus, Marlon went on some kind of fishing trip or something, totally removed from everybody and everything. He couldn't be reached if the world was about to end."

Jilly's smile had turned sardonic. "I suspect your next conversation with Gene is going to be a bit awkward."

"Whenever it happens," Leon said. "I've tried him a few times since we got back and he's not picking up."

How about his partner, Venuto?"

"I tried her as well. She's not picking up either."

"Beyond the dog," Dan chimed in. "Vickers' attempt on Barnfeather and the hit on Rybus and the other guy. Is there a connection?"

"It's tenuous," Leon said. "From what we know, it doesn't make a lot of sense that Vickers would be trying to pull a takeover. According to Dougie, Vickers was firmly entrenched as the new number two guy, and Rybus was back in charge in the flesh. There wasn't a lot to gain by trying a coup. He would have had advantages to staying in Rybus's camp, at the very least to bide his time. It seems that he was trying to eliminate Barnfeather as a potential embarrassment and solidify his position with the boss. I just don't see the two incidents being related."

"On the other hand," offered Jilly, "there's a very small window of opportunity for someone else to grab power. Given more time, Rybus could have recovered his hold over everything, We can't rule out the two incidents being coordinated."

"That could mean further *incidents* to come," said Art glumly.

"It's like we're outside looking in on what's going on with Rybus's people," said Dan. "We'll need to talk to someone with better intel on the organization."

"I'll reach out to someone else at Narco," Jilly said. "But I've got a feeling they're in as much chaos about all this as we are right now."

Art laughed. To be fair, it was more of a cough than a laugh, but it was enough to cause the other three detectives to all turn their heads toward him.

"Is that actually possible?"

* * * *

Narcotics detectives, as it turned out, were in an equal state of confusion, compounded by reports they were receiving from far downstate: two separate incidents, in two separate downstate communities, involving violent attacks on other known associates of Yancey Rybus. If some kind of war had started, it was spreading over a larger geographic area. It was going to take considerably more time and effort for them to consolidate and absorb what little information was coming in. *Chaos* was definitely the current operative word throughout Narco; the four Personal Crimes detectives weren't going to find any help from that direction. Maybe SID or the Coroner's Office would provide some help as they gradually produced information. There was little else for them to do but to return to their desks and once again pore over what they already knew in hopes of finding something they'd missed.

Jilly and Dan were doing just that when the phone call came through to Jilly. The conversation was short, and very animated on her end. Before she'd finished talking, she was on her feet, grabbing her bag, and waving to Dan to join her.

"What's up?" he asked as he followed suit, clearly clueless. To make it all the more mystifying, he could distinctly hear Jilly utter "Oh shit" twice in succession as she rang off and jammed the cell phone back into her bag.

Jilly, like the Lou, wasn't one to fall back on profanity. Dan could literally have counted on one hand the number of times he'd heard the expletive out of his partner in the entire time he'd been in Personal Crimes.

"First Castillo, now you," he called after her. "That's like, your quota of four-letter words for the month, if I heard right."

"Yeah, well, wait'll you hear the story. I'll tell you on the way."

"The way where?" Dan called after her, running to catch up with her.

"Medical Center!" Jilly yelled back as she reached the stairs.

* * * *

"He just called me out of the blue. I hadn't heard word one from him since this morning when he texted me saying he had some personal business to take care of. I had no idea where he'd gone or what he was up to. Not a damn clue. To be honest, I'd decided I'd had it with him and was going to put in for a new partner."

Olivia Venuto tossed the cigarette butt on the pavement of the hospital parking lot, ground it out with the toe of her shoe, and reflexively had the pack out of her pocket instantly.

"I'd given these damned things up," she muttered, sardonically laughing as she lit up again, looking at the cigarette between her fingers and then down at the three butts at her feet. She kept moving her head and hands, constantly dragging on the coffin nail, unable to stand still. "You know that old disaster-comedy where the guy keeps saying he picked the wrong week to give up everything?"

"So, all this you're telling us about, just started, just like that?" Jilly asked.

She and Dan were standing close with the Narco detective, in a corner of the lot where nobody could hear them converse. She'd met them at the entrance and told them Gene was in surgery, walked them outside and proceeded to tell them as much of the story as she'd heard, which was plenty. They were still struggling to wrap their heads around it.

"Yeah. No word all morning, then, about noon, I get the call. I started to lace into him, and he interrupted me. He said, 'Livvy, I fucked up big time.' No, 'Major.' That was the exact word he used. 'I fucked up, major.' That stopped me in my tracks. I asked him where he was. He didn't sound so good. His words were labored, and he was kind of wheezing. He said, 'I think I might be in trouble here.' Okay, the guy's been an asshole lately.

Well, he's always been something of an asshole; I can kinda see why you guys let him transfer out of Personal. He's not exactly a get-along guy in the best of times. But recently he's really *really* been a major pain in the ass. Secretive shit. Going and coming, not letting me in on what's going on." She spat out a cloud of smoke in exasperation.

"But in the end, no matter how much *he's* disrespected the partnership, the guy's still my partner, and he was in trouble of some kind, and I'm *not* an asshole, whatever other things you could say about me. You don't leave your partner out in the cold. Not ever, certainly not when it sounds like life and death. No matter how big a douchebag he's been. So, I put the anger on hold and just told him to tell me where he was. And on the way, I stayed on the phone with him since he started sounding like he was circling the drain, and I had him keep talking, to tell me what had happened."

"That's when he told you he shot Rybus?"

"Yeah. And Rybus's bodyguard. In the process, I guess the bodyguard caught him back with a couple shots, even after Gene nailed him. Bad ass, for sure. Gene didn't even think he was hit seriously until he got back to his car and saw how much he was bleeding. Somehow, he got himself to a cheap hideaway motel while he tried to assess the damage. He finally realized it was serious and called me. The damn fool could have died."

"So, you went and got him at the motel."

"Sure, right away. On the way, I called for an ambulance, stat, and then some unis to come cover the scene and his car. They were there when I arrived. I rode with him in the ambulance over here and he was able to talk a bit. I tried to get him to just rest and be quiet, but it seems he really wanted to tell me more about everything that had gone down. I guess he was worried he was going to die without telling the story to someone."

"I still don't get it," Jilly said. "Gene mixed up with Rybus? That's crazy."

Venuto shook her head. "God knows who that scumbag owns—make that *owned*—in the unit. I'm sure there are others. There's no real way of knowing. But Gene? I would never have pegged Gene to be dirty. Shit, he used to be a drunk, no big surprise there given what we do, right? But unlike most of them, he'd gotten sober! He'd gotten his family back together. His daughter's in college, for God's sake!" She dropped and stubbed out the half-smoked cigarette. "Turns out Rybus must have been the one paying for the girl's tuition and who knows what else. Son of a bitch."

"You said Rybus had something on him that started all this. What is it exactly?"

"He told me most of the story. Back when he was partners with Marlon Morrison on your unit, he got involved with some dancer or hostess or somebody. Some case involving a robbery of a mobbed-up club that never got solved."

"I think I remember the case," Jilly said. "That goes back quite a way. I don't think any of us had any idea he'd gotten tangled up with anyone."

"Gene told me as much. It was all on the down low. She turned out to be the girlfriend of a major local operator. Remember the guy they used to call the Baron?"

"Sure. Suave slimebag. Liked to banter with the press and the cops. Real Teflon guy, nothing could stick to him. Claimed to be a legit business-man while he was running every racket imaginable. One of the many fac-tions co-opted when Rybus took over."

"And if memory serves," Dan chimed in, "he disappeared sometime thereafter. And left behind a lot of unsolved stuff that will probably never be unraveled."

Jilly nodded grimly. "The only sad note to our losing him."

Venuto continued. "That's the son of a bitch. The Baron got word of his girlfriend messing around with him, killed her and arranged to frame Gene. Did something like slipped him a roofie and got his prints on the weapon. Some stupid shit he let himself get caught up in by thinking with his little brain instead of his big one." She shook her head at the thought. "Just an asshole situation. A Gene situation, just a particularly extreme one this time. It was messy all around for him with no apparent way out, so of course he chose to go and make it even worse. He figured if he did a couple favors for the guy, he could make it go away. Can you say 'wishful think-ing'? That's when he transferred to Narco and partnered up with me. And then he started taking the Baron's money, apparently in big amounts."

"Down the rabbit hole," Jilly said.

"And some rabbit hole. He was putting his life back in order. He had a bank account and was attending to his family. Everything was just sweet-ness and light. And that's when Rybus started absorbing everybody, in-cluding our big piece of crap the Baron, and inherited Gene's little fuckup contract. Rybus was a different sort of boss, wanting lots more from him. By that time Gene was in so deep, there was no way out."

Jilly thought back to the stories she'd recently heard from Marlon, complaining about how Gene had been coming around, trying to cozy up to him, asking strange questions. She remembered Leon's account of his own recent encounters with Gene. At least some things were fitting together and making sense.

"Well," Venuto continued, reaching again for the pack in her pocket, and then stopping, "I guess he figured there was one way out. Rybus was secretive and mistrustful even around his own people; Gene always dealt with him directly, nobody else. It was a good bet that if Rybus went away, so would the evidence on Gene. Hence the Old West style ambush. It was a calculated risk by a desperate man. Might have worked, too, if he hadn't gotten himself shot in the process."

"Is he going to be okay?" Jilly asked.

"Oh, the docs say he'll fully recover. Physically, anyway. He lost a lot of blood, and he's got some long hard recovery in front of him, but he was lucky. I'm not so sure how good he's going to be in other ways. I made sure that when they removed the slugs, they'd be saved as evidence. And there are two unis up there to baby sit him once he's out of the OR. I assume you two better take over this case from here."

"Yeah. I wish we didn't have to. I'm sure it'll ultimately go to Internal Affairs. Thanks for the call, Olivia."

"My goddamned partner sure gave us the gift that's going to keep on giving. At least with Rybus, we knew what we were dealing with. He had everyone in line. With him dead, all hell is going to break loose. Freelancers back out on the corners, renegades, all kinds of new players bringing in their shit. There'll be a deluge of contaminated crap on the streets. And it won't be just the regular organization coming apart. He had a lot of the younger gangs under his control. They're going to go nuts now. And with the recent budget freezes and attrition, we've got a total of six Narco detectives on our shift now." She shot a glare up at the higher floors of the hospital. "No, make that five."

Jilly fully understood the implications. When the inevitable violence began, the chaos was going to slop over to Personal Crimes as well.

"I'm sorry you had to go through all this. I guess we'll go upstairs and wait for them to bring Gene out."

"One thing," Venuto said. "I left my car back at the motel. If I could get a lift back from one of you?" She started to pull her pack of cigarettes out of her bag, then put it back. "I promise I won't smoke in your car. Aggravations or no aggravations, I gotta stop this nasty habit."

Jilly looked quizzically at Dan, as if to ask which task he'd rather take. It was an easy choice. Dan had already decided he was no great fan of Olivia Venuto but far less a one of Gene Gehm.

He already had the car keys out. "Sure. Let's go, Olivia."

TWENTY-SIX

Doug Barnfeather's apartment was, to employ an overused expression, a true pigsty.

A search warrant had been approved without a hitch and Thursday morning, Leon, Art and two uniformed officers waited for a sullen off-site manager to show up with his keys and let them into the second-floor walk-up. They walked into an impressive accumulation of pizza boxes and fast-food wrappers strewn about the floor and tables, along with pungent food scraps and beer and soda cans.

"Looks like our friend went to the mattresses," Art observed, stepping to avoid a cockroach skittering by. "Literally."

Incongruously, the cramped three-room apartment was also packed with high end audio and video gear. A large flat screen filled one wall; several remotes and game consoles lay scattered beneath a pizza box on the couch across from it. Various unopened boxes of more electronics were stacked in the corners. In the tiny kitchenette they found still more piles of sealed boxes, labeled as various auto parts. All of this would undoubtedly be of great interest to someone in Property Crimes, but not to Art and Leon at the moment.

It didn't take long to root through the cramped little place. Art found several baggies of powder, probably methamphetamine, in a dresser draw-er, along with a shoebox full of marijuana buds. There was plenty to in-criminate Dougie in several matters, but they uncovered no weapons, am-munition, or anything else that might tie him to the Donner murders. They directed the officers to seal and tape off the apartment and trudged out of the building, dejected. Not only had they not found anything of value to their case; picking through the life of a guy like Dougie was just depressing as hell.

Leon checked his email on his phone as they walked down the street from the apartment. For once, the lab had been right on the spot and had sent through a preliminary ballistics report. He exhaled heavily.

"What?" asked Art.

"Not a match. Dougie's gun didn't kill the Donners."

"We kinda figured that, didn't we?"

"So what's our next move?"

They reached their cruiser and Art, who was once again driving, paused before unlocking the driver's side door. He stared down at the hood for a long time.

"So, are you gonna open my door, or what?"

Art, acting as if he hadn't heard a word Leon had said, looked up at him across the roof of the car.

"It finally occurred to me. I might have something."

"You *might?* Well, do you or don't you?"

"Remember something Dougie said, about that old junker of a Camaro he passed that night? Funny he'd mention that."

Leon shrugged. "He's a car nut. That old Firebird of his. I had a gearhead friend who used to call Firebirds and Camaros 'cousins' so I guess he'd notice things like that. Why? Who do we know who's got an old Camaro?"

"It's a bit of a long shot," Art said absently. "But damn, what else do we have right now?"

* * * *

"Gotta admit, it fits the bill." Art gestured grandly over the oxidizing silvery-grey Chevy Camaro sitting in the driveway as they walked around it towards the small back house.

Leon stopped and squatted next to the front wheel. "The tires are fairly bare but there's mud and gravel caught in what's left of the tread."

"The day's young. Let's hope our friend is still sober." Art rapped on the window of the front door.

The red-nosed individual who opened the door half smiled. "Hey, you're that detective guy, right?"

"Hello, Mr. Mercer. Right, Detective Dowdy. This is my partner, Detective Simpkins. I've just got a few more questions. Can we come in?"

Mercer lazily waved the beer can in his free hand. "Sure, come on in. Can I get you guys a brewsky?"

"No, thank you," Art said as he and Leon stepped past him into the little house.

Compared to Doug Barnfeather's, the Mercer residence, while of a similar size, was a definite upgrade. For one thing, there was only one old pizza box to be seen, over in a corner. There was a small living room area that opened on one side into an even smaller bedroom and on the other side to a kitchenette. The current popular domestic mainstay, a flat screen television, took up part of one wall but the rest of the walls were covered with actual framed pictures and photographs. There were several mismatched old chairs, but their upholstery wasn't as torn and faded as Dougie's, and while they were covered with debris, at least there was no old food.

What dominated the living room was the large cage in one corner, a good six feet high. Its door was wide open and perched atop the cage, staring at them with some mixture of curiosity and disdain, was a fuzzy, bright tan Capuchin monkey.

"Hello, Gummy," muttered Art.

Mercer closed the front door and went over to sweep magazines and other articles from a couple of them, then motioned for them to be seated. He picked up what looked like a dismantled television cable box off one of the chairs.

'My cable's been out all week. Trying to get in touch with the company so I can watch my TV again. Can you imagine not having TV for five days now?"

As they cautiously lowered themselves into two of the grotty chairs, the monkey stood up and rotated its head back and forth between them. Mercer laughed. "That's right, you met Gummy the other day. Master of the house. He needs to know what's going on with every new visitor who comes here. Make yourselves at home. I'm just gonna get another beer from the kitchen. Sure I can't get you guys anything? No?"

Mercer returned a moment later, fresh beer can in hand and plopped himself into the open seat. Gummy jumped down into his lap and began to inspect the can before letting Mercer take a swig. "So I hope you still don't think Abby had anything to do with all this."

Art, having already made Mercer's acquaintance, was the logical one to continue the conversation. "We're still looking at everything and everyone. We thought you might be able to help us clear up a few things."

"Like I told you before, Abby was out of town last Sunday night when that crazy Donner woman and her husband got killed. She's still out of town. You can't possibly think she did it."

"We're tending toward believing you're right, sir." Art looked out the window and pointed to the car in the driveway. "That's your Camaro out there? Looks like a classic."

Leon suppressed a smile. Art was in fine form. And the monkey was everything he'd promised.

"Yeah, it's seen better days, but it's a nice '92 RS model. Even got a V-8 under the hood. Needs work. I figure, one of these days I'll find the inspiration to clean it up." He wagged a finger at Gummy, who climbed around on his arm.

"Do you drive it much?"

"Not all that much. Haven't taken it out of the driveway in some time now. You know the old joke, right? They told me 'If you drink, don't drive.' So I left my car." This struck him as particularly funny, and he guffawed. "Mainly I just go hang out with my boys, Roy and Duane, and I can walk to their places easy enough. Or I trudge on over to the local market. I order in a lot of my meals;"

"So you didn't drive anywhere during the recent rain then?"

"Nope. Got kinda wet walking over to Duane's but I don't mind."

Art looked around at the various photos and pictures framed haphazardly on the walls. They were mostly old family photos, probably with his wife Ruth and a very young daughter Abigail, many of them on what looked like camping or fishing trips, alongside a sign that proclaimed in large caps BLESS THIS MESS. "So you're interested in cars, obviously, and it looks like you hunt and fish?"

"A bit now and then. Well, I used to, Haven't in a while now. Since the family's gone, no more campouts. Those were fun." He frowned. Gummy seemed to pick up on the changed mood and mugged a forlorn face that looked a lot like Craig's own.

"You still have any guns here by any chance?"

"Used to have a couple rifles and a shotgun. Sold 'em a while back. Same with my fishing gear."

"I've never been a fisherman myself, but I did do some shooting. You seem like a guy who knows his way around firearms pretty well."

"Yeah, back in the day. Not so much in a while now."

"Any chance you still own any handguns?"

"Nah. I had a pistol, mostly just to go the range and practice, but I got rid of it. Hadn't fired it in years."

"Is that right? What'd you have?"

"Oh hell, it was just an old Smith and Wesson .22. Not sure why I'd even kept it as long as I did."

"When did you get rid of it?"

"I don't know, sometime last year, maybe. Sold it at a gun show."

"And you've got the paperwork for the sale, I assume."

"Oh, somewhere around this dump, yeah." Mercer waved an arm around the disheveled abode. "My filing system needs a little bit of an update, you know?" He stopped and stared back and forth at Leon and Art. "Wait a minute. Why are you asking all these questions?"

As if on cue, Gummy leapt down from Mercer's lap and bound over to Art, jumping into his lap. It was the last thing he'd expected, and he awkwardly juggled the monkey, who started climbing and tugging on the sleeve of his jacket.

"Mr. Mercer, a minute ago you referred to the murders of the other day. You said your daughter couldn't possibly have killed them."

"That's right. She couldn't, and she didn't."

"You said *them*."

"Well, yeah. The bitch who was trying to sue Abby, and her husband."

"And when we last spoke, you expressed surprise when I told you she was dead and had been murdered."

"Well, sure. Hit me like a ton of bricks. I had no idea! I mean, they were miserable excuses for human beings, but that shouldn't happen to anybody. Oh, hey, don't worry 'bout Gummy, Detective, he's friendly, just boisterous."

That last comment was directed at Leon. Gummy had decided he was bored with Art, who wasn't letting him inspect the inside of his jacket, and had taken a bound across to Leon, who caught him in his arms, looking a bit concerned that he might get a bite taken out of him. The monkey actually settled into Leon's arms like a baby and started making soft chattering noises. Leon tried to ignore it all and pay attention to Art as he continued his line of discussion. *You're on a roll, partner.*

"Mr. Mercer, when I was here talking to you Tuesday, I only mentioned that Halley Donner had been killed."

"What do you mean?"

"I didn't mention anybody else. Just her."

Leon had caught on to what Art was doing. He could almost smell Mercer's foggy brain trying to shift into gear all of a sudden. "You, you must've mentioned it. How else would I know her and her husband were both killed?"

"You tell me."

"You musta told us! I can call Roy and Duane, they'll remember!"

"Mr. Mercer, I definitely did not mention anyone but Halley Donner, and I didn't mention her by name either."

"Well, hell, of course I knew her name. She was trying to ruin Abby's life. You can be damned sure I knew her name!"

"But how did you know about her husband?"

It was clearly an effort for Craig Mercer to keep track of his thoughts. The anxiety in his face grew as the gravity of his situation sank in. Even Gummy seemed to pick up on the mood and slumped down, staring over Leon's forearm at his friend and protector.

"Maybe I saw it on the news. It's been all over the news, right?"

"How would you have watched the news when your cable TV is out of service?"

Mercer stared down at the palms of his open hands as if they somehow held some kind of answer to get him out of this spot.

"The guys must've told me. I mean, I knew there were two of them *somehow.* That must've been it."

Art leaned in. "We can keep doing this, if that's what you want. But I think I know what really happened. And I think it might be better all around if you were to just tell us."

Craig Mercer's shoulders sagged, and his entire body deflated. Keeping this up was all too much for him. He dropped his hands to his knees and bowed his head, shaking it back and forth, as if he could just negate it all away. Gummy imitated the gesture, slumping down in Leon's arms and shaking his head back and forth.

"Aw shit," he sighed. "I was just trying to help."

* * * *

"Maybe I better put Gummy back in his cage," Mercer said quietly, putting his beer on the floor and motioning for the monkey to come to him. Leon stood and watched him as he carried Gummy, talking softly to him the whole time, into his cage and latched it shut. He turned around, silently returned to his seat, and then just sat there, unmoving, staring down at the ground.

Art and Leon tried to wait him out, see what he'd choose to say in his own time. It took a while.

Mercer rested his forearms across his legs, lacing his fingers, and jiggled his feet nervously, making his arms bounce up and down. It seemed to go on and on and on.

Finally, Leon gently said, "Craig, are you saying that you killed Jack and Halley Donner?"

That brought it on.

"Well… I didn't necessarily plan to do that."

"What do you mean?"

"I went there to have a talk with them, see if I could convince Halley to drop her lawsuit against Abigail and Wayne. But I set it up so nobody would know I'd gone there, just in case."

"Seems as if you went to considerable effort to do that."

"You know the hardest part? It was the not drinking, not since the day before. Well, I did keep a can of beer going during the day, just to keep the shakes from coming on, you know? I knew Duane was going to have me and Roy over that Sunday and I knew there'd be a fair amount of drinking and other stuff going on and if I stayed sober, I could sneak out once they got kinda hammered. It was actually a pretty good alibi."

"You didn't worry one of them would notice you weren't drinking along with them as usual?"

"Oh hell, Detective, don't tell me you haven't noticed, when serious drinkers get down to it, they pay no attention to what anybody else's doing. You play it cool, hold a can or a bottle in your hand, nobody *cares* if you're drinking. They just, you know, presume you're keeping up. I just acted my usual low-energy self, talking and moving sludgy, or just not moving at all. We got ourselves going fairly early, and before long, Duane and Roy were both pretty heavily into their cups. Duane's got a decent sized house, not like this little hideaway of mine. I just let it be known I was going downstairs to his basement den and nod out. Not exactly the first time I or someone else had done that. His den's popular because it's got a couch and it's also got a bathroom, in case you have to pee or get sick. But the den's also small, so the first guy to claim it gets to have some privacy. Best of all for my purposes, it's got a back door and a set of stairs out through his yard. To be cautious, I flopped myself out on his couch and played possum, waited a while, to see if Duane or Roy would come down to check on me, but it got quiet upstairs. Finally I figured it was safe enough for me to sneak out the back. I'd left my raincoat up on his back porch when I first got there. By now it was starting to rain harder.

"I'd told Duane that I'd walked over to his place. That's not unusual since, like I said, I'm usually in no condition to drive for a long time afterwards, and it's not all that far a walk home. And like I said, I don't mind walking in the rain when there's a drinking fest at the other end. But I'd parked my car a block or so away. So, I walked in the rain back to my car and I drove over to the Donner house. That must have been around, I don't know, maybe seven?"

Art rejoined the conversation. "You brought a gun along with you, is that right?"

"Yeah, I did."

"The one you told us you'd gotten rid of?"

"Yep."

"Did you wear some kind of gloves?"

"I did. Thin ones, kinda transparent. Got 'em at the drug store. You couldn't really tell I was wearing them as long as I kept my hands in my pockets or kept them moving."

Art rubbed his temple. "Forgive me for saying so, Craig, but it seems to me you didn't really think you were just going to be able to talk them out of anything. Sounds to me like you knew how the evening was going to go from the outset."

"Well, hell. Detective, did you *know* that bitch Halley Donner? She didn't care what she did to other people. She was making a living off other people's misery, she and that ambulance chasing horse's ass Applegate. It was truly my intention to give her a chance to do the right thing, it really was. But, yeah, I suppose I kind of knew how the meeting was going to go down. She wanted to take Abby and Wayne's home away from them. I wasn't going to let that happen."

There was a long awkward pause. Mercer seemed to be slipping back into some kind of reverie. Leon prompted him. "Anyway, please go on. So, you drove to the Donner home."

"Man, was the rain coming down. I didn't want my car to be seen, so I parked it about halfway along their driveway, under the trees. Between the rain and the dark, it couldn't be seen either from the street or from their house. Then I walked up and knocked on their door. They were just sitting in their front room drinking beer. Jack answered the door and I asked if I could come in and talk with them. He didn't really want me to, this strange soaking wet guy standing in the rain like a fool, but Halley called out to him to let me in. She knew who I was. No formalities like a handshake, he just stepped back to let me in and went and sat down again. They just sat there and looked at me, didn't offer me any kind of hospitality, but I hadn't really expected them to— so I pulled up a chair. I don't think they were real happy about my tracking water in on their floor, but the place was such a dump, I didn't see how it made a difference. The whole place reeked of whatever they'd been cooking, onions and chiles and shit, and of the joint they'd been smoking. I didn't really give a crap if they thought I was messing up their household. I just sat down and proceeded to make my case."

"How did they react?"

"About like you'd figure. Halley just laughed and said it was just Abby's tough luck to have left herself open for a liability suit. She made some wiseass comment about daddy coming to try to save his stupid little girl or some shit like that."

Mercer paused and ran a hand through his greying hair, as if he was getting to the difficult part of the story. But he was rolling, and he wasn't going to stop now. "That's when I pulled out the gun from under my raincoat and kinda just held it up, casual like. All of a sudden, they noticed I was wearing the gloves and put it all together. That shut them up quick. Real rocket scientists, those two. They just looked at each other for a while, with big eyes. I think they both swallowed a bunch, like *gulp,* you know? Then they both started babbling, offering me all manner of things to not shoot them. Halley said they had a lot of drugs in the closet I could have. I think she mentioned coke and speed and weed. She might have even said they had money back there she could give me. She started to stand up as if to go to the closet, but I told her to sit the fuck back down. I knew she had it in mind to go for those gun racks I could see toward the back, or maybe she had a gun in the closet. I told them they couldn't buy me: there was only one thing they could do to save themselves and that was to call off the lawsuit. Halley started babbling that she'd write anything I wanted, just give her a pen and paper.

"You know, maybe when I first planned this out, I honestly believed I could get them to pull out, but at that point I knew that was total bullshit. They were just saying anything that they thought would get then off the hook. There was this moment of clarity, you know? Maybe I'd realized it all along. I had to do what I'd had in the back of my mind all along.

"That's when I shot each of them, once in the chest. That likely left them each alive so then I got up, walked over, and gave each of them a head shot at close range."

"It didn't bother you to do that?" Leon asked. "Had you ever killed someone before?"

"Nope. Never. Just, you know, hunting, birds and rabbits and stuff. To be honest, I wasn't sure I was going to be able to do it. But I knew it was the only way, they wouldn't have let it go. Funny thing, it was like nothing, like I wasn't shooting human beings. They were just scumbag predators, a waste of oxygen. The world was gonna be better off without them.

"I remember thinking it was weird, but it didn't bother me at all, seeing them both lying back shot dead and all. It was like I was watching myself and the whole thing in a movie, you know? It wasn't all that hard to stay calm and in the moment. I wasn't worried about being heard. Their house was pretty removed from any of their neighbors and the rain was loud. I could take my time and finish up proper. I looked around for anything that would indicate I'd been there. Then I went over and opened the closet she'd mentioned. It was a mess, filled with her fake casts and crutches and all that crap from her miserable scams. Stuff just tumbled out of it. And, yep, there was a handgun she'd no doubt intended to make a grab for if I'd let her. And then there was the box that they kept their drugs in, this big ornate carved wooden box that would have hollered at you from across the room. They were a special kind of stupid, those two. Zip-lock bags of white powder, that I knew wasn't sugar. I brought the box back to the table, opened a bag and and spilled a little around to look haphazard, then sealed it up and pocketed the rest. I wasn't interested in the drugs; it was just to make it look like the killings were from a drug deal gone bad. Nobody would doubt for a second that Halley and Jack Donner had been involved in something like that.

"I made sure the whole arrangement looked right and let myself out. I walked down the driveway and back to my car.

"Then I drove up to that little lake in that little park near the botanical gardens. As I figured, it was deserted in the rain. Nobody saw me park in the shadows and walk out to that curved bridge, the one that all the kids put the love padlocks on. And I tossed the gun, the gloves, and the drugs into the lake. Then I drove back to where I'd parked earlier and walked back to Duane's. I had no problem sneaking back in through the back door. Everything was dark and really quiet, except for the TV going upstairs, so I figured Roy and Duane were still passed out up there in the living room, like they usually did when they partied hearty. The only problem was that

I'd been walking around in the rain, and there was some mud on my shoes and the bottoms of my jeans. And I was a little worried that I'd got some of the drug residue or some blood on me somewhere, or something like that. So I threw my coat, all my clothes and my shoes into the shower and ran the water, cleaned them off and let it all go down the drain. Then I stuck my wet coat out back where I'd left it earlier. I figured I could tell them I'd gotten sick on myself and just jumped into the shower, clothes and all. Sure enough, they bought it, even thought it was downright funny. Didn't even occur to them why my coat was still soaking wet back up on the porch. After I went home that morning, I burned all of it just to be absolutely sure."

"Whatever you might say, to us or even to yourself," said Art, staring directly at Mercer, "it seems pretty clear to me. You had it planned out. Right from the outset, you were going there to kill them."

Craig shrugged, a dumb half-smile curling up in the corners of his mouth. "I guess so. Maybe I wanted to fool myself into thinking I wasn't a killer." He heaved a sigh of resignation. "But I suppose it was clear in the back of my mind somewhere, the only way to end that whole nightmare for Abby was going to be if they were no longer around."

"And you had no problem, going through with that."

"I expected I would have a lot of a problem, which is maybe why the reality of doing it didn't sink in before I got there. Like I said, I never killed anybody before in my whole life. I thought it was gonna be hard, maybe impossible. But it wasn't, you know?" He looked back and forth at both of them. "It wasn't."

"You killed them both, without any hesitation."

"I had to. It was for Abby. I've been a shit father. She wants nothing to do with me, and I can't blame her for that. I mean, look at me. This was kind of my way of starting to make up for it. And that's all it was, was a start." Craig wiped the corner of his eye. "I would've done anything to try to make it up to her, but like I said earlier, the very worst part of the whole thing was not drinking, staying sober, that entire day."

Leon and Art both rose from their chairs. Everyone understood what came next. Mercer looked back and forth at both of them.

"Can you do me one favor? I'm not gonna be here for Gummy any more. I couldn't stand to see the little guy cast adrift somewhere. Can you make sure he gets taken to a good home?"

* * * *

They stood where the driveway met the street and watched as the uniformed officers loaded a handcuffed Craig Mercer into the back of their cruiser. He gave them a glum look as he was driven off.

"We need to call SID and have them come over and process the joint," Art sighed. "I'll get the tape from the car to close it off."

Leon nodded. "And we'll have to get divers in the lake to see if we can find Mercer's gun. By the way, nice work on that one. You were an absolute joy to watch in action."

Art's face was sour. "Monkey and all. That wasn't too much of a distraction or anything."

"I feel bad that we couldn't guarantee him that the monkey would be all right. I don't know what animal control is going to do when they show up. Gummy's an illegal animal. But maybe there's something I can do."

* * * *

"I can't believe you've spent close to an hour on the phone over that damned stupid monkey!"

Leon just raised his eyebrows, cradling the receiver of the phone on his shoulder, and stared across the desks at Art.

"Uh huh," he spoke into the phone. "Great. Thank you." He replaced the receiver on the desk set. "And it looks like it paid off. There's an animal rescue that specializes in contraband animals that's going to take Gummy. In fact they've got another capuchin."

"Maybe they can teach the critter some manners. Like not jumping onto strangers' laps and going through their pockets."

"Capuchins are illegal to own in this state. Plus, as I've just found out, they don't generally make good pets. They're unhappy in a home environment and can become dangerously aggressive."

"Lucky for Gummy he seemed to have gotten along just fine with Craig Mercer."

"They're also prone to serious health problems and they're happiest around other capuchins. This should work out better for the little guy. I promised Craig I'd try and I lucked out. Hey, it's not Gummy's fault he's in this situation. There was the possibility he would have been, you know," Leon zipped his finger across his throat.

"At least someone's going to come out okay in all this clusterfuck," Art muttered.

"And I wasn't only calling about the monkey."

"Is that so? What other good deeds were you doing to earn your merit badge?"

"Just helping Myra Wambsgans connect a few dots and get her Beatrice back. Hey, what's with the look? The dog didn't do anything either; it's not her fault she had to go through all this with all those knuckleheads."

"Leon, I'll be sure to let you know if the SPCA calls wanting to award you a medal."

Leon's phone rang and he picked it up and spoke tersely for a second before hanging up and pushing his chair back to rise.

"What's up?" Art asked.

"Desk sergeant. Seems I've got a visitor downstairs."

Leon opted for the stairs and when he got to the front door, he saw a familiar uniformed figure standing at the base of the steps, waiting for him.

"Officer Ochida." Leon cast a look around, but she was alone.

"Dom's not with me."

"Okay." They stepped to the side to avoid any incoming or outgoing foot traffic. Leon crossed his arms. "So what's up?"

"I thought you'd want to know. Dom Radley resigned this morning."

Leon, taken aback, took a moment to reply. "Is that so."

"He doesn't think I knew about everything that's been going on. I know about him and Halley Donner. I know about how he stepped over the line to try to protect her. I guess he decided there was enough there that he'll be into serious trouble and could maybe take others with him."

Leon nodded.

"I guess he's a pretty private guy. All I knew about him until pretty recently was that Dom's a good cop. He's been a great training officer. He's made me a tougher and smarter officer already. And, yeah, he made mistakes. He just lost his wife after a hellacious battle with cancer, for God's sake."

Leon held his tongue, just took it all in as she continued.

"I know you suspected him of having something to do with what went down on Mockingbird Lane. There's no way in hell. I'm sure of that."

"We know that now. We got the guy who did it."

"You strike me as the kind of guy who won't feel comfortable leaving the rest of this alone. The reason I came here is to ask you to just let it all lie. He's leaving. Nothing good can come of the whole story coming out."

"I'll take that into consideration, Officer Ochida."

"That's all I'm asking. By the way, my name's Paige. I don't think Dom has ever called me by that. I was always just Ochida."

"Okay, Paige. I'm Leon."

"Yeah, I knew that."

"Good luck. So now what happens to you?"

"They're assigning me a new training officer to finish up my probation period. Whoever they are, I hope they're anywhere near as good as Dom was."

Leon still held his tongue.

TWENTY-SEVEN

Why in holy hell would anyone choose to live here?

Theo pondered the question still one more time as he sat nursing his cappuccino, keeping an eye out the window of the coffee shop at the post office across the street. Talk about a one-horse town. Crystalline for the most part consisted of the main highway and an intersecting avenue, each having a long strip sparsely dotted with various businesses: stores, a couple restaurants and bars, a motel, and weirdly enough, a library. Two small malls had things like a supermarket, a smaller-scale outlet of a big-box store, and a movie theater. A gas station, of course, with a mechanic's bay packed with Jeeps and junkers. A few apartment houses and rickety old homes a little farther out. And that was it. It had to be a complete bore to be stuck here long term, not to mention, being out here in the desert, it was hot as hell.

He wasn't sure how this little town had even sprung up. Had it been a pit mining town back in the day, or a water stop for a stagecoach, or what? Maybe this was one of those places where millennials decided to start a music festival or something. For sure there was plenty of open space around here, maybe for campgrounds or some kind of RV park or something. The few people he'd seen looked like retirees, urban refugees, or antisocial hermits, with a sprinkling of those millennials. There were plenty of beards on the males and just about everyone wore shorts or other desert wear.

This was Nowhere Central. Musgrave—or whatever his real name was—must have chosen this as a safe, out of the way place to lay low until Lydia could get free and come join him. But that would have been *before* she got a murder rap pinned on her. He must have learned about the murder charge, but it was possible he hadn't found out about Lydia's death as yet. In any case, Theo figured, this was a temporary way station for Musgrave and now he'd have no reason to remain much longer.

Theo wasn't sure why he felt so totally sure that Musgrave really was still here. It was just pure instinct. Over the years he'd found himself in lots of situations where he'd had to make a decision and crucial things—even his life—had depended on it. He'd so far made the right ones often enough that he'd learned to trust his gut. His gut told him the guy was still here.

When he'd arrived in Crystalline early Tuesday afternoon, the first thing he did was to grab a motel room, then scout out his surroundings. He realized he stood out amidst the small population here, so he'd made a visit to the box store to buy some new clothes. Theo was a natural role player; he could figure out how best to blend in anywhere quickly, right down to mimicking patterns of speech. Clothing was usually an easy call for him. A couple pairs of cargo shorts and light shirts fit the bill—and of course a good hat.

The only clue he had about Musgrave's whereabouts was the post office box provided by his old employer at the Parks Department, so Theo's best move seemed to be to keep an eye on it. If Musgrave was still under the impression he'd be hearing from Lydia, or if he was expecting a severance check from his old job, he'd likely come by here. There was clearly some reason he'd given a forwarding address. In any case, it was all that Theo had to go on.

Luckily the coffee shop was directly across the street, and Theo figured he looked like any other new denizen around here, sitting with his laptop and his cappuccino for a good part of the day. If anybody tried to strike up a conversation with him he had a readymade story, devoid of too much detail, about being a writer on sabbatical looking for inspiration. Writers, as he figured it, were eccentric enough that it would cover his behavior, and he kind of enjoyed playing his little roles. But it was hardly a suspicious community, what there was of it, nor was it exactly gregarious. He could well be invisible. He'd get up and move around a few times during the day, always staying close enough to observe the post office while not being conspicuous. He could grab food to go at a diner a couple doors down and sit on various benches nearby. Luckily there were shade trees, and the businesses were air conditioned, because that sun was insane. The few other people who ventured out into the searing heat paid him no mind whatever.

The next problem he'd had to solve was to figure out just who he was looking for. What did this guy look like? One of his first moves was to walk into the post office and find the box number he'd been given by Karlotta Fields. He'd lucked out there. The boxes were along a back wall and were faced by a large window. Musgrave's box was in the very top row. From his vantage point in the coffee shop, he could see the entire section.

The post office didn't seem to get all that much traffic, maybe a handful of people each day, and it was almost entirely people driving up and into the small parking lot. There were almost no walk-ups. The patrons that came in to check their boxes hardly ever came anywhere near the box he was watching.

His biggest problem might well be terminal boredom. He didn't know how long he could keep this up. He'd been there the remainder of Tuesday, Wednesday from the time the post office opened in the morning until it closed in the evening, and now today. Dealing with the heat compounded the challenge.

Over the past two days he'd spent a lot of time trying to come up with an alternate plan. No way the guy would be stupid enough to use the Webster Musgrave name here; he could be calling himself anything. Theo had checked online directories anyway but there was nobody by that name in the area. He'd debated dropping the name in a few inquiries but decided that there was more of a chance that would tip off his prey than yield any information.

He only had the most basic idea of what this Musgrave guy looked like, as he had been described to him once: a skinny white guy, of indeterminate age but not really old, with mussy hair. A lot of the white guys he'd seen could have matched that description. Of course, by now Musgrave's hair could be cut short, restyled, or shaved off. And for all he knew, the dude had put on some pounds in the ensuing weeks as well. So basically, he was looking for an adult white guy who was not yet geriatric, a demographic which was in no short supply here in Crystalline.

This was really a needle in a haystack kind of situation, but for some reason he knew, just *knew,* the money was here, and that meant one million reasons for searching for that needle. Not to mention, it was the principle of the thing. This Musgrave, along with his old girlfriend Lydia, had betrayed him, put him in deep shit with his employer Yancey, and gotten him arrested in the process. Lydia might be in the grave, but Theo still required payback. Musgrave joining her would be a start. He couldn't return to Yancey's territory—not yet, at any rate, and maybe not for some time—but a million dollars would facilitate getting pretty far away and setting him up for his comeback.

What it all came down to was this: he had to stay. He had to find this character, whatever he was now calling himself, and this insane stake-out was his only recourse. Well, what else was there to do?

At least he was safe here. He'd eliminated the people sent by Yancey to intercept him. He had a burner phone and credit cards under a different name. He was virtually anonymous. Nobody could possibly know where he was.

Meanwhile, Theo figured, back at home, Yancey's organization was probably in turmoil. There was nobody who could step in and take his place as number two; he was the real reason behind the Ice Man's success. Probably a handful of fools were jockeying for position in the boss's favor, likely knocking each other off. Suspicions would be running high, and backstabbing would be the order of the day. Yancey would be even more paranoid and distrustful than ever now; there would be chaos. Some day soon, he might actually be able to return and take over, like he'd earlier envisioned, if it still suited him.

But first, the money. And that meant the wait.

The hours crawled by. Theo regularly checked his watch until it was six. He could see the lights going off inside the post office and a postal employee coming to the door to lock it from the inside. Another day down the drain.

He decided he was hungry, so he stopped at the diner and ordered a steak, fries and a beer. It wasn't very good, but it was filling, and the beer was icy cold. He found himself looking forward to getting out of this wasteland and going someplace where he could get a truly decent meal. Soon enough.

The waitress was friendly enough to him, downright flirtatious, noting his laptop on the seat next to him and asking how his writing was going. He naturally slid into the character he'd invented, having some fun with her, acting the part of an urban hipster enjoying his stay in the awesome desert. He even flirted back. *Man, I should have been in movies.* He found himself relaxing just a bit, his mind wandering off into new areas.

He kept trying to come up with some other way he could search for Musgrave. There just didn't seem to be any alternative. Theo put himself in the guy's shoes: if it were he, he'd hole up, showing his face only when necessary. He'd have the money stashed somewhere nearby but safe. There was a small bank here, but would someone as slick as Musgrave trust a safe deposit box? There's no way he'd open an account and leave a paper trail.

Just like Theo, Musgrave was off the radar and safe in these Godforsaken boonies. If he sat tight, he and his money would be safe, or so it stood to reason to Theo. Once again, he concluded that what he was doing was the only thing he could do. He had to stay the course.

When he finished his meal, paid his check, and smiled goodbye to the waitress after leaving her a good tip, dusk was falling. It was considerably cooler as the sun went down; bacon might actually not grill on the sidewalk anymore. Theo did have to admit, the desert sunset was beautiful, all sorts of colors. At least, with a full stomach, he could feel a little more human. He was almost serene as he reached his Camry parked at the curb, started it up, and and pulled out onto the quiet highway. His motel was another quarter mile or so down the road. He yawned. Despite not really doing anything, he was pretty beat. A good night's sleep sounded good, and he'd be up again early to resume his stakeout.

How did cops do this kind of shit all the time? It must drive them nuts.

There was a side street that led back to the parking lot behind the motel, not very well lit. He turned off to see a car stopped, partway off the road, a Mustang, with the hood up. A dark figure in coveralls was bent over the engine under the hood. At the approach of Theo's lights, the figure stood up and waved both hands back and forth.

Some guy in a mechanic's uniform and cap. Theo slowed down as the guy stepped out in front of his Camry, still waving his hands.

Theo stopped, lowered his window, turned down the AC to a dull roar, and began to ask, "What's the trouble?" He didn't get the entire second word out of his mouth before the barrel of an automatic was being shoved into his face.

"Turn off the car and get the fuck out."

This was no guy. This was a woman. What in hell was going on? Was this some kind of carjack?

He glanced over at the floor of the passenger seat. The woman with the gun hissed, "I see the weapon under the seat. Don't even think of it."

Theo unlocked his car door, and she yanked it open with her free hand, keeping the automatic trained on him.

"Look, if you really want the car…" he began, starting to ease out of the car, his hands raised.

"Shut the hell up and start walking down the street."

Beyond the entrance to the motel parking lot, the road ran maybe another few hundred yards. Theo couldn't really be sure if there was anything back there. It looked like just scrub brush. She seemed to be herding him back off the street that way.

Who was this bizarre creature in a wrinkled, baggy mechanic's coverall, cap pulled way down over her eyes, who vaguely smelled? Back in the city he would have pegged her for a street person looking for a handout, except of course for the gun. What kind of a fucked-up robbery was this? Was this the kind of people that hung around this town? He had to get an advantage here somehow.

"Look, you want money or my car? Whatever it is you want—"

"I said to shut up."

They reached the end of the road and continued to trudge out into the darkening desert. Finally, Theo just stopped and turned around. If he was going to get shot, he at least wanted a chance to defend himself, and he had one advantage that she didn't suspect. His captor, about four paces behind him, her gun arm extended, pulled up short.

"Okay, what the hell is this all about?" he shouted.

"What the hell this is all about," she said, "is I want my fucking money."

"Wait a minute." He stared at her, unbelieving. Could it be?

She pulled off the cap. The short hair and burns on the face threw him off for a second. Then it registered.

"How in hell? You're—"

"Dead? Surprise, motherfucker! Did you miss me?"

"Lydia?"

"Aw, that's sweet. You didn't forget your old girlfriend."

"How—?"

"In the flesh. Kinda burnt flesh. What was it the guy said, rumors of my death have been greatly exaggerated? A nice little piece of luck. If you can call getting smacked up in a collision with a truck that catches fire and having to fight for your life with a vicious little gangster girl *luck*."

"Wait a minute. There was another prisoner. You switched with her?"

"Hey, you're still as smart as ever, Theo. Can you believe she had a knife on her? Just a prison shiv, a long hunk of metal she'd filed down and snuck out. She was smart. And tough. But I was tougher, which came as a surprise to her. You would have loved the scene. Two girls fighting to the death in a flame-burning van. Girls in manacles, no less! Is that somebody's idea of a fantasy? Put those mixed martial arts shows to shame."

"They said it was you they found."

"They found a barbecued body wearing that necklace you gave me, remember that? Came in handy. I got burnt good all over, but I came out better than her. And talk about luck, one of the deputies was nice enough to get the van unlocked for us before he collapsed. A regular fucking hero, that man."

"How in hell did you get here?"

"Well duh, I staked out your hiding place and then followed you. Not exactly hard. I knew your secret crib and it was just a matter of waiting until you took off. For a smart guy, you did leave a big trail. I had to take some of your old boss's muscle out of the chase on the way. You did know there were two cars on your tail, didn't you?" She jiggled the gun slightly. "Took this off one of the guys in the car. He wasn't going to be needing it anymore."

Theo had to admit, he'd had no idea of any other cars but Felix following him. He cursed his own overconfidence. "You were following me the whole way?"

"Didn't see me, huh? Aren't you proud of how well I've turned out? A Mustang's a pretty common car, I guess, just blends in. Oh yeah, I got the mechanic's duds along with the car."

"You've been here in Crystalline the whole time I've been here?"

"Is that what this piece of crap is called? After two days of living in my car in these stinking clothes in this heat, just keeping an eye on you to figure out the best place to grab you, I've had enough of this joint for the rest of my life. Why here?"

"You know damn well why."

"So, the money is here. Where?"

"What do you mean, where? Your boyfriend Webster has it."

"Are you still trying to get off on that Webster bullshit? Come on, Theo. Nobody has ever bought that fairy tale. You took the money. My money."

"Why in hell, by any stretch of the imagination, is it *your* money, Lydia, whoever's got it? It came from Yancey."

"I have it coming, for all the shit I took from you and him. I got it from him fair and square."

"By kidnapping his fucking dog? That's fair and square? Man, you are a piece of work."

"Says the drug dealer and murderer himself, the kingpin's right-hand man."

"So, what are you going to do, shoot me, here, out in the open?"

"First, you're going to take me to the money. Cooperate and you won't suffer before I kill you." She lowered the barrel of the automatic. "Otherwise, I'll just start putting a few slugs into you where it hurts. You know I'll do it."

Theo nodded slowly, keeping his eyes on hers, his mind churning with possible moves to make very quickly. He had to keep her occupied as long as he could, hoping for an opening. "I'm sure you will. But let's at least drop this charade. We both know about you and Musgrave. We three might be the only ones who do. Why can't you just admit that at least, and humor me with an explanation: why you two decided to meet up here in the boondocks? You've had two days so I assume he knows you're alive and here?"

"How about *you* drop the charade, Theo? You and I and the whole fucking world know there's no Musgrave, never has been."

"Come on, Lydia, game's up. I found the guy. He was working at the Parks Department under his Musgrave name. I talked to his supervisor. She even told me the PO box he's got down here."

"You've really had time to come up with some story, I'll give you that. Now, last time before I take out your knee: where's the money?"

There was a sudden cacophony and a blaze of light, bathing them in illumination. Some kind of big off-road vehicle with gigantic headlights had turned down the side street with a roar, sweeping with a screech around the two cars parked in the roadway. There were only a few seconds before it turned into the motel parking lot and everything reverted to quiet darkness, but it was all the distraction Theo needed. He yanked the Beretta from under his shirt, quickly stepping to his right. Lydia reflexively had fired but the shot was far off. She swiveled as her eyes strove to accustom back to the dark. What she saw was Theo in a two-hand stance pointing his weapon directly at her.

"Where the fuck did you get that!" she might have howled. And Theo might have been obliging enough to inform her that the automatic she'd spied on the floor of his car was one of those he'd grabbed from Felix and Nate after plugging them, and that he'd been driving the short distance back to his motel with his own gun in the holster clipped to his belt under his shirt.

But there was no time for any of that to happen. The both of them, their eyes still recovering from the blast of light, started firing away at one another in the dark on the lonely stretch of desert scrub. The shots clamored across the landscape for several seconds, then died away in a sudden deep silence.

TWENTY-EIGHT

This, thought Alex, *is totally fucked.*

For two days now he'd been stuck in detention down here in wherever he was, with no word from Barclay, who'd promised to get someone down to help him out. The few phone calls he'd been allowed, to Barclay and then a couple other members of his crew, had gone unanswered and unreturned.

It sure looked like he'd been hung out to dry.

Alex wasn't even sure what they were holding him for. Every now and then he'd be interviewed by some local cop or other, asked a lot of questions about what he and Antoine were doing at that gas station at four in the morning, who else might have been there, all kinds of other things. Different individuals kept coming in, men and women, soft and harsh, dark and light, yet they were always the same, throwing the same questions at him, rephrased and recast. He kept giving them the same story about the innocent road trip that had somehow gotten upended by the attack of some maniac.

Alex also learned that Antoine hadn't made it. So now he was involved in an active murder case.

One thing was becoming clearer by the moment: he was on his own. Nobody was coming to help him out of this jam.

He knew the car was clean; there were no weapons or contraband. Aside from his being a material witness on the scene, there was nothing he could figure that they had on him. He wasn't sure what to do, but he figured if he waited them out, didn't raise any suspicion, they'd have to let him go. So he stayed the course.

As he sat one more time in another grey interview room, at a grey slab of a table, staring at the grey light coming through a frosted window covered with a grey metal grille, awaiting one more grey-looking cop or detective or whatever to ask him the same questions still one more time, Alex came to a decision.

Every cop seemed to know where he and Antoine had come from, that they were part of Yancey's crews. If there was anything that could be pinned on him, it would have to be something he and Antoine did back home with the crew, as Barclay's guys. Barclay was their mentor, and they'd put all their faith in him and followed his directions to the letter, and now he'd screwed them over.

Somehow, Alex reasoned, it was Barclay's fault that his cousin was dead. He'd never be able to get that nightmare scene out of his head of Antoine falling out of the car drenched in blood. It was Barclay's fault that he was rotting in this detention center today.

His one chance, Alex had decided, was to get up from under the bus where he'd been thrown and toss Barclay down there instead.

The code said not to rat, no matter what. Fuck the code. It was survival time.

The metal door opened with a clank and someone new walked in, a mean looking dude whose fat pressed against his uniform shirt like it was going to burst it at the seams. Following him in were an unfamiliar man and woman in civilian garb, both scowling.

"These are detectives from your hometown, sport, come down just to pick you up and bring you home. Lucky you. Lucky us, too."

"I'll make a deal," Alex exclaimed to them. "I know stuff. I can give you a major player. Give me a deal."

They looked at each other and back at him, eyebrows raised expectantly.

* * * *

Felix opened his eyes to see someone grinning across the room at him. He smiled weakly back.

"Hello, youngster. They haven't let you out of here yet?"

"They're saying I'm not ready yet."

"Yeah, I can believe that. You look like shit."

Actually, Nate didn't look all that bad to him. He still had a lot of bandages, and one arm was in a sling. He was actually up and moving around, slow and uneasy as he seemed to be. He was able to come visit Felix in his own room. Good signs for the walking dead.

"You wanna see shit, you should see yourself, old man. How you feeling?"

"Like somebody pumped a couple of slugs into me at close range and left me to bleed out. How the hell do you think I feel?"

"You're out of ICU now, you understand? Docs are saying you're gonna make it. You following what I'm saying? They've kept you pretty pumped up."

Felix actually felt fairly coherent, which was a new feeling after recent days. There were still tubes and wires running all over between him and all sorts of bags and meters and things.

"How long we been here," he sighed with effort, "wherever *here* is?"

"We're in something called County General, whatever county it is. I'm not exactly sure, but we've been here a few days."

"You sound pretty together. Haven't had the curiosity to ask?"

Nate tried to shrug but it made him wince. "Tell you the truth, Felix, I don't care. I got nowhere to go. There are some cops, I don't know, maybe state cops? They been coming around asking questions. I told 'em you and me, we were just on a day trip, like we talked about in the car in case we got stopped. You remember all that?"

"Kinda. Much as I remember anything right now."

"They weren't totally buying it. They pegged us as what they called Known Associates. Seems there's been some major shit going down back at home with Yancey and the crews. They wouldn't tell me anymore, but it sounds pretty crazy. I just kept saying I had no idea about any of it. Luckily, they didn't find any weapons or other shit in the car. It was pretty well burned out. They don't seem to be able to pin anything on us, but they're suspicious. They mighta contacted the police back in the city to come down and talk to us."

T.C. must have taken the guns, before he dragged him and Nate out onto the pavement and set the car on fire. It was crazy, but the only thing that made sense to his addled brain right now.

"Stay the course," muttered Felix, feeling very tired. "We got our story, We know nothin'. They got nothin' on us, and their investigation of this shooting is going to hit a dead end quick."

"Think Yancey will send down a lawyer if we need it?"

"I'm thinking we're on our own. If I had to take a guess, I'd say Yancey's a dead end from here on out."

He had no idea how right he might be, but he had a strong suspicion.

Nate nodded. "I been thinking, too. I don't really wanta go back anyway if I can help it."

Felix closed his eyes. "First time you been shot, young man, am I right?" He'd taken a few slugs in his life, been torn up, just never quite so lethal and scary as this time. He remembered how terrifying that initial experience had been, when he was still so young and had fought mightily to not show his terror. T.C. had been with him. They went back together that far.

He labored to think about it. Thinking was still coming slowly, but this was the first time in a while he could actually do it with some rationality. His medication was wearing off, which also was why the pain was starting to return. He wanted to make some sense of everything while he could.

It had all started with that damned stupid dog of Yancey's. That's what caused the ransom, and the money to go missing, and for both T.C. and Yancey to go balls-up shitass crazy. Up until then, they'd all had a good thing going. After that, everything was just *wrong*. T.C. must have taken the money and turned on everyone. That had to be what happened. Those last days that Felix had been with him, it was clear that he was out of his mind.

Yancey's organization was never going to be the same again without a sane and steady T.C. keeping things running smoothly, but Barclay had been right. He had to go. It was him or the rest of them. Felix had known that, and for sure T.C. knew that.

T.C. was as efficient a killer as he knew. When the man wanted people dead, they got dead and stayed that way. And yet he and Nate were in a hospital instead of a morgue.

He could remember, pretty close at least, the last words he'd said to T.C.

Only one of us gets out alive. It's the life. We both know it's you or me.

The man had killed plenty, without hesitation or regret. Felix had been present for some of them. But for some reason T.C. hadn't been able to finish it with him or Nate. This was no mistake. He gave them both a chance and left it up to fate.

T.C. must have figured he was done with the life. He for sure was moving on to something else. Nothing else made sense.

Felix vaguely remembered gunshots, and pain, and then the EMT talking to him. They'd arrived in the nick of time, on an anonymous call by a passing driver. Couldn't miss the burning car. Fate had smiled on them both.

It all made a weird sense to him, while at the same time it didn't make any sense at all. It ran contrary to the severe but necessary code by which they all lived, but at least this time what his own grandmother had told him when he was a kid actually seemed to hold true. Blood for once really was thicker than water.

T.C., you muffug, I didn't see this one coming.

It had been a long time since Felix had been in a church or said a prayer. In the life he'd chosen, there wasn't a lot of room for anybody upstairs, not a lot of relevance. Maybe it was his foggy state, but he found himself saying a silent prayer for T.C., that he'd made it out safe, with the money. Who really gave a shit about Yancey's money anyway?

He snapped back foggily to the present, to his question to Nate, who was nodding his head, almost sheepish. It was indeed the first time he'd taken a bullet. Felix realized how young the kid really still was. He'd been a willing apprentice, ready to learn, but somehow, he hadn't totally gone down the dark hole yet. He could still have his doubts.

"I mean, I got some family there," Nate was saying. "But no big loss, you know? Nobody who really cares. Not much back there but trouble."

"I hear you, my friend. I think it might be wise for both of us to not go back there if we can help it."

Would they even have a choice, if their own local cops showed up to take them back? He was tired, the thinking was getting muddier and the pain getting worse. He saw the unclear shape of what might be a nurse coming in to administer his meds, and he told himself he'd think about all that later.

TWENTY-NINE

Marlon Morrison, ever the master of multi-tasking, shook his head, took a gulp of his coffee, and swiped his free hand in the direction of a stack of folders on his desk, all in one jerky motion. And then he commenced to wailing.

"So I come back from my vacation and before I can even get myself settled, the Lou tosses three new murders on me! And now you tell me, while I've been gone all bloody hell has been breaking loose? It's like the city went to hell in a handbasket!"

It was Monday morning, Marlon's first day back on the job, and he was already in full complaint mode, to the barely concealed amusement of the gathering—Leon, Art, Jilly and Dan—who had assembled to fill him in on the events of the past week.

Marlon, slapping a palm on the top folder, continued his hard-luck diatribe.

"First up, I got some kid named, um," he moaned, peeking inside the folder, "Alex LaShay. Our own Narco folks picked him up downstate. He and his cousin, I think his name was Anthony or Antoine or something, apparently got assaulted driving around early morning last Wednesday. The cousin's dead. After a day or so, the local genius cops finally deduced the kids were both Rybus crew, so they called our Narco, who sent a couple people down. No sooner did they get there than this Alex starts singing his head off about dirty deeds he's aware of, trying to wheedle a deal for himself. Seems he knows where bodies are buried, and I mean literally. They bring him back with them, and Narco is only too happy to hand it all off to Personal, first thing this morning, and guess who gets it?" He again swept his hand dramatically over the papers in front of him and took another gulp of coffee. "I'm so close to retirement I can smell it, but there's still time to get a stress ulcer."

"Great timing," Jilly said, unable to suppress a smile. "Some guys are just lucky."

Marlon pressed on. "So now you tell me it's been an amusement park shooting gallery around here this past week, but with no stuffed animal prizes? All the losers I arrested got themselves killed this past week? Not that it couldn't have happened to a nicer bunch of degenerates, mind you, but what are the odds?"

"Not quite all of them," Leon corrected him. "Famoaana, the enforcer, is still alive, but he's not going to be going anywhere except Falcon Island Penitentiary. He got the ball rolling on all this by confessing to every single charge dropped on any of them. He took one for the team, and let the rest of them fly the coop."

"Rybus got him to do that? That's nuts." Marlon shook his head.

"All except Lydia Montgomery," Jilly jumped back in. "She escaped custody in a fluke collision, while being transported back to Costa County to face murder charges."

"And in the process," Dan added, "she killed another prisoner, Yvette St. Cloud. and switched identities with her. She had us in knots for a while. She swiped a car and disappeared completely."

"For a while, anyway," Dan interjected. "Thursday night she turned up, along with your pal Theo Charles, way downstate, in a desert town called Crystalline. What the two of them were doing there, nobody's got any idea yet, but it seems they killed each other in an armed shoot-out in the street."

"What is this?" Marlon wailed. "The friggin' Wild West?"

"She had swiped some mechanic's tools," Dan continued, "and they were still in the car she'd lifted. Forensics techs down there found blood on them. Apparently, she had more than one run-in during her escape."

Marlon started rubbing his forehead. "What a goddamn crazy quilt. I'm not sure I'm making sense out of all of this."

"Join the club," Art interjected.

"And then," Marlon continued, "you said that Gene Gehm killed Rybus? *Gene?* What in hell is up with that?"

Jilly picked up the thread again. "Long story short..."

"Please," Marlon interrupted. "By all means, short version. I'm already crazy here."

"Rybus had something on Gene to keep him in line and was upping the pressure on him to feed him information. Gene wanted out so he set him up and laid in wait. With a shotgun. Took him out along with his bodyguard, who in the process shot Gene."

"He was dirty? In bed with Rybus? That son of a bitch. That's why he'd been working me. I knew something was up. And it was on account of that dog. That dog's nothing but trouble."

"We learned some more," Jilly continued. She glanced at the yellow pad she was carrying where she'd been jotting down notes since she first got there that morning. "Your boys the LaShay cousins were doing a lot of clean-up work for Barclay Vickers—"

"Hold on," Marlon raised a hand, looking totally at sea. "Vickers, he's the guy you said had become Rybus's number two, right?"

"Right. He replaced Theo Charles."

"And he's dead now too, you said. Is that right?"

"Right. He was killed by the guy who stole Rybus's dog back."

"The dog again! I'm not following almost any of this, but what I do get is, even *more* stiffs. Damnation!"

"And we're not finished yet." Jilly took a deep breath, gave her notes another look, and went on. "That Wednesday that the LaShays got attacked, another hundred or so miles down the Interstate, two more of Rybus's associates got attacked in their car in a rest stop. Someone pumped some slugs into them and set their car on fire. They somehow survived, although one of them you'll recognize, Felix Sykes, was in critical condition and is still recovering."

"Sykes! The big guy?"

"He'd only been out of custody a day or two," Dan mused, "and he was back in trouble."

"Sykes," Marlon muttered, thinking back to his confrontation on the street with a pack of apparently stark raving insane, heavily armed gangsters who had all become the players in this bizarre tale: Rybus, Theo Charles, Lydia, the gigantic Felix Sykes and the even bigger Tiny Famoaana. It was a memory he'd now rather forget.

Jilly took a quick look at her notes. "The county sheriff's office down there contacted us wondering if we had interest in them. They had nothing to really hold them on. Before they could get an answer, the younger guy, Nathaniel Brand, checked himself out AMA and disappeared."

"I'm guessing," added Dan, "nobody's going to see a reason to bring Sykes back up here when he's able to be transported. It remains to be seen."

"So, wait." Marlon started counting on his fingers in dramatic fashion. "Yancey Rybus is dead. So is Rybus's bodyguard, whoever he was. Theo Charles. Lydia the dognapper. This LaShay kid. This Barclay Vickers dude. And this St. Cloud gal? Did I miss anybody? Have I got 'em all? All in the past week. A goddamned massacre."

"And you weren't even here for any of it," Leon smiled wryly. "You missed all the action, Marlon."

"I wish that were true," Marlon said sadly. "If I'd just stayed away a couple more days." He slapped the top of the stack of folders one more time. "On top of that, there's all the fallout from that other LaShay kid covering his ass and dropping a dime on this Vickers knucklehead. Lord knows how many more DBs I'll wind up tracking down."

Sensing their moment was coming to an end, the detectives began to rise and disperse. Marlon moved to his summation.

"And why do I still think that this whole mess is the fault of that damned dog of Rybus's? This all started with the dog. It kept turning up here, there, all over. I can't help but feel, it's all because of the dog."

"We haven't told him about the monkey yet," Art said to Leon with a smirk.

"A monkey now? A *monkey?* Do me a favor and *don't* tell me about the monkey. But tell me that the dog has been placed somewhere where it can't cause any more mischief."

"That," said Leon, eyebrows raised, "is something I haven't had the chance to look into just yet."

THIRTY

It was a typical, glorious desert morning. The sun beamed warm brightness out of a cloudless, azure sky over a beautiful display of flora and fauna. The distant hills shimmered like fabulous mirages. The individual in the khaki shirt and shorts who'd stopped his jeep on the access road paused a long moment to take it all in before stepping out of his vehicle. There were people, he reflected, who thought the desert was lifeless. How wrong they were. It was full of life and wonder.

He picked his computer tablet up off the passenger seat and tapped up the information that he needed. This was a remote corner of the Downstate Desert Conservancy, a three hundred square mile expanse, and many was the day that would go by without his seeing a single person out here. That was fine with him. He'd learned he wasn't what you'd call a people person. He far preferred the company of birds and animals, and he'd come to learn that he especially preferred the ones that kept their own counsel as well, so working out here in the desert suited him very well indeed.

Of course it was going to be a nice day today; to him, they all were. The heat didn't bother him a bit. He had plenty of water, a good hat and sunscreen to protect his ruddy skin, and it was always bone dry, so he felt comfortable in the high temperatures out here. The fact of the matter was, this was his ideal environment. He couldn't imagine any place on earth that would suit him better. What great fortune that he'd been offered this job in this wondrous place.

Things had worked out, he considered, pretty darned good. It had been a good six months now since he'd found his way down here, and nobody seemed to have followed him or come after him. He remained wary and careful, but every day he could breathe a little easier. The box of money remained tucked away safely under the floorboards of the house he rented, and he was judicious in how he spent it, taking a hundred-dollar bill out only now and then to augment the paycheck he got from the Conservancy. Nobody looked twice at a hundred dollar bill these days, not even down here. He'd use it on a trip to the big-box store, going through the self-checkout, and it went smoothly every single time. As long as he kept a low profile, he should be okay, and that was the lifestyle that definitely suited him. He'd come to realize that he was a desert rat at heart.

Now and then it would occur to him that the rental on his post office box was about to expire, and he'd already decided he'd just give it up. The only reason he'd taken it was to have someplace for his old supervisor Karly to send him his severance check from Parks, Recreation and Wildlife, and she'd gotten that out to him promptly. He hadn't even seen a reason to stop in at the post office to check the box after that. In fact, he'd gotten so involved in his new job that he found little reason to do much else at all. He seldom drove into Crystalline proper except to get supplies.

His views on people hadn't been changed by things he'd heard about crazy tourists, partying millennials, and the altercations of local drinkers. The desert did tend to attract outliers and many of them were of the nasty sort. There was even that incident a while back where those two crazy drunks, some kind of feuding gang members or something, had gotten into a road rage argument one night, pulled out guns, and killed each other. He was happy to stay at his place out in the desert and occupy his time with the Conservancy, which filled up the day free of undue stress. The handful of people who kept the Conservancy going were decent sorts, hands-off in outlook like himself. He didn't have a television or radio, never listened to the news, and had not yet even set up his computer or looked for an internet connection. The desert and its natural denizens were all he needed.

But back to the matter at hand.

He walked a way off the road to a berm that had been built up. The rescued tortoise they had recently brought in had constructed a nice burrow. It looked as if she was going to adapt nicely to her new home. That made him very happy. He noted that the flora and the ground formations themselves seemed undisturbed.

After entering some data, he headed back to his jeep and started it up. The next stop on his route was the Turkle Cactus Oasis, a garden of plants that flanked a natural spring. It had once been the home of a hermit prospector named Wild Sam Turkle, a guy, he'd decided, was definitely after his own heart.

There was a small parking area at the garden, marked by a sign. He was surprised to see an old van parked there. He pulled in near the van and saw two figures strolling along the gravel paths among the cacti and yucca, a woman and a big white dog. The woman was tall, dressed in light white linen shirt and pants, with a large straw hat. She turned and smiled as he approached her.

"Good morning," she said. He noted that her dog was leashed, as regulations required on the Conservancy land, and seemed well behaved. She scratched the dog behind its ears.

"Good morning," he replied, nodding and returning the smile. "You're certainly out here early."

"I assumed it was okay," she said. "I love the desert, and I've been wanting to see the Cactus Oasis for so long. We're on a vacation and I made a point to get up early today to come out and see it."

"Oh, you're fine, Ma'am. The whole park is open to the public at sunrise. It's just not often we actually see people out here this early."

"I don't understand why. It's magnificent, just magnificent." She spread her arms to encompass the vista before them. "When you're out here, it's like there couldn't be anything wrong with the world."

He knew exactly what she meant. It wasn't often he felt he could relate to another human being.

Her dog, a big pit bull, sniffed at him.

"Don't worry, she's friendly. In fact, she's a total sweetheart."

He came closer and cautiously extended a hand for the dog to sniff further, then squatted down and rubbed the animal behind its ears. "She's a real beauty. What's her name?"

"Beatrice. She's a rescue. She's the love of my life." She looked at the name on his uniform shirt. "And you're Ranger Musgrave?"

"They don't call us rangers. I guess my official title is conservator. You can just call me Web."

"Hello, Web. I'm Myra. We're a long way from home, Beatrice and me. Just two girls on a road trip adventure. We're visiting some of the state and national parks."

"Nice to meet you both. I hope you enjoy the desert preserve here. Have you checked out the Visitors' Center yet?"

"As a matter of fact, that's how I found out about the Cactus Oasis. And so much more that we want to see today."

Beatrice had decided she liked Web and was happily nuzzling her nose against him as he patted her.

He laughed. "She seems like such a sweet dog."

"Oh, she is. She's my sweet girl."

"A lot of people are afraid of pit bulls. When they're treated right, they can be really nice dogs."

"And you know, she's had such a terrible life. She was owned by a bunch of drug dealers or some such, then she was stolen away a couple of times. They even stole her from me once, after I adopted her, but I got her back."

"Wow, that's quite a story. And yet, look at her, she seems so happy to be around people."

"The right people, yes. She can sense when someone's a nice person. You're clearly someone who loves and respects animals."

"You've got that right."

"This must be a nice place to work."

"It's great. A lot of people who come here don't seem to get that. Sometimes they tell me they can't understand why I'd want to be stuck out here in the Godforsaken desert. That's the term they always use."

"Are you serious? They're crazy. They really don't get it, what a wonderful place this is? Why, just look around us! This is blessed, not forsaken."

"I'm glad to meet someone else who sees that, Myra."

"Well, I'd better let you get to your work. Very nice to talk to you, Web. You're so lucky to be out here. I hope you realize how special you are, and may you have much health and happiness."

Web gave Beatrice a final pat on the neck, standing up. "Nice to talk to you too, Myra. I hope you and Beatrice enjoy the rest of your trip, and maybe you'll come back and see us again."

"I think that's very possible. And when we do, we'll be sure to look you up, if we might."

"Sure. I'd like that. I'll be here."

When he returned to his jeep and started the engine, Webster saw Myra waving to him from the cactus garden and waved back. It was the first time in a while that he'd actually enjoyed interaction with another human being. It felt strange.

Funny, he told himself as he headed back down the access road, that out here in the middle of nowhere two people could still come together, who had no conceivable connections to one another. He'd often felt that this place had some kind of mystical thing going on, that it was fraught with possibilities. Anything could happen here; witness his own experience so far.

He really did hope that Myra and Beatrice would come back one day and look him up again